BARKBELLY

Cat Weatherill

BARKBELLY

illustrated by Peter Brown

ALFRED A. KNOPF 🐎 NEW YORK

THIS IS A BORZOI BOOK PUBLISHED BY ALFRED A. KNOPF

www.randomhouse.com/kids

Educators and librarians, for a variety of teaching tools, visit us at
www.randomhouse.com/teachers

Library of Congress Cataloging-in-Publication Data
Weatherill, Cat.
Barkbelly / by Cat Weatherill ; illustrated by Peter Brown. — 1st American ed.
p.   cm.
SUMMARY: A wooden boy who is being raised by loving human parents flees after accidentally killing a playmate and begins a quest for his real home and family.
ISBN-10: 0-375-83327-7 (trade) — ISBN-10: 0-375-93327-1 (lib. bdg.)
ISBN-13: 978-0-375-83327-4 (trade) — ISBN-13: 978-0-375-93327-1 (lib. bdg.)
[1. Fantasy.] I. Brown, Peter, ill. II. Title.
PZ7.W35395Bar   2006
[Fic]—dc22   2005011065

Printed in the United States of America
June 2006
10 9 8 7 6 5 4 3 2 1
First American Edition

To Ray, for holding on to the dream

To my mum, for simply holding on

And to my dad, who would have been so proud

The Beginning

The flying machine bumbled on through the night, humming like a fat bee. Above, the sky was freckled with stars. Below, the blue hills slipped by unseen. On board, the star sailor swayed in his hammock, dreaming of gold. Nothing disturbed his sleep. Nothing told him that some of his precious cargo was about to be stolen.

The thief clung to the rigging, eyeing the bag of wooden eggs. She tilted her head. She peered. She pondered. She judged the distance between her perch and the string bag and calculated the degree of sway. Then she flew down between the spinning feather blades, caught hold of the bag with beak and claws, and dangled acrobatically beneath. She breathed in. *Silver stars! What a tantalizing scent!* She opened her mouth and wrapped her beak round one of the eggs. Her black tongue wriggled over its surface. She tasted salt and sand, forest and fern.

The parrot wondered what kind of nuts they were. She had never seen anything like them before. The shells were unbelievably hard. Could she crack one open? No, not in the bag. She would have to get one onto the deck and then hold it between her feet. If she chewed through the string, one would slip out easily enough. . . .

"Bella! Leave the cargo alone!"

The star sailor, Moontar, was wandering across the deck to the navigation crystals. Bella knew he would soon return to his hammock. If she didn't move, perhaps he would forget she was there.

"Bella! Come down!" Moontar yawned and rubbed his gummy eyes. "I can see you, you know! Come down! Those eggs are worth money. If you chew through the bag, they'll go everywhere. Come on now. Leave them!"

But Bella didn't leave them. She dangled like a bat and glared at Moontar. How dare he intrude like this? She was a Purple-Plumed Night Parrot. The night belonged to her. *To her.* Moontar was trespassing. How dare he? This was her time to fly, to explore, to eat. She would do what she liked. Let him wait till morning.

Bella returned to her chewing. The thin string was wet and weak. Her tongue wormed the fibers looser.

"Bella. . . ."

Moontar was walking toward her. She chewed on.

"I'm warning you."

He was pointing a finger at her. *Oh, the cheek of the man!* She watched him with one cold eye. She could feel an egg starting to push through the hole she was making.

"Bella!"

The star sailor lunged toward her but she was gone, flying off into the darkness she loved. His fingers closed round nothing but the bag.

"Seven seas!" he muttered. "She's more trouble than a monkey. And that's saying something."

Moontar realized he would have to unhook the bag from the rigging. Bella couldn't be trusted. She would return as soon as he was below deck, and the eggs were valuable cargo. With a grunt, he pulled over a crate, clambered up and unhooked the bag. But as he did, one shiny egg slipped out through the hole Bella had made and fell down, down, down through the midnight sky. Down to the shadowland below, where it thudded into a farmer's field. And there it lay, hidden from human eyes, while the wheat grew up around it. Mice built their nests in the stalks above it. Slugs gathered in the damp soil beneath it. Rain soaked it. Mud spattered it. Summer sun dried it. Weeks went by and still it lay there unnoticed.

But then the harvesters came.

PART ONE

Chapter 1

ish Patterson pulled out a grubby handkerchief and mopped his brow. It was still early, but already he could feel the heat rising. Sunbeams were dancing on the roofs in Pumbleditch.

I should be down at the river on a day like this, he thought, *not stuck in a field with the oldies.* But everyone had to help with the harvest. That was the rule. For two exhausting weeks, every Pumbleditcher had to sweat and heave and tie and truss until the fields were stubbly as chins.

His mates were already at work—if shoving wheat stalks down someone's shirt could be called work. Moth, Dipper, Log: they were all there, over on the far side of the field. Even at this distance Fish could hear Moth's protests. He was writhing around on the ground, shouting and laughing in turn. Poor Moth. Always the victim.

Fish felt someone tugging at his sweater, as if it weren't baggy enough already. He knew it was Little Pan Evans before he heard his voice.

"Fish! Fish!"

"What?" He looked down onto a face as eager as a puppy's.

"One of the harness rats is being real nasty," said Pan, hopping from foot to foot. "In the next field. I'm going to tell the lads." He sprinted away.

Fish thought for a moment. Did he really want to watch someone fighting a rat as big as a lion, with teeth like penknives and claws like daggers? Yes. Oh, yes!

Fish sped into the next field.

The harness rats powered the tractors. They were devils to handle if they were angry, and this morning one was. The handlers had it trapped in a corner of the field. They had ropes, but Fish could see that the rat wasn't going to be harnessed without a fight. It bared its teeth and gripped the earth with polished claws.

"He's wicked," said a familiar voice at his side. Moth Williams. "Look at those eyes. They'll never get him in the wheelcage."

"Course they will," said Dipper Dean, coming up behind. "They just need to get those ropes round his neck, then they can haul him in. They'll have to mind his tail, though."

The gang watched as the men positioned themselves. Boot Marlow, the head rat handler, was a brawny man with watery eyes and a beard like a hawthorn hedge. Next to him was Sock Samuels, a thin man with patched trousers and foul feet. And lastly, Rag Weaver, the youngest of the three—little more than a lad, with a thatch of yellow hair and a gap-toothed grin. He wasn't smiling now, though. He was terrified. The rope dangled in his hands like a dead adder.

"I think they should forget about the ropes," said Log Worthing, last to arrive as usual. "If Sock Samuels took off his shoes, they could hold him like a battering ram and the stink from his feet would stun that rat."

Fish grinned. "That's too cruel! I like this rat. Look at it his way. Once he's in that wheelcage, he'll have to run round and round all day. I'd put up a fight too."

But the rat didn't have time to fight. Suddenly three ropes dropped over his head and the nooses tightened as the men pulled. The rat reared up on his back legs, but the men held him fast and others ran to join them. The rat was dragged along the ground. His claws furrowed the earth. He thrashed his tail, but the men were expecting that and kept well clear. He hissed uselessly. Big as he was, there were just too many of them.

The lads watched as he was bullied into an empty wheelcage. The men closed the door and slipped the ropes off his head. The rat sniffed the air. There was a rat in the other wheelcage—he could smell its misery. Then the men pushed the tractor from behind and the wheelcages began to turn. The rat started to run; he had no choice. The wheelcages turned faster and faster as the tractor gathered momentum and then they settled into a steady rhythmic roll. Another day's work had begun.

"Poor thing didn't stand a chance," said Moth.

"Never do," said Dipper.

"I like rats," said Little Pan Evans, though he knew no one would be listening to him.

"We should be getting back now," said Log. "We'll be missed."

They started to walk off. In the other field, they saw Gable Gantry, the village carpenter, mending a broken wheelcage. He nodded to them as they passed.

"I like him," said Moth while they walked on.

"Yes, he's all right," said Fish.

"Stand back!" said Log.

A tractor was rumbling toward them, driven by Farmer Gubbin. There was a shushing of blades as it scythed past, then—*thuud!*—the blades struck something hard. Whatever it was went hurtling through the air toward Gable Gantry and—*uurgh!*—smacked him hard on the head. He went down like a bowling pin.

"Whoa!" said Fish. "Old man down!"

The gang whooped and whistled and ran over for a closer look. But when they reached him, Gable Gantry was scary. He wasn't moving. Thick, dark blood dripped from the wound in his forehead.

"He's dead!" cried Little Pan Evans.

"He can't be," said Fish. He knelt down and put his ear close to the old man's face. He listened. He frowned.

"Is he dead?" whispered Moth. There was no reply. "Fish! Is he dead?"

Fish looked up. His face was pale as paper. "I can hear him breathing," he said gravely. Then he grinned and Little Pan Evans punched him.

People started running over from all parts of the field. They made a ring round the old man, still holding the tools they had been working with. They nudged each other, whispered, shuffled closer like cows. Suddenly Gable shuddered and screwed up his face. Then he opened his eyes and found himself surrounded by villagers. Some of them were trying to help him up. Some of them were telling him to lie down. His head ached and his sight was fuzzy.

"What happened?" he croaked.

"You were hit by this," said Fish, and he gave him a lump of mud.

Gable rubbed the object between his fingers. The mud

started to flake off. It looked like an egg. A wooden egg, no larger than a goose egg, but much heavier. "What on earth is it?" he said.

"Goodness knows!" said Farmer Gubbin, climbing down from his tractor. "It was just lying there on the ground. I've never seen anything like it before. I doubt if anyone here has!"

He was right. No one had.

"Well," said Gable, offering the egg to the farmer, "if it was on your land, happen it's yours by right."

"Eh, no!" cried Farmer Gubbin. "I don't want it! You keep it, Gable! To remind you of your adventure!"

So Gable wrapped the egg in his handkerchief and took it home to show his wife.

Chapter 2

*H*ome for Gable Gantry was a small stone cottage with mullioned windows and a moss-green door. It was hidden among the trees of Ferny Wood, but the path to it was well trodden. In the Gantry house, any visitor was welcome: young or old, feathered or furred. Many a stray cat had found a warm hearth beyond the green door. The stove, like the kettle, was never allowed to go cold. All day long, smoke curled out of the cottage chimney like apple peel.

Pumpkin Gantry was at home, making lunch for the harvesters. *Green pea soup!* Gable could smell it from the garden gate. He smiled and let himself in.

"Oh, my!" said Pumpkin when she saw him. "Whatever has happened?"

"I've had a bit of a morning," said Gable, sinking into his favorite chair.

"I can see that! Look at your head! Oh! Let me wipe away that blood." She wet a cloth at the sink and started dabbing at the wound.

"Something hit me," said Gable. "It was thrown up by a tractor."

"It must have been pretty hard, whatever it was," said Pumpkin. "This is a nasty cut."

Gable fished in his pocket and brought out the egg. "It was this."

Pumpkin took it to the sink. She washed it clean and dried it on her apron. "Look at this pattern," she said. She traced the grain with a fleshy finger. "It's ever so lovely. Is it sycamore wood?"

Gable took it back. "No, it's not sycamore. I reckon it's ash."

"I wonder where it came from," said Pumpkin. "Do you think something laid it? Some kind of bird?"

"No," said Gable. "I know it looks like an egg, but it's solid. There's nothing inside it. See?" He knocked it hard on the table.

"Don't do that!" cried Pumpkin. "You'll dent it!" But when she took it from him, she found that the egg was as smooth as it had ever been. "I want to keep it," she said. "It's so pretty. I'm going to put it on the window ledge."

And she did. She put it between the potted plant and the porcelain cat. And there it lay, gathering dust, until one winter's night, when a troublesome fire changed everything.

It was bitterly cold. The wind was prowling round the cottage, rattling the doors and window frames. Gable had been struggling for hours, trying to coax life into the fire. It just wouldn't burn properly. The wood smoked miserably and no amount of kindling made any difference.

"It's got no heart," he grumbled as he tempted the flames with dried potato peelings. "A fire must have a heart! This is nothing but a bundle of bones."

Pumpkin smiled and put down her sewing. Gable was so patient! She would have lost her temper long ago. She pulled herself out of her chair and went to the window ledge. There was the wooden egg: dull, dusty, long forgotten.

"Here," she said, handing it to her husband. "Try this."

"No! Not that! You like it."

"I do," said Pumpkin. "It's such a pretty thing. But it's just lying there. There's not much you can do with a wooden egg, is there? Look—it's covered in dust. No, put it on the fire, and if it gets a blaze going, we can sit together and watch the flames."

Gable wiped the egg and gazed for one last time at the wonderful patterns in the wood. Then he sighed and threw it into the fire. The flames started to lick at it, but they didn't burn brighter. If anything, they seemed to dwindle even more.

"Perhaps it won't burn," said Pumpkin, disappointed. "It's very hard wood."

She made a fresh pot of tea and buttered some scones. Then the old couple settled themselves to watch. At first it seemed that Pumpkin was right. The egg simply wouldn't burn. But then it started to smolder and a thick, bark-brown smoke spiraled lazily up the chimney.

"There it goes," said Pumpkin happily. "It'll burn now!"

But the egg didn't burn. Instead, it started to move.

It began slowly at first, with a gentle rhythmic rocking. Then it started to twist, as if something was stirring inside it. Then it shuddered, and with a great BANG! it cannonballed out of the fire, smashed the teapot on the table, ricocheted across the room, hit the milk pail, shot back toward the fire and landed on the cat.

The cat ran up the curtains. Pumpkin tried to calm the cat.

Gable tried to catch the egg. The egg bounced onto the best rug.

And there it lay, quite still.

The old couple watched, owl-eyed. They hardly dared to breathe. The egg was starting to grow. It grew bigger and bigger, till it was the size of an old leather football. Then it started to stretch. *There was something inside it.* And whatever it was, it was trying to get out. The leathery egg strained and bulged—and out came a leg. A fat little wooden leg, with wriggling toes. Then out came a second leg. And a fat arm. And another fat arm. The egg wasn't an egg now. It was a body, with a round belly and arms and legs—but no head. It rolled helplessly on its back, like a beetle. Its wooden fingers curled into two angry little fists that beat at the air. Then it managed to flop over onto its belly. The arms pushed down on the ground, the toes dug into the rug and the creature rose unsteadily to its feet. Then the hands took hold of the empty place where the head should have been and they tugged and tugged—and out popped a head. And there stood a perfect wooden baby, with an angry, crumpled face.

He peered at the old couple. He screwed up his wooden eyes and opened his wooden mouth. They saw a wooden tongue and two rows of sharp wooden teeth.

"Waaaaaa!" he bawled, and the whole house rattled.

Gable and Pumpkin stared at the new arrival. Then they stared at each other and back at the baby.

The wooden baby looked from one moon face to the other. He frowned. Who were these people? Didn't they understand?

"Mamaaa!" he wailed. "Papaaa! Feeeed meeee!"

"Ah!" cried Gable in horror. "It can talk!"

"He called me Mama," said Pumpkin in a small voice. "He called me Mama."

Gable looked at his wife. Her eyes were bright with tears.

"We have a son," said Pumpkin. "After years of waiting—years of disappointment—we have a son, Gable. *We have a son.*"

She reached out to the wooden baby and gathered him into her arms. Instantly he was calm. He gazed at her with warm wooden eyes. Pumpkin thought they looked just like hazelnuts. She smiled and started rocking her new son.

"Mama," he said again, quietly now. "Mama."

Gable watched his wife with the child. So much tenderness. So much joy. Gable felt love purring in his heart like a warm cat.

"Happen the little chap will need a name," he said gently. "What would you like to call him, my sweet?"

Pumpkin looked at the baby carefully. He was pale, with a fine wood-grain pattern on his limbs. He had strong little arms and legs. And such a potbelly! It was hard and round like a piglet's, with wood grain swirling all over it. Pumpkin stroked it and the wooden baby gurgled with pleasure.

"My love?" said Gable again. "Do you have a name for him?"

Pumpkin smiled. "I do," she said. "I think we should call him Barkbelly."

Chapter 3

$\mathcal{B}$arkbelly didn't grow like other children. He shot up like a string bean. Within an hour, he was walking. Within a day, he had grown to the size of a two-year-old. Within a week, he looked like a five-year-old.

Pumpkin started to worry. Would he live out the whole of his life within a year? Would he age and wither before her eyes? Would she see him dead and buried in Mound Meadow? *No mother should outlive her child. It isn't right.*

By the end of the month, Barkbelly was as big as a ten-year-old boy, and a hefty one at that. But then he stopped growing. In the month that followed, he became stronger and his use of language improved, but he didn't grow any taller. And Pumpkin finally stopped worrying. She felt sure he would live a long and happy life.

But much as she loved her wooden boy, Pumpkin had to admit that he could be quite a handful at times. He was headstrong. And this, combined with his fearsome physical strength, was a worry to her.

"He needs to go to school," she told herself one day. "He'll soon learn that he has to bend a little if he wants to get on with people. The other lads will teach him that—if they accept him." She frowned. "It's that tall lad he'll have to please, Fish Patterson. All the other boys follow him like sheep. They'll be in the same class. But there's nothing I can do. Bark will have to take care of himself. I can't hold his hand. He isn't a baby!"

But he *was* a baby in so many ways, and Pumpkin knew it. For all his size and strength, Barkbelly was completely unworldly. He knew the cottage and the garden. He had ventured a little way into Ferny Wood. But he had never been into the village and he hadn't played with any children. Sometimes they called to him from the gate, but he never replied. He wasn't shy; he simply wasn't interested. He was so happily absorbed in his own games, he didn't need company.

Pumpkin felt like a pigeon, pushing her chick out of the nest before it was ready to fly. But she knew she had to do it. Barkbelly had to learn about life.

And so, when Barkbelly was ten weeks old, Pumpkin sent him to school.

Barkbelly stood by the teacher's desk and stared boldly at his new classmates. Big ones, tall ones, fat ones, small ones. . . . There were all kinds, but no one was wooden. And no one was smiling. Except Miss Dillwater, who was introducing him. She was a brisk young woman with a long snake of hair coiled on the back of her head.

"This is Barkbelly," she said, "as I'm sure you all know." She put her hand reassuringly on his shoulder. "He will be joining our class starting today, so I want you all to be nice to him." She paused just long enough to take a breath, but Barkbelly felt she was looking at the extraordinarily pretty girl

in the front row. The one with the silver curls and the dark, mischievous eyes. "Make him feel welcome. Do you hear me?"

"Yes, Miss Dillwater," said the class.

"Good." She glanced at the wall clock. "It's a little early, but I think we can have break now. You can use the extra minutes to get to know your new friend. Ring the bell, Sweet Pea."

A haughty girl with shiny shoes picked up the bell and left the room. Soon a deafening clang rattled the schoolhouse windows. Chairs scraped, desks slammed, boots thudded and doors banged. Play began.

Outside in the playground, Barkbelly found himself surrounded by curious classmates. Candy Pie, the one with the silver curls, elbowed her way to the front. Her two best friends flanked her: Pillow Anderson, a pale girl with pink ribbons, and Sweet Pea Nicholson, the girl who had rung the bell. All three of them peered shamelessly at him, studying his bare legs and hands. Then Candy Pie leaned forward and touched him. Her eyes widened. She fingered his wooden curls. Then she rapped him hard on the cheek with her knuckles.

"So, Barkbrain," she said, "are you wooden all over?"

"Yes," said Barkbelly.

Candy Pie smiled. "Really? You're wooden *all over?*"

Her girlfriends giggled. Barkbelly frowned, and glared at her.

Candy Pie's dark eyes were challenging and defiant. Barkbelly was speechless. Someone started sniggering.

Then the ring was jostled from behind and Fish Patterson burst through, followed by Moth Williams, Log Worthing and Dipper Dean.

"Oi," said Fish, pointing his finger accusingly at Candy Pie. "I hope you're not threatening him."

"What if I am?" snapped Candy. She knocked his finger away. "What's it to you?"

"Boys first," said Fish.

Candy's eyes narrowed.

"You know the rules," said Dipper. He was right behind her.

Candy wavered. Fish Patterson wouldn't hit a girl but Dipper Dean would. "Have him," she said at last. "With my blessing. I have *real* friends. I don't need to play with puppets." She linked arms with Pillow and Sweet Pea and they flounced off.

Fish moved closer to Barkbelly. "So, new boy, what's the answer?"

Barkbelly studied Fish. He was tall and scrawny, but he looked like he could fight if he wanted to. "I don't understand," he said.

"The girl asked you a question," said Fish. "But we never heard your answer. Are you wooden all over?"

Dipper Dean sniggered.

"Yes," said Barkbelly warily. "I'm exactly the same as you."

"Ah, but you're not the same, are you?" said Fish. He stroked Barkbelly's wooden arm with a mucky finger.

"I am!" said Barkbelly defiantly. "But where you have flesh, I have wood."

"Well, that's not the same, is it?" Fish started to circle him. "Do you bleed?"

"Don't know."

"Do you break?"

"Don't know."

"Do you feel pain?"

"No."

"Then you won't feel this," hissed Dipper Dean, and he pushed Barkbelly to the ground and started kicking him.

Barkbelly was bewildered. Instinct closed his eyes and curled him up into a ball, but it couldn't close his ears. Shouts and jeers hammered him like fists: four, five, six voices or more. And there was more than one pair of boots kicking him, he could tell. Kick followed kick in a volley of violence.

But Barkbelly wasn't hurting. Suddenly he realized they could kick him all day and he would be just as strong as when they started. They would be the ones going home with bruises. But his clothes . . . his fine new clothes! His smart jacket and his best britches . . . muddied and torn! His new boots . . . his new, shiny, grown-up boots . . . scuffed and grimed! Mama had taken money from the savings pot to buy them. Hard-earned money.

Barkbelly exploded into a flurry of fists and feet. He grabbed Dipper Dean by the ankles, pulled him down and thumped him. He thumped him again. He pulled his hair. He squashed his nose into his face. He twisted his ears. Dipper called for help. Log Worthing tried to pin Barkbelly's arms from behind; Barkbelly elbowed him in the guts. Moth Williams grabbed a leg; Barkbelly booted him away with the other one. Dipper was yelling now; Barkbelly was on top of him, pinning him down. Barkbelly's knees were burrowing into the tender flesh of his upper arms.

"You were right," snarled Barkbelly. "I am not the same as you. I am stronger than you will ever be. I will not break. I will not bleed. And do you want to know something else? I will not cry. So you can call me all the names you want. You will not hurt me. *Do you understand?*"

"Yes," replied Dipper through clenched teeth.

"I didn't hear you."

"Yes!"

"Do you give in?"

Dipper squirmed. Barkbelly dug his knees in even harder.

"Do you give in?"

"Yes! Yes! Flamin' yes!"

Barkbelly felt his heart somersault inside him. "Good," he said, and rolled off.

Dipper groaned. He tried to sit up, but it felt as if he had been run over by a tractor.

"Do you know how to play Bull Run?" Fish Patterson was leaning against the playground wall. He hadn't been involved in the fight at all.

Barkbelly grunted. "What?"

"Do you know how to play Bull Run?"

Barkbelly shook his head. "No. I don't."

"Then I'll teach you," said Fish. "You can't be in the gang if you don't know how to play."

Barkbelly stared at him. "You want me to be in your gang?"

"Yeah. If you're not in my gang, you'll be in Tie Donahue's, and that would be infinitely worse," said Fish. "You can fight. I want you with me, not against me."

"And why would I want to be in your gang?"

"It's the best," said Fish, grinning.

Barkbelly didn't want to ask, but he had to know. "What would I have to do to join?"

"Nothing," said Fish. "You've done it already. Dipper has the bruises to prove it."

Dipper grunted and rubbed his ribs.

"So—what do you say? Are you in?"

Barkbelly shook his head in amazement. What a strange world it was. "Yes," he said at last. "I'm in."

Chapter 4

*B*arkbelly swallowed the last mouthful of sausage roll and
wiped his hands on his britches. He wished he could
have another, but he wasn't allowed. His mother had banned
him from the kitchen. It was the first day of spring and the
Gantrys were throwing a Blossom Party. Pumpkin wanted the
food to be perfect but Barkbelly kept dipping his finger into
the bowls. No wonder she wanted him outside.

Barkbelly found his father sitting in the back garden,
sharpening an ax. An untidy pile of logs and branches
sprawled on the ground at his feet.

"I'll split the logs," said Gable, "but you can help with the
branches. If we saw them down a bit, we can build a bonfire for
tonight. I'll saw, you hold. It won't take long."

It didn't. Twenty minutes later, all the branches had been
sawed and the bonfire had been built. Only the logs remained.
They had been sawed already, but they were too bulky to fit
into the kitchen stove. They needed splitting.

"I'll do these," said Gable. "You go inside. Start getting
cleaned up." He picked up a log and stood it on the chopping
block. Then he took up his ax, swung it in the air and—

26

smack!—the blade thumped down onto the log, splitting it into four clean pieces. Gable winced with pain.

"Are you all right, Papa?"

"Aye, I'm fine," said Gable heavily. "It's just a bit of an ache. You can't work all day and not feel an ache or two. Not at my age!" He bent down slowly and picked up another log.

"Let me help," said Barkbelly. "If I feed you the logs, you won't have to bend down."

Gable leaned on his ax. "I suppose it makes sense," he said at last. "It would save my old bones."

So they started. Barkbelly knelt at Gable's feet, and as soon as a log was split, he put another one onto the chopping block. Father and son made a good team. They soon settled into an easy rhythm and the pile of logs shrank rapidly. Barkbelly felt incredibly happy. How could he feel otherwise? It was a gloriously sunny day, he was helping his father, they were having fireworks later . . . and there was a fox behind the apple tree! He could see it out of the corner of his eye. It was eating something.

And before Barkbelly knew what he was doing, he was turning his head to look, and he didn't pull his hands away, and the old man was getting tired, and he didn't see and—*smack!*—the ax chopped Barkbelly's hand right off! It shot through the air and landed in the wood basket.

"*Ohhh!*" cried Barkbelly. "*Ohhh! My hand! Papa! My hand!*"

Gable dropped the ax and looked down in horror. "Ohhh! Blessed monkeys!" he cried. "What have I done? What have I done? Oh, my poor boy!" He sank to his knees and took Barkbelly into his arms. "Oh, I'm a stupid old man! A stupid old man! You should never have been doing that! Oh! Oh!"

He hugged Barkbelly so tight, the boy could barely breathe. "Are you in pain?" he asked. "Son! Are you in pain?"

"No," said Barkbelly. "No. No pain." But he did feel faint. His chest started to heave. He thought he would cry, but no tears came.

"What's to be done?" cried Gable. "What's to be done? Oh, I'm a stupid old man!" He rocked Barkbelly like a baby, back and forth.

"Papa," said Barkbelly, "look."

But Gable wasn't listening. His mind was whirring like beetle wings. "What's to be done?" he said again. "What's to be done? Think. Think!"

"Papa!" said Barkbelly urgently, pulling himself free. "Papa! Look!"

Gable looked. Barkbelly was holding up the stump of his arm. It was oozing a strange white sap. But it was also vibrating—so fast, it showed only as a shimmer over the cut surface.

"Is that hurting?" whispered Gable.

"No," said Barkbelly. "It's tingling. Oh!"

"What's . . . Oh, my!"

The hand was growing back. As they watched, the stump seemed to stretch and four knobbly bits appeared at the end. From these new knuckles grew four new fingers. Then a fifth knobble appeared on the side of the hand and out came a new thumb. From beginning to end it had taken barely two minutes, but the new hand was perfect. Barkbelly wiggled his fingers. They all worked. No one would ever guess it wasn't the hand he was born with.

"I can't believe it," said Gable. "I saw it with my own eyes, but still I can't believe it. What an extraordinary thing!"

"Where's my old hand?" said Barkbelly, suddenly remembering. "I think I saw it go into the wood basket."

They tipped out the logs, but the hand wasn't in there. They searched the ground, moved every log, but it had vanished.

"How will I explain this to your mother?" said Gable. "First you have a hand—then you don't—then you do—and then we lose one altogether! Oh, she is going to be devilish annoyed with me. I should never have let you help in the first place. It's all my fault."

"Do we have to tell her?" said Barkbelly. "She would be so upset. The hand has grown back. She need never know."

Gable shook his head. "I don't like keeping secrets and that's a fact. But I don't like hurting your mother either. And today, well . . . it's a special day. I can't tell you how much she loves her Blossom Parties! Every year I say to her, 'We'll just have a few friends round this time,' and before I know it, she's invited the whole village, planned the food and ordered the fireworks! She was up before the cockerel this morning, ready to start baking. Couldn't sleep, she was that excited. Something like this would ruin her day. Really, it would."

"So we'll keep it quiet, then?" said Barkbelly.

"Aye," Gable agreed. "We'll keep it quiet. Then we can have the best party that Pumbleditch has ever seen!"

And they did. That night, the sky was aflame with fireworks. The air was sweet with song. The ground rumbled with the tumble of dancing feet and every plate was licked clean. And the secret was kept between them, like a leaf pressed in the pages of a book.

Chapter 5

*B*arkbelly lay in bed, listening. It was the middle of the night, but something was happening outside. He peered out of the window. It was dark. Heavy clouds were hiding the moon. But he could see shapes. Huge creatures pulling long covered wagons. Figures walking beside them, muffled and caped. Lights flickering and swaying like smugglers' lamps. A magical, silent, otherworldly procession was disappearing into the darkness, heading for the village. Carmenero's Circus had arrived.

On his way to school, Barkbelly saw the camp. It was on Farmer Gubbin's land. There were dozens of painted wagons with golden tassels that swung in the breeze. There were animal cages with glistening silver bars and ornate roofs. There were elephants, ankle-tethered with golden chains. There were campfires with steaming kettles and pans of porridge slung over the flames. And there were people—wild, exotic circus folk with embroidered waistcoats and extravagant cloaks. Women with pinned-up hair and easy smiles. Men with dark eyes and gray chins. Children in hand-me-down costumes with unwashed faces and hands full of toasted buns.

Barkbelly was speechless with the wonder of it all.

*　　*　　*

By evening, the circus was ready to open. Barkbelly left the cottage at dusk and cut through the orchard toward Farmer Gubbin's land. A low mist was rising. The air was still and curiously charged. He walked on, his heart drumming with excitement. And when he emerged from the shadow of the trees and saw the massive Stardust Palace rising from the mist like an Eastern temple, he caught his breath and bit his lip. It was too wonderful for words. As he walked through the long grass, his legs grew damp and sticky with seeds, but he didn't notice. He was looking at the lanterns, bright as beads, strung between the wagons. He could hear the hum of the crowd, the roar of a lion, the crack of a whip.

As he drew closer, he could smell cotton candy and hot honeyed nuts. Sausages. Soap. Wood smoke. Tobacco smoke. Sharp, sulfurous *gun* smoke!

Barkbelly was lost in a joyous, bewildering chaos of color and sensation. His fingers closed round the money in his pocket. Three precious coins that would buy a ticket into the heart of this paradise.

"There y'are, Bark!" cried Fish Patterson, emerging from the crowd with his gang dancing behind him. "Where've you been? We were starting to think you weren't coming! What've you been doing?"

"Just looking," said Barkbelly, and they all nodded. Nothing more needed to be said.

"Let's buy our tickets," said Moth. "Then we can be ready to get the best seats when they start letting people in."

Half an hour later, Barkbelly was sitting in a ringside seat, with the pink scent of his cotton candy mingling with the raw smell of sawdust. Above him, he saw the rigging for the trapeze

artists: a riot of ropes, knots, ladders and platforms. At the back of the ring there was a velvet curtain: midnight blue with golden tassels. Two circus girls stood nearby, waiting to open and close it: long-limbed beauties with painted faces and curled hair. Just above the curtain was a carved wooden platform with lanterns dangling from it. They jiggled as the musicians climbed on. And what a raggle-taggle band they were! Mismatched costumes with a scrap of velvet here and a bit of brocade there; silver buttons and feathered caps; waxed mustaches and clipped beards. Barkbelly thought they were fantastic.

Suddenly the lamps hanging round the tent were being turned down. The audience was settling. The band was playing. The beautiful girls were pulling the curtain aside . . . and out came a pig! A giant curly-coated pig, ridden by a monkey in a shiny top hat. The pig tore round the ring, then skidded to a halt, spun round and round, and reared up on its back legs. The monkey took off its hat and waved. The audience gasped, but there was no time for anyone to catch their breath because the curtain was whisked aside again and in raced a dozen more pigs! The ring was full of snorts and snouts and trotters and tails. Sawdust swirled at their feet; sweat beads flew like crystal flies. The musicians played louder and faster, while the platform swayed and shuddered beneath them.

The crowd hollered in a frenzy of excitement and then—*crash!*—the mighty cymbals rang, the pigs trotted out and, to the sound of a single violin, a young girl entered the ring. She curtsied and smiled—and everyone fell in love with her. She was exquisite: as perfect as a dewdrop. A single rope ladder fell from above and she began to climb up, up, up toward the dark roof of the tent, where lanterns shone like stars in heaven. Once she reached the top, she climbed onto a tiny platform and pirouetted, while everyone below stomped and cheered. Then she started dancing across a silver tightrope that ran between the tent poles.

Down below, Barkbelly was spellbound.

She shimmered.

She shone.

She danced like a snowflake.

She was brave.

She was wonderful.

She was *falling*. . . .

She fell like rain from the darkness above. A scrap of white, like a dove with a broken wing. People screamed, covered their mouths with their hands and stared in horror. Barkbelly jumped to his feet and yelled, "*No-o-o-o-o-o-o!*"

. . . and she opened an umbrella and started to float down to earth. Light as thistledown, she landed on her feet without even disturbing the sawdust.

The crowd went wild. The roar was so loud that the girl was almost blown over by it. Everyone shouted and screamed at once—in excitement, in relief, in sheer wonder at the brilliance of it all.

Barkbelly glanced across the ring and saw Candy Pie. She was bouncing up and down in her seat, hugging herself in delight. And three rows behind her, Freckle Flannagan was in tears. *Freckle Flannagan! In tears!* It was unbelievable. Everyone thought Freckle was a boy. She had cropped hair, never wore dresses and could spit farther than Moth Williams. No one would have dreamed she could cry like a girl, but there she was, sitting in a daze, with tears shining on her cheeks.

Barkbelly wondered how the show could possibly get any better, but it did. Carmenero's Circus was as sensational as its posters promised. Act followed act in an endlessly entertaining spectacle. There were acrobats, jugglers and fire-eaters. Trapeze artists who scythed the air like swallows. Shadow lions with ghost-gray coats and tasseled tails. A strong man who wrestled with iron bars, bending them into horseshoes round his neck while his veins bulged blue. A human cannonball who flew to the top of the tent and nose-dived down into a net. And there was a clown called Slippers who fired a bubble gun straight at Farmer Bunkum, soaking his pants, while everyone howled with laughter and said he couldn't have chosen a better target.

All too soon, Carmenero strode into the ring and announced the finale. The band, dripping with sweat, played a circus march and all the performers stomped round the ring. They waved, smiled, blew kisses to the crowd. Then someone screamed. The performers scattered—and in ran ten skunks with blue ribbons round their necks.

They charged across the ring in all directions, jumped up onto the little wooden wall that surrounded it, pointed their bottoms at the audience, lifted their tails and—*pssss!*—long streams of stink arced through the air and showered the crowd. Everyone squealed and squirmed in their seats. But the air was filled with the smell of roses! A warm, glorious scent, like a garden on a warm summer's evening. And everyone sighed, and laughed, and hugged each other, and the show was over.

Chapter 6

fterward—when the crowd had gone home, the costumes had been hung up, the makeup washed off, the
popcorn swept up, the animals fed—Barkbelly sat on the steps
of a wagon and listened to circus tales. Jewel, the storyteller,
was the oldest woman he had ever seen. Her face was nothing
but wrinkles. Her hair was as silver as the rings on her twisted
fingers. But her eyes shone like a girl's as she told him about
her days as a trapeze artist.

"I performed with my sisters," she said. "We were called
the Dragonflies. We wore spangled costumes—dark purple,
blue, green—and when we flew through the air, we were a
beautiful sight. Have you ever watched dragonflies? You know
the way they hang in the air? As if there's nothing holding
them up except their own joy of flying? That's how we looked.
Especially my little sister, Rain. When she flew, people forgot
to breathe. She was so lovely." The old woman smiled and
sipped her tea. "You remember Gossamer—the girl who
danced on the high wire tonight? She's Rain's great-
granddaughter. She's got something of Rain's spirit in her,
that's for sure."

Jewel paused and peered into the darkness. She beckoned. "Come! Come! Don't be shy. Everyone's welcome here."

Freckle Flannagan slid out of the shadows and joined them. Barkbelly saw a strange glow on her face that he'd never seen before. She looked quite different: suddenly grown up and yet very young, both at the same time.

They sat outside the wagon until well past midnight, Barkbelly the wooden boy and Freckle the reluctant girl. Above them, the constellations grazed across the night sky. Beneath them, the grass grew damp with dew. But still they sat on, listening to Jewel's tales. They were stories she had told a hundred times before, but her smile suggested she'd happily tell them a hundred times more.

Her words flowed like wild honey, and Barkbelly and Freckle feasted like forest bears. For three magical nights, when the show was over they came to listen. On the final night, Jewel talked about her love of the circus.

"In this life," she said, "I have been blessed. I have had the love of two families: my real family and my circus family—all the people you see around you now. The circus is a magical place to be. It doesn't matter who you are or where you come from; you are what you are and that's all that matters. And if you want to be something else—well, you can! Circus folk are like caterpillars. Every night, we put on our glitter and our spangles. We paint our faces. We smile. And out we come like butterflies. And just for those few minutes when we're in the ring, with the lanterns shining down on us, we are whatever we want to be. That is an amazing thing.

"There's a lot of love here. On the road, traveling around, we all work together. We have to. And sometimes it's hard work, and sometimes it rains and you're soaked to the skin, but you go on. Because you know there will be better times. Magical times. On the trapeze, when you see the faces looking up at you like daisies in a field. Or late at night, when the campfires are burning and you're sitting under the stars, and all the people you love are around you. . . . Oh, those are very special moments and I wouldn't have missed them for the world. Not for anything."

By morning, the camp had disappeared. Barkbelly saw an empty space where the great tent had been. Flattened grass where the wagons had stood. Flame-blackened circles where the cooking fires had glowed. All that remained of the circus was a forgotten poster, clinging damply to a tree. Everything seemed gray, forlorn and desperately ordinary.

But Fish was still breathless with excitement.

"Have you heard?" he gasped, running into the playground. "Someone's run off with the circus!"

"No!" cried the gang in unison. "Who?"

"I don't know," said Fish, coughing as he tried to catch his breath. "But I do know it's a girl."

Barkbelly closed his eyes and saw Freckle, sitting on the wagon step beside him. He could remember the look on her face: her shining eyes, with that faraway, lost look; her glowing cheeks, pink with excitement; her teeth, biting her bottom lip as she dreamed of running away.

"It's Freckle Flannagan," he said.

"Can't be," said Log. "She's there—look."

Freckle was walking in through the playground gates, swinging her bag and singing one of the circus tunes.

Barkbelly ran over to her.

"I thought you'd run away with the circus!" he said.

"Why?" asked Freckle.

"Because someone has," explained Barkbelly.

"No—why me?" said Freckle. "Why did you think it was *me?*"

"Because—" He stopped in a fluster, realizing that his reasons weren't entirely complimentary.

"Because you think I'm a *misfit?*" pressed Freckle, reading his mind. "You think that speech about wanting to be someone else would appeal to me?"

Barkbelly squirmed. Freckle smiled and went on, enjoying herself.

"You think I want to be a boy? And if I ran away with the circus, I could pretend to be one? Listen. As much as I loved Jewel, as much as I loved the stories and the things she told us, I would never run off with the circus. *Never.* I want to be a doctor. I have to study. And I don't want to be a boy, I want to be an adult. But at the moment I'm not. And if I'm looking for company, well, I prefer boys. I don't really like girly things. I don't like dressing up, or fiddling with hair, or whispering in corners, or telling secrets. And let's face it, the world doesn't need another Candy Pie. Incidentally, she's the one who's run off with the circus."

"Candy Pie? Are you sure?"

"Absolutely," said Freckle. "I saw her mother leaving their house this morning. She's going after her."

The bell rang. Barkbelly and Freckle went into school and the day began. Life was back to normal. It was as if the circus had never been there at all. Except there was one empty chair in the classroom and one empty hook in the cloakroom. And there was silence when Miss Dillwater reached Candy Pie's name on the register.

Chapter 7

*B*arkbelly sat on the fence outside the cottage, watching his father plant cabbages. School was over for summer. Ahead of him stretched the long, empty holidays, with nothing to do but laze and dream.

"Son," said Gable Gantry, "a big strapping lad like you can't sit in the sun all day for weeks, doing nothing. It'll addle your brain. You need a job. A proper job, working with men. And—" He paused dramatically. "I've got you one!"

Barkbelly couldn't believe what he was hearing. This was terrible news.

"You start tomorrow," said Gable proudly. "Working for Farmer Muckledown. Helping with the urchins."

"What's an urchin?"

"What's an urchin? Bless me, son, don't you know? What do they teach you at that school? It's a hedgehog! That's what an urchin is. But Farmer Muckledown doesn't keep ordinary ones, like you find in a hedgerow. Oh, no! His are much grander than that."

"What will I be doing?"

"Oh, fetching and carrying. Cleaning the sheds. Things like that."

"Will he be paying me?"

"Of course he'll be paying you! It's a proper job, like I said. Anyway, you'll find out all these things tomorrow."

Muckledown Farm lay on the far side of Ferny Wood, so Barkbelly had to start out early. The mist was still ribboning across the fields when he saw the sign:

MUCKLEDOWN FARM
~ HOME OF CHAMPION URCHINS ~
Proprietor: Farmer Mallet Muckledown

Beyond the gates, a long gravel path led straight to a farmhouse surrounded by barns and sheds. But Barkbelly was more interested in the activity to the left of the path. A man was driving a herd of hedgehogs toward a small leafy copse and they were *huge*. As big as pigs! They were ambling along, snorting and snuffling, completely ignoring the farm dogs that snapped impatiently at their heels.

The hedgehogs disappeared into the trees and the man waved at Barkbelly. "That's them settled," he said, coming over. "Plenty of worms and such in there."

"I had no idea they were so big," said Barkbelly. "They're enormous."

"Oh, they're not *all* that big," said Farmer Muckledown. "They come in different sizes for different kinds of jobs. Some of them are no bigger than my thumb."

"But what do you use them for?" asked Barkbelly as they walked into the farmyard. "And why do you need different sizes?"

Farmer Muckledown laughed out loud and slapped him on the back. "You've got a lot to learn, m'lad! But you couldn't ask for a better teacher. No one knows more about urchins than me and that's a fact! Here on this farm, I breed the best urchins in the whole of the country. It's true! Champion urchins, they are. You've heard of the Urchin Cup?"

Barkbelly shook his head.

"No? It's famous! Every year in Fieldhaven they hold the Urchin Show and people come from all over Lindenland, bringing the best animals they have. There are lots of prizes to be won, and I've won them all at one time or another, but the one that everyone wants to win is the Urchin Cup. Now, to win that you must have the finest urchin in the show. And, my young friend, I am proud to say that I have won that cup every year for the last ten years. And *this* beauty is the one I hope to win with this year."

Farmer Muckledown opened a barn door and the stiff smell of urchin punched Barkbelly in the face. As his eyes grew accustomed to the gloom, he could see a peat-filled pen with a water dish, a bowl full of worms—and a huge pile of sleeping spikes.

"Isn't she gorgeous?" whispered the farmer. "She's called Bramble."

Barkbelly nodded, slack-jawed.

The urchin was massive. Her spikes were as long as arrows, glossy black and tipped with amber. She was fast asleep, curled up in a tight ball.

Barkbelly sighed. "She's *magnificent*."

"Aye, she is," said Farmer Muckledown, puffed up with pride. "Just wait till you see her face."

With that, he made a strange cooing sound and the urchin

43

began to uncurl. Barkbelly saw a long furry snout with a glistening black nose, twitching whiskers and eyes as dark as destiny.

"There now," said the farmer. "Isn't she just fine?"

Barkbelly nodded. But those eyes . . . Beautiful though they were, they were full of sadness. And just for a moment Barkbelly had a vision of a forest. Of trees and snow. Secret, silent spaces. Wild freedom. And suddenly he knew what the urchin had lost, because it was something he had lost too. But until that moment he hadn't known he had lost it.

Farmer Muckledown took Barkbelly into other barns to show him more urchins. They came in all sizes and colors, from babies like little pink toothbrushes to boars as big as beer barrels.

Behind the barns were the workshops, where a team of inventors worked on new designs and ideas—all made from urchin spikes. Barkbelly was drawn to the display cases. Inside there were all kinds of brushes and gadgets, and a machine for picking up fallen leaves. It was like a bicycle: pedal-powered, with a high seat, handlebars and extra-wide wheels studded with spikes. Beside the cabinets he found a strange contraption—a long brush attached lengthways to a post in the ground.

"Cow scratcher," said Farmer Muckledown. "We make all kinds of things here! But enough of this." He slapped Barkbelly heavily on the back. "I'm sure you're wondering what you'll be doing, eh?"

Barkbelly nodded.

"Well," he said, "when your father told me all about you— about how, er, *special* you are—I was mighty keen to have you. Mighty keen!"

"Why?" said Barkbelly with a frown. "I have no experience working with urchins. I have no experience at all. This is my first job."

"But you are—how can I put this?—*exceptionally qualified* for the job. You're wooden, my lad! Wooden! You won't feel the spikes. You'll be able to handle urchins as if they were no more bother than fluffy chicks."

"So I'll be working with the urchins? I thought I would be cleaning dirty sheds."

"Bless me, no!" laughed Farmer Muckledown. "You won't be cleaning! I want you on Spike Extraction, first thing in the morning. In fact, you might as well run off home now. Get some rest before tomorrow. You'll need it."

Barkbelly went home. He spent the afternoon making a kite, but he had no desire to fly it. He had an early night, but he didn't sleep. His head was full of questions. What on earth was *spike extraction?* Obviously it meant getting the spikes out of the urchins, but how did they do it? Sometimes, in class, Fish would lean forward and pull a single hair from Pillow Anderson's head. She would cry out in pain, her eyes brimming with tears, and that was just one hair. How much more pain must there be for an urchin, having its prickles yanked out? It would be excru-ciating. Surely they didn't just sit there and take it? No. They would be furious. They would ram and butt, slash and tear. No wonder Farmer Muckledown was interested in him. He would probably be given the biggest boars on the farm and he would have to pull out all their spikes, one by one.

Sleep finally came. A muddled sleep full of spikes, teeth and enormous metal tweezers. When he eventually woke up, exhausted and confused, the sun was already high. It was time to go.

Chapter 8

*B*arkbelly heard the screams long before he entered the farmyard. Then he saw farmhands running back and forth with poles and pitchforks, their faces blanched with fear.

The shed at the center of the commotion was a low, pine-clad building with the words SPIKE EXTRACTION painted on a sign outside. He went in. The noise was deafening: a wild, animal wail and, beneath it, a muffled moan. Men were crowding round one of the pens. He edged closer, peered between shoulders and saw a nightmarish scene.

In the pen was an immense black urchin. He was rubbing himself up against the shed wall, as if he were scratching an itch, and the moan was coming from the wall. Barkbelly suddenly realized why. The urchin had a man trapped against it and was driving his spikes into him. The farm workers were frantically pushing poles between man and beast, trying to pry them apart. They were succeeding but it was taking too long.

"Aha!" cried a gruff voice, and Barkbelly found himself grabbed roughly by the shoulders. "Just the man!"

Farmer Muckledown pulled Barkbelly behind him with

one hand and opened a gate into the pen with the other. "You pull Brick out of there. *Now, m'lad, now!*"

He pushed Barkbelly into the pen.

Barkbelly had no time to think. Brains gave way to instinct. He grabbed hold of the injured farmhand and dragged him over to the far side of the pen, where waiting hands lifted him out, placed him on a makeshift stretcher and carried him away. For him, the drama was over. But not for Barkbelly.

The urchin was furious. It squealed and spat and pushed against the restraining poles.

"We can't hold him!" shouted one of the men. "Get out while you can!"

Barkbelly tried to move but he couldn't. His legs wouldn't work.

"He's going!"

The boar smashed through the poles, lowered his head and charged. *Oof!* A long black snout slammed into Barkbelly's backside and tossed him into the air, out of the pen, over the men and into a pile of doings.

"Mud and moonbeams!" cried Farmer Muckledown, pulling him to his feet. "I thought we'd lost you! Have you broken anything?"

"Er—no," said Barkbelly. "There's nothing to break. I feel a bit woozy, though."

"Aye, you will. That was a belter of a blow. I don't know how you're still standing. Well done, m'lad. Well done! And well done, the rest of you too. Pot—get that kettle on! Shoe? Be a good lad and run to the kitchen. Ask Missus Muckledown for a carrot cake, eh?"

The farmer threw his arm round Barkbelly's shoulders and beamed at him. "I reckon we've all earned a piece."

And with a mopping of brows and a shaking of hands, the men swaggered to the canteen with Barkbelly counted among them.

"Will he be all right?" asked Barkbelly. He licked his finger and dabbed at the cake crumbs on his empty plate.

"Course he will," said Saddle Yates from the next chair. "He's a strong lad, is Brick Pullman. He'll be fine when the blisters heal."

"Blisters?"

"Oh, aye," said Weasel Watkins, standing by the window. "That was no ordinary urchin back there, you know. He's a Black-Backed Highland Hunting Hog. Very dangerous. Those spikes of his are poisonous—if they prick flesh, they cause blisters. Giant, pus-filled blisters."

"And they smell," chipped in Shoe Mercer, who had fetched the cake.

"Aye, they smell. The doctor has to clean them before they burst. First he pricks them with a long, *long* pin"—he held up his hands to show Barkbelly just how long he meant—"then he squeezes them and out comes this stuff. . . . Oh, you would not believe the smell. It could turn up the toes on a dead man."

"Do you *have* to go to the doctor?" asked Barkbelly, fascinated.

"No," said Saddle. "You don't *have* to go to him. But if you don't, the blisters burst anyway and they make a terrible mess."

"Once there was a man here called Hammer Rowland," said Nail Adams, a gnomish man sitting on an upturned barrel. "He was blistered. Said he didn't want the doctor. And when they burst, the mess was so bad that they had to burn the bed."

"And the carpet."

"And the curtains."

"And the wallpaper. The pus splattered everywhere and it . . . *soaked in.*" Nail scrunched up his nose in disgust. "The smell was awful. They just couldn't get rid of it."

"Time to get back to work, lads!" boomed Farmer Muckledown, coming into the canteen. "Barkbelly, I want you to carry on with Blister."

"*Blister?*" said Barkbelly. "You don't mean . . ."

"I do! That big boar we've just been wrestling with. Blister, he's called. S'pose the men told you why?" His eyes were twinkling. Barkbelly suddenly thought of Fish and his wicked teasing.

He relaxed. "Were they pulling my leg?"

"Oh, no! They were telling the truth!" Farmer Muckledown grinned. "That old boar can cause grievous damage, make no mistake. But not to *you,* boy! Not to you! You're wooden, see?" And he rapped his knuckles against Barkbelly's arm.

"But he's vicious!" wailed Barkbelly in a panic. "He *attacked* Brick Pullman."

But the farmer wasn't listening. He marched Barkbelly back into the extraction shed, despite his frenzied pleading.

"Listen," he said when they reached the boar's pen. "He's calmed down now. You go in there, I'll switch on the machine and you just move this nozzle all over his body. See?"

Barkbelly saw that Farmer Muckledown was holding a long tube with a copper funnel at one end and a flat leather bag at the other. He had no idea how it worked.

"Ready? In you go," said the farmer, and he opened the gate and pushed Barkbelly forward. Then he handed him the funnel end of the strange contraption, bent down, flicked a switch somewhere and—*wooooofff!*—the leather bag inflated like bagpipes as wind rushed through. When Barkbelly put his fingers over the top of the funnel, he could feel the suction at work.

At the sound of the machine, the great urchin opened a dark eye and scanned the pen. He had been dozing in the shadows, grunting musically to himself, but now it seemed he was being disturbed again.

He peered at the intruder. He sniffed the air. Wood? This was something new. He heaved himself onto his feet slowly, heavily. The spines along his back mountained into a black ridge. He sniffed again and shifted his great bristly bulk, steadying himself. He waited for the wooden one to move.

And Barkbelly did move, but very, *very* slowly. He inched his way forward, not even lifting his feet. He just slid them toward the terrible Blister, hoping the urchin wouldn't notice. As he drew closer, his hand started to shake. The long tube felt slippery in his grip. He was going to drop it. He curled his fingers tighter and started to stretch out his arm. Closer, closer . . . the funnel was almost touching the beast's flank. Closer . . . closer . . . contact! He felt the funnel seal tight against the boar's hide; the suction took hold. Any second now, Blister would feel the pain as his spikes were ripped out. The screams would begin. Barkbelly closed his eyes and braced himself for the attack.

But then a curious thing happened. Barkbelly heard a giggle. A high-pitched, girly sort of giggle. A bit like Candy Pie's. Surely she wasn't here to see this!

His eyes snapped open in horror at the thought. But it wasn't Candy. It was the urchin. The terrifying, ferocious

Blister was *giggling* as the funnel sucked. Barkbelly saw the bristles were being pulled out at the root—where the funnel had been there was nothing but a line of smooth, tawny skin.

But Blister wasn't feeling any pain. He felt he was being tickled all over. Within seconds, his giggle had turned into a warm, throaty hum.

Barkbelly found he was smiling. He couldn't help it. And when the great beast flopped down onto his side and started kicking his legs in the air, he laughed out loud, though whether in pleasure or relief he didn't know.

"He likes it!" he cried over his shoulder to Farmer Muckledown. "He really likes it!"

"Of course he does!" shouted the farmer over the wheezing of the extraction machine. "They all do!"

Too soon it was over. The farmer switched off the machine. Barkbelly climbed out of the pen and saw that the leather bag was bulging with spikes. Blister, on the other hand, was completely bald. The huge, naked dome of his body shone even in the dull gloom of the shed, but he was rolling around in the dirt quite happily, coating himself in dust and muck.

"I can't believe it!" said Barkbelly. "I can't believe it was that easy. I thought it was going to hurt him. I thought he would attack me."

"No! Not old Blister. He's soft as snow most of the time."

"But he attacked Brick Pullman!"

"Aye, he did," agreed the farmer. "But that had nothing to do with the spike extraction. Listen. Urchins love having their prickles out. These aren't ordinary wild urchins we've got here, you know! They're specially bred. Every summer they shed their spines, soon as it gets hot. We could leave them to get on with it naturally, like, but they would shed them one at a time, all over the place. We'd have to spend hours collecting them and sorting them. This way, with the machine, we get them all out in one go and they just need bundling together. And, as you can see, the urchins feel a whole lot better without them. It's cooler for them, and they can get rid of their fleas and ticks. And urchins have a ton of those, believe me! And with the spikes out of the way, they can roll in the dust and that seems to kill the little blighters. That's what he's doing now, ain't you, boy?"

"But Brick Pullman . . . ," Barkbelly persisted.

"Brick Pullman is a great hulking lump of a lad. Good-hearted, mind, but clumsy. So, in he goes with his big fat feet, in his heavy boots, not looking—and he stands on Blister's foot. Well, Blister turned on him. I think that's fair enough. I wouldn't like it if Brick Pullman stomped on my foot, would you?"

Barkbelly leaned on the bars of the pen and gazed at the great boar. It rolled and grunted like a baby with its diaper off. "No," he said with a smile. "I wouldn't like it either."

Chapter 9

*B*arkbelly adored his job. He loved walking to the farm through the morning mist. He loved walking home along lanes heavy with pollen and humming with bees. He loved the urchins, and Farmer Muckledown kept his word: Barkbelly was never sent to clean the sheds. Most days he worked on Spike Extraction and Grading. All the spikes had to be inspected, sorted, bundled and tied after extraction, and with his wooden fingers, Barkbelly could do this in a fraction of the time it took the others.

In his spare moments, he liked to inspect the prize hogs. The Urchin Cup was approaching and everyone wanted Farmer Muckledown to win it again. His best hope this year was Bramble, the sad-eyed sow. She was a Golden-Spiked Far Forest Hog—a rare, ancient breed from the Northern Wilderness. Mostly her spikes were black, but nestling between her ears were a handful of short golden ones. They were gorgeous. But what were they used for? Barkbelly knew that every spike had a particular use on Muckledown Farm but he couldn't remember seeing anything golden in the display cabinets.

When the time came to extract Bramble's spikes, she

purred like a cat and tilted her head so he could get every last prickle. Then she rolled happily in the dirt while he went to the sorting shed to empty the extractor bag. But when he opened the bag, all the spikes were black. The golden ones were missing.

Barkbelly was horrified. Those were surely the most precious spikes of any urchin and he had lost them! Farmer Muckledown would be furious.

He ran back to the extraction shed to examine Bramble. The spikes had been pulled, no doubt about that. The skin between her ears was quite smooth. The spikes must have gone into the bag. They couldn't go anywhere else.

Barkbelly went back to the sorting table and frantically turned the bag inside out. But the spikes weren't there. They had gone. What if Farmer Muckledown thought he had stolen them? It was too horrible to think about.

Just then, Barkbelly felt a hand on his shoulder. *Farmer Muckledown!* No. Pot Williamson, the oldest worker on the farm. He was a kindly man who seemed to do nothing but smoke his pipe and drink tea, but Barkbelly knew the other men revered him. Pot had worked with urchins for seventy years ("Bred 'em, fed 'em and wed 'em," according to his wife, Plum). What he didn't know about urchins wasn't worth knowing.

"Made you jump, did I, boy?" laughed the old man. "Got something to hide?"

"Oh, Mister Williamson, sir, something terrible's happened!" wailed Barkbelly. "I've lost Bramble's golden spikes! I know I extracted them. I know I did. But they're not in the bag. I've lost them!" Barkbelly held his head in his hands and trembled with the worry of it all.

Pot smiled. "You can't lose what you never had," he said.

"But I did have them!" cried Barkbelly. "They were in this bag!"

"Oh, no, they weren't," chuckled the old man. "And I'll tell you why. They never left her head."

Barkbelly stared at him, struggling to make sense of what he had just heard.

"Those spikes are still there," said Pot. "Deep inside Bramble's head. She pulled them in as soon as you started extracting. *Pulled them in*, like little snails going back into their shells. I know it's true—I've seen her do it myself. And when the rest of her spikes start growing back, well, those golden ones will grow right alongside them."

Barkbelly was speechless. If it weren't for the fact that the golden spikes had disappeared into thin air, he never would have believed it.

"Has no one ever managed to extract the golden spikes?" he asked.

"Not on this farm," said Pot, filling his pipe. "But I did hear tell of a young chap over at Westmeadow some years ago. Seems he gave a Golden-Spike a sleeping potion of some kind, and when she was asleep, he pulled one out with a pair of pliers. Well, she didn't stay asleep for long! She woke up in a real fury and bit him in the leg, right through to the bone. And it was a strange wound. Wouldn't heal. The whole leg went black within days and had to be cut off."

"But he got the spike out?" Barkbelly persisted.

"Yes, but . . ." The old man paused, savoring the moment. "The spike didn't last more than a couple of minutes. It turned to dust and blew away on the wind."

"Is that a true story?"

"Yes," said the old man. "It is! And if you go to the Urchin Show this year, you'll probably see that young fella there. Rope Daniels, he's called. Course, he's not so young now, but he's still got the leg missing. You ask him, if you don't believe me."

"Oh, it's not that I don't believe you," said Barkbelly hurriedly. "It's just so strange. If the spikes can't be *pulled* out, do the urchins ever shed them?"

"Well, I've never found one," said the old man. "But that doesn't mean they don't. Perhaps they turn to dust even when they're shed. But there's something special about those golden spikes. Way up north, in the Far Forest, there are caves. Explorers found them years ago. And they do say that a whole race of people lived in those caves once, but who they were no one knows. Anyway, the walls of those caves are covered in paintings, and I did hear that one of them shows an urchin just like our Bramble. And she's holding a golden spike in her mouth, as if she's planning to do something with it. Strange, eh? So perhaps the golden spikes *can* be shed at will. Instead of pulling them in, they just push them out for some special reason. And those spikes *don't* turn to dust. At least, not straightaway."

The old man cracked his knuckles. "So don't worry! You've done nothing wrong! Tell you what. I'll help you bundle these spikes and then we'll take Bramble over to the copse. And we won't hurry back."

Barkbelly gathered the first bundle while Pot fetched the string. What curious things these spikes were! With their sleek black shafts and amber tips, they looked like wizards' wands. But the power of a wizard was nothing compared to this pure, primal power. Bramble was a young animal, but her spikes held ancestral knowledge. Ancient secrets passed down through the generations, from urchin to urchin. Just touching them, Barkbelly could feel their potency.

"Pot," he said, "what are these black spikes used for?"

"Furniture, mostly. High-quality stuff. Nothing we could afford. Chair seats, mainly."

Barkbelly gasped. That such beautiful, magical things should be flattened by fat backsides in posh houses . . . What an ignorant world it was.

Chapter 10

Summer was nearly over. Barkbelly could hardly believe it, but when he looked at Bramble, there was the proof. Her spikes had regrown, as long and as lustrous as ever. And now, with the Urchin Show just one week away, Farmer Muckledown had given him the task of preparing Bramble for showing. Every day, he had to inspect her for fleas and ticks. Bramble enjoyed the attention. She would nuzzle him and sniff at his pockets for the mushrooms he brought her. But although she was friendly and clearly pleased to see him, Bramble never lost the sadness in her eyes, and Barkbelly couldn't help feeling she belonged in a forest, not a sty, no matter how well cared for she was.

One morning, Barkbelly was walking to work through the woods when he heard something heavy moving in the undergrowth. Entire bushes were shaking as it brushed by, snuffling and wheezing. Suddenly it stopped behind a mound of tangled briar.

Barkbelly crouched down, crept closer and peered through the greenery. It was Bramble! She had escaped! But how? Last night, he had locked her into her sty. He clearly remembered checking that the bolt was secure. So how . . . But looking again, he saw that this urchin was bigger, and its spikes were smoky gray instead of shadow black. And when the urchin turned and stared at him with hostile eyes, he knew this was an altogether wilder creature. A creature of wood and forest, mountain and stream.

Barkbelly froze, not daring to turn his back on the huge urchin in case it decided to charge. He wasn't worried for himself—he was indestructible!—but the urchin was strong, and if instinct took over . . . He didn't want to hurt the urchin. So he walked away backward, with his eyes downcast, until he regained the path. Then he turned and walked on, wondering whether to tell Farmer Muckledown. He would definitely be interested—Golden-Spiked Far Forest Hogs were rare, after all—but he would almost certainly want to capture it. Barkbelly couldn't bear that. He would keep his news secret.

That afternoon, Barkbelly was given the job of polishing all the medals, cups and trophies that Farmer Muckledown had won over the years at the Urchin Show. The farmer was planning to display them on his trade stand, so they had to shine. To Barkbelly's delight, he found that Pot was working alongside him. The old man talked for nearly an hour about past winners and losers at the show. Then he mentioned Bramble and started considering her chances.

Barkbelly seized his opportunity.

"Where did Bramble come from?" he asked. "Was she captured in Ferny Wood?"

"No, lad!" laughed Pot. "They don't live round here! All the big hogs—Golden-Spiked Far Forests, Black-Backed Highlands, Silver Ridgebacks, Mountain Bristlers, Coastal Long Snouts and what have you—they all come from the

Northern Wilderness. And that's a wild, unknowable place! The forests there are home to many a strange beast. Thumping great rabbits with feet like fence posts. Vicious great squirrels with teeth that'll take your hand off! You know the harness rats? They came from there originally. For some reason, animals in the Northern Wilderness grow to a massive size. Not all of them, mind. I believe the insects are pretty normal. It's mostly the furry ones. But what was I saying before I started on that?"

"I asked you where Bramble came from."

"So you did!" said Pot. "You asked me if she was caught in Ferny Wood. And no, she wasn't. She was bred right here on the farm." He spat on a medal and polished hard.

"So Farmer Muckledown used to have other Golden-Spikes?"

"Oh, yes," said Pot. "And all of them were champions." He picked a medal out of the pile still to be polished. "This one here was won by Blackbriar, Bramble's mother. And this one"—he fished out another—"was won by her father, Quill."

"Where are they now? Bramble's parents?"

Pot's eyes clouded. He put down the medals and fumbled in his pocket for his pipe. He filled it and lit it and puffed in silence awhile.

"They're gone," he said at last. "There was a sickness came across the land. No one knew what it was or where it came from. It fell like a shadow. It didn't affect all the urchins, mind—just certain breeds. The Golden-Spikes seemed to be especially vulnerable, and Muckledown had about thirty of them at the time: a couple of boars, a dozen breeding sows and loads of newborn hoglets. They all died, one by one, except for Bramble and Thorn." The old man sighed and sucked hard upon his pipe. "I don't know how those two survived, but they did. A right pair of fighters, they were!"

"Was Thorn Bramble's brother?" asked Barkbelly.

"No. Thorn was from another litter. He was her mate. They were inseparable. And I have to say, he was the finest urchin I have ever seen. He was *glorious*. And what a champion! He was unstoppable. Thorn won the Urchin Cup five years running. He won it last year. And he would win it again this year, easy, if he were still here."

"Did he die?" Barkbelly held his breath, waiting for the answer.

"Die? No, lad! He escaped!"

Chapter 11

*I*t was a disappointing day. Instead of the promised sun-shine, the sky was sodden with rain. Barkbelly hurried to work through the dripping wood with his shoulders hunched, his head down and his hands in his pockets. He was walking so fast that he had collided with the urchin before he knew it was there. He staggered back. Thorn bristled, his treacherous spikes rising like lances. His piggy eyes glittered.

Barkbelly stood quite still. Pot was right. Thorn was glorious: the most magnificent urchin Barkbelly had ever seen. He was leaner than Bramble and a shade lighter, but other than that he looked like her twin.

Thorn snorted and ambled closer. Then he did a curious thing. He put his snout into Barkbelly's palm and rubbed it up and down. He started to dribble, but still he rubbed, until the thick spittle was smeared all over Barkbelly's fingers. Then he sneezed, looked Barkbelly straight in the eyes and wandered off into the greenwood.

Barkbelly walked on. Thoughts whirred around his wooden head. Here was a dilemma! He wanted to ask Pot to explain the urchin's strange behavior, but then the secret would be out. Thorn would be hunted down before the day was through.

He was still lost in thought when he reached the farm. His first job of the day was Flea Inspection. Without even thinking what he was doing, he went straight to Bramble's pen, reached out to stroke her furry nose and—*thump!*—hit the floor with Bramble on top of him. She was whimpering and snorting, pummeling him with her paws, licking his hand over and over and over, delirious with the scent of her beloved Thorn.

Barkbelly started to giggle. Any other boy would have been crushed by her heftiness, but he was just tickled. He could hear her purring and humming, and when he suddenly cried out, "Enough! Enough!" and she stopped, he saw that the sadness had gone from her eyes. They shone, like the sun bursting through the clouds on a gray day. What was lost had been found.

And in that moment, Barkbelly saw that she was so beautiful and so wild, so desperate and so caged. And he felt his heart thumping against his wooden chest like a bear in a barrel.

He knew what he had to do.

Chapter 12

The cloud cover thickened throughout the day and by nightfall the temperature had plummeted. It seemed that nature too was plotting, keeping everyone indoors, far away from the sties.

Barkbelly clambered out of his bedroom window while his parents sat below, hugging the fire. He slunk through Ferny Wood, listening for sounds coming from the under-growth, but there was nothing unusual. Just falling leaves and restless rooks. But Barkbelly knew his every move was being shadowed by Thorn. He was out there, watching and waiting.

Muckledown Farm was asleep. The farmer and his family, the workers—everyone. Only the farm dogs stirred as Barkbelly approached, and as soon as they saw who it was, they wagged their tails and dropped their heads back onto their paws.

Barkbelly crept toward the urchin sties. Every door had a painted nameplate: Thistle . . . Prickler . . . Spike . . . Blister . . . Conker . . . Teasel . . . Bramble. Barkbelly slid back the bolt on Bramble's door, eased it open and there she was, anxiously sniffing the air. But then she caught a scent—long remembered, much loved—and suddenly she ran, across the yard and into the wood.

Barkbelly shut the sty door and slid back the bolt, then he too slipped into the shadows.

Halfway home, the clouds parted to reveal a silver moon, pale as a coin. Suddenly the wood was bathed in light. Shadows were caught behind every tree. And ahead on the path the urchins were waiting. Their eyes glittered, and Barkbelly saw that Bramble's eyes now had the same wild defiance as Thorn's. Fleetingly they seemed to soften, and Barkbelly couldn't be sure whether it was just a trick of the moonlight, but Bramble seemed to nod at him. Then both urchins pattered off into the shadows and were gone.

When Barkbelly arrived at work the next day, he found the place in chaos. Brick, Shoe and Saddle had been sent to search the woods. Nail was examining the mud in the lane for footprints. Missus Muckledown was putting a dish of Bramble's favorite food into her sty, hoping it would tempt her back. Farmer Muckledown was stomping around with dust storms at his heels. Pot was brewing up endless tea. Barkbelly was sent to feed the hoglets, with orders to return at ten o'clock sharp for a meeting in the hay barn.

At the meeting, Farmer Muckledown shared his thoughts. "I reckon Bramble was stolen," he said grimly. "I know it's hard to believe, but what other explanation is there? I inspected the sties myself, just before I turned in for the night. That was around eleven o'clock. Every sty

was secured; every bolt was fastened. *So you, Barkbelly"*—he pointed a thick finger and Barkbelly was trapped like a moth in a light beam—*"you have nothing to feel guilty about.* I know you were the last one in the sty with her, but you *did* slide the bolt back firmly. I checked. No, my friends, Bramble didn't push her way out. Someone *let* her out. There are plenty of people around here who know that Bramble is my best hope of winning the Urchin Cup, and plenty who are tired of my winning, year after year. And people will do *dark deeds* in the pursuit of glory. That's all I'm saying."

"What are you going to do if she's gone for good?" said Nail Adams.

"Well, we'll still be going to the show, m'lads! Don't you worry about that! We still have Thistle and Prickler. They can both win Best of Breed. They won't win the cup—you need something really special for that—but they're good urchins. And I have high hopes for little Tiddler winning Hoglet of the Year. So even without Bramble, we'll still have a good time at the show."

And they did. Thistle won Best of Breed. Little Tiddler won Hoglet of the Year. Farmer Muckledown was consoled for the loss of Bramble with several free pints of nettle beer in the refreshment tent. Barkbelly even saw Rope Daniels, the man with one leg.

Finally the time came to award the Urchin Cup. It went to Rapier, a magnificent Sable-Spiked Wood Hog from the famous Marshgold Farm. Barkbelly was standing beside Farmer Muckledown when the cup was presented.

"He's a first-class specimen, that Rapier," said the farmer. "I can't deny it. But my Bramble was even better. And I can't think of anywhere I would rather see her right now than standing up there with a winner's rosette on her. Can you?"

Barkbelly closed his eyes. He could picture her in the forest with Thorn by her side. She was dappled with sunlight and munching a mouthful of acorns.

"No," he said. "I can't." And he smiled.

Chapter 13

*S*ummer was over. The long golden descent into winter had begun. A troublesome wind whipped across the playground and rattled the leaves in the lane. The bell rang to signal the start of playtime and everyone stormed out.

In one corner of the playground, the tinies started their singing games, skipping in happy circles. Behind the wood store, the older girls were giggling like imps. Petticoat Palmer had stolen her sister's diary and was sharing its secrets. Missus O'Leary was on duty, but as usual she was living up to her nickname. She closed her eyes and leaned against the wall. She sighed. She sipped tea. She ignored the little ones tugging at her skirt. Nothing mattered to Weary O'Leary when she was on duty.

The boys were playing Bull Run and were already on their third round. Fish had been on first, followed by Dipper. Tie Donahue was on next, but as Tie stepped forward, Barkbelly declared that *he* wanted to be on.

"It's my turn," said Tie, a stocky lad with tousled hair and a coat held together with string. "You'll get your turn later."

"Ah, but I won't, will I?" growled Barkbelly. "I won't. *You* will. And Moth . . . and Ham . . . and Log . . . even Little Pan Evans. But I won't, because I never do."

"C'mon, Bark," said Fish, trying to calm things down. "You know why. It wouldn't be fair. We wouldn't stand a chance. Especially not these." He pointed at Sprout Wallace and Little Pan Evans.

"But it's not fair to *me*," Barkbelly complained. "I know I'm stronger than the rest of you—"

"It takes all of us to bring you down!" interrupted Tie, wanting to get on with it.

"But I can tone it down a bit. Not try too hard. What do you think?"

Everyone looked at him. He was so hopeful, so puppyish, that no one had the heart to tell him what they were thinking.

"What do you think, Fish?" asked Little Pan Evans.

"Don't bring me into this!" cried Fish. "I'm not saying a word. I'm biased. He's my best mate."

"Am I?" said Barkbelly. "Wow. Thanks, Fish."

"So you think he should have a go?" said Tie.

"I didn't say that!" said Fish.

"You didn't have to," said Ham Malone. "We know what you're thinking."

"Then why are you asking me?" cried Fish. "Honestly!" He shook his head and started to walk away, but then he came back. "If you don't get on with it, there won't be any time left for another round."

This was true.

"Well . . . ," said Moth slowly. "You could have just one go. . . ."

"*Yes!*" cried Barkbelly triumphantly.

"*No!*" wailed Tie. "That's not fair. It was my turn!" And he stormed off and started kicking the bench, muttering angrily to himself.

The lads ignored him and lined up: Moth Williams, Sprout Wallace, Fish Patterson, Spoon Hardy, Needle Morgan, Ham Malone, Log Worthing, Dipper Dean and Little Pan Evans.

Barkbelly faced them, barring the way. He crouched down like a wrestler and stretched out his arms, ready to tackle the runners. The lads looked at him, worried. Barkbelly seemed deadly serious. There was no sign of him toning it down. He was like an enormous wooden crab, with snapping pincers and glittering eyes. They were minnows, swimming into the jaws of death. They braced themselves.

"Bull Run!" cried Barkbelly, and they were off, running wildly across the pitch toward the safety of the wall, swerving round his terrible wooden fists, vaulting over his loggy legs.

But Moth was caught. He struggled. He fought. He pummeled his fists against Barkbelly's chest. He kicked his wooden shins, but it was no use. He surrendered.

So now there were two of them on. The lads lined up again. Barkbelly and Moth huddled together, whispering and plotting. Then they crouched down and cried, "Bull Run!" and everyone ran.

They went straight for Dipper. He didn't stand a chance. Moth butted him like an angry ram, winding him completely, and while Dipper stood there gasping, Barkbelly grabbed his arms. He had to give in.

More whispering and plotting. The chasers chose their next victim. Barkbelly crouched, flanked now by Dipper and Moth.

"Bull Run!" they cried in unison, and the Bull Runners ran.

71

In an instant, it was clear they wanted Log. They ran at him from all sides: six arms, six legs, three bodies, with only one brain between them. Their eyes burned. Their arms pumped. Their feet pounded. Barkbelly was in front, wild with excitement, thundering on blindly, not seeing—not seeing Little Pan Evans. Little Pan Evans, running to the faraway safety of the wall. Head down, sightless, determined.

Barkbelly hit him like a hammer.

Little Pan Evans soared through the air and fell like a sack of potatoes. The gang heard the deadly crack of a skull against gravel, a stomach-turning thud as his head hit the ground. Then silence.

The game stopped. Everyone gathered round. Little Pan Evans was lying facedown, completely still. No one said anything. Dipper squatted and turned the body over. There was blood. Endless blood. Someone screamed.

"He's dead," said Dipper. "He's dead. You've killed him."

Barkbelly stared in horror. He couldn't speak. He couldn't move. Little Pan Evans was dead.

Suddenly the playground was in chaos. There were screams and shouts. People pointing and crying. Missus O'Leary was coming over.

"You've killed him," said Dipper again. He stood up. There was blood on his hands and on his coat. His face was twisting into a mask of anger. "He's dead!" he shouted, and he pushed Barkbelly away from the body. "He's dead, you murderin' freak!"

Still Barkbelly said nothing. He saw heads turning away from the body, toward him. He saw glazed faces. Tears and terror. Fear and mistrust.

"Run," whispered a voice beside him. Fish. "Run."

Barkbelly didn't move. He couldn't.

"Run!" Fish grabbed hold of Barkbelly's arm and shook it violently. *"Run!"* he wailed, and Barkbelly heard the desperation in his voice. *"Go! Before they come."*

Barkbelly turned and looked into his friend's eyes. He saw panic and fear.

"Where can I go?" he asked stupidly.

"I don't know!" cried Fish. "Just go! Run! Now! *Please!*"

And as Barkbelly gazed at Fish, he felt a sudden sharp pain cutting deep into his chest. His heart was splintering.

"I don't want to go," he whispered.

"You *must*. They won't understand. They'll say you're a murderer. Dipper's doing it already and he's supposed to be your friend. Please, Bark, just go. Do it for me. *Please.*"

So Barkbelly turned, and he ran.

PART TWO

Chapter 14

*B*arkbelly ran on through the afternoon. He ran through woods and over fields, across streams and over stiles. He didn't stop. If he stopped, he would think, and that was something he didn't want to do.

When dusk fell, he was in rich farmland. The fields were fat with cows and there was a farm ahead with a jumble of outbuildings. He could find food there if he was careful. The farm dogs wouldn't catch him. He had no human smell to color the wind.

He waited till it was truly dark, then crept closer. Very quietly, he opened a wooden door and entered. He was in a dairy with white tiled walls and a well-swept floor. A cool marble slab, piled high with butter and cheeses, ran along one side of the room. There were silver pails covered with thick wooden lids. Lifting one, he found milk, yellowy with cream.

He began to drink. The milk was good; he could feel the strength returning to his spent legs. But it reminded him of home. Of his mother, singing softly as she milked the family cow. Of his father, drinking straight from the pail, his mustache dripping with milk drops. And, there in the dark,

Barkbelly suddenly longed to cry. He rubbed his eyes and held his breath—but the tears refused to fall. Why? When he wanted them so badly? They could roll down his cheeks, splash into the milk and salt the sweet goodness—he wouldn't care as long as they washed away the pain of being a murderer: lost, alone and far from home.

But even murderers need to sleep. And eat! Barkbelly was ravenous. He took two round cheeses and retired to the milking shed next door. There he slept, curled up on a pile of hay.

When morning came, the sound of opening doors woke him, and as the cows ambled in, pearled with dew, he slipped out of a side door and disappeared into the morning mist.

Barkbelly ran for seven days and nights. Sometimes he worried he was running round in circles, like a rat in a wheelcage. Farms, roads, barns . . . they all looked endlessly familiar. He was desperately tired, and scared that in his weariness he would blunder back into his own village. But he couldn't sleep. He was haunted by nightmares of Little Pan Evans, lying in a pool of blood. Even when he ran there was no real escape. Running reminded him of the playground and Bull Run and . . . Little Pan Evans. How he had loved to play alongside the bigger boys! Fish had always told him, "Pan, you're too small to play with us. You'll get hurt one day." But he wouldn't listen. And now he was dead.

On the eighth day, Barkbelly found he couldn't run any farther. He still had the strength, but the will to run had gone. He had slept fitfully all night, and when he awoke, his head was throbbing with questions. Where was he running to? Should he stop? Had he run far enough?

He didn't know, but sitting in the morning sunshine, he listened to his heart. And it seemed to say yes. *Yes, you have run far enough. You are tired of running. Stop now. You can't run forever.*

He stood up and stretched. He was halfway up a hill. *I might as well go up as down.*

He began to climb. The hill was steeper than it looked and he was panting and cursing as he reached the summit. But when he saw the view, the curses died on his tongue. The land fell away into an immense floodplain, ringed by mountains. A river shimmered through it like a dropped necklace. But his eyes were drawn to something far more interesting: a boomtown. A great gray mass of factories and homes, built on hope and ambition. Roads riddled it. Furnaces fired it. A thick pall of smoke hovered over the sprawl like an avenging ghost.

Barkbelly knew of this place. Travelers told tales about a dark town where people lived in squalor and labored like harness rats. Every Pumbleditcher had heard them. But they were just stories, weren't they? No one believed such a place could exist.

But it did. Barkbelly was looking at it.

This was Tythingtown.

Chapter 15

ythingtown was a huddle of houses and factories. High walls funneled the sky. Smoke belched from spiral chimneys. Water ran down the streets in greasy gullies. Dogs and children scavenged in the alleys, side by side. The townsfolk had pale faces. Watery eyes. Hacking coughs and savage sneezes. But they would survive—Barkbelly could see that. These people were determined to flourish. He saw builders sawing and hammering. Crowds of factory workers packing the streets like sheep being driven to market. Street vendors selling sausages, pickled fish, hot soup, cheese rolls, cream buns—everything a hungry boy could desire. The air was thick with language and the smell of cooking. So many people! It was perfect. He could melt into the crowd and no one would ever find him.

But could he make a living? Wooden or not, he needed to eat and that would cost money. He wanted a bed too. He wouldn't sleep on the street like a dog. He needed a job.

He didn't have to search long. Tythingtown was expanding like a balloon. There were factories, workshops and jobs aplenty. That afternoon, he found a fine pair of golden gates, and above them a sign, arching like a rainbow:

TYTHING & SON
Jam Makers

Tied to the gate was a handwritten card:

HELP WANTED
ASK AT THE GATEHOUSE

The gatehouse was a tiny redbrick building with a grimy window. Barkbelly peered in and saw a little old man with more whiskers than face. He was reading a newspaper and twisting his finger in his ear, winkling wax.

Barkbelly tapped on the window. The gatekeeper put down his newspaper, slid back a panel and peered at him through thick spectacles.

"Yes?" he hissed.

"I saw the sign," said Barkbelly, "and I'd like to apply for a job."

"Well, of course you would," said the gatekeeper, screwing up his face. "Shabby little scrap of nothing like yourself, walking through a dirty town with neither money in your pockets nor food in your belly. Looking, looking, looking for any opening, any kind of salvation, any shaft of sunlight cutting through the clouds of despair and desperation, promising the crumbs of a meal, the comfort of a bed, some shelter from this world of sin and sorrow, and the hope, just the hope, that there might be a better future for those who work hard for it, in a place where work is available for those who see the sign, and spontaneously act upon it and ask, just ask at the gatehouse."

The gatekeeper closed the window panel and returned to his copy of the *Daily Truth*.

Barkbelly was completely flummoxed. He looked around to see if there was another gatehouse he could ask at, but there wasn't. He tapped on the window a second time.

"Yes?" hissed the gatekeeper again, sliding the window panel open.

"As I said, I saw the sign and would like to apply for a job."

"Then you must be interviewed," said the gatekeeper. "For while it is true that those who ask might well be given, they most certainly will *not* be given without an interview. And an interview, before you ask, which you almost certainly will, because boys like you always do, coming not infrequently from the countryside where such formalities are not considered necessary for the furtherance of business, an interview is a *meeting*. Nothing more, nothing less. A meeting—albeit a rather formal one—in which you will be questioned by Young Master Tything and expected to answer in return. And again, before you ask, Young Master Tything is indeed the son in Tything and *Son*—that is, son of Sir Blunderbuss Tything, owner and founder of the magnificent factory you now stand before, humbled by its glory and dwarfed by its immensity. Before this factory, you are *nothing*. Nothing but an outsider, a bystander, an observer, a scavenging, beggarly dog, grateful for the meanest of scraps dropped from the lowest of tables, but inside this factory, beyond these golden gates, *you can be something*. You can be *a worker*. You can have money and food and a roof over your head. You can have the companionship of friends and the satisfaction of knowing that in every jar of Tything's jam there is something of you. Without you, that jam would not exist. You are an essential part of the process. You could be proud of that, could you not?"

"Oh, y-yes," stammered Barkbelly, quite overcome by the enormousness of it all.

"Then it shall be yours. Yours for the asking. Wait there."

The gatekeeper closed the window panel and disappeared from view, then reappeared from the back of the gatehouse, jangling an enormous bunch of keys. He shuffled over to the golden gates, paused, held the keys up to his spectacles, squinted hard, chose the right one, slid it into the lock and turned it till it clicked, and then the gates silently opened and Barkbelly walked through.

The gatekeeper led him along corridors and through archways, up staircases and down into cellars, across cobbled courtyards and round corners until they reached an office with a wall of windows. The gatekeeper stopped and knocked. Barkbelly read the polished sign on the door:

MASTER TEAK TYTHING
FACTORY MANAGER

The door opened and there stood a tall young man with a freckled face and a tangle of red hair. He smiled and brushed his bangs away from his forehead.

"Ah, Dogger," he said, "I'll be with you in just a minute." He pointed to a wooden bench in the corridor. "Take a seat."

They sat down and Barkbelly found himself looking through the office windows. The young man was talking to someone in a high-backed chair and he was clearly enjoying the company. He laughed and listened and laughed again. Suddenly the visitor stood up and turned—and Barkbelly gasped. The room shimmered with the radiance of a beautiful young woman in a yellow dress. Barkbelly knew instantly that she was the young man's sister. Her red hair, tied up in yellow ribbons, was as curly as his and her heart-shaped face had the same freckles.

"Who is that?" he whispered.

"Miss Taffeta Tything," said the gatekeeper. "Beloved daughter of Old Master Tything and sister to Young Master Tything."

"Does she work in the factory?"

"Of course. Though not in the sense that you or I work in the factory, it has to be said, since in truth she is not a worker but an owner, and that is a completely different thing, but nevertheless, she does work in the factory, or, shall we say, she bears certain responsibilities within it, namely *stores*. It is her job to ensure that the storerooms contain sufficient fruit and sugar to make jam in accordance with both the season and the production schedule."

"She's very beautiful."

"Yes," agreed the gatekeeper, and surprisingly said no more.

At that moment the office door opened again and out ran a small dog. It yapped and danced and twirled around upon its hind legs, clearly excited to be outside again.

"Shush!" cried a buttery voice, and out came Miss Taffeta. "Now, you promise you won't be late?" she said as she paused in the doorway. "You know how Daddy hates to be kept waiting—especially on his birthday!" She giggled. "Shush!" she said again, wagging a finger at the dancing dog. "I'm coming!" She kissed her brother on the cheek and skipped away.

Barkbelly watched her go. She breezed down the corridor with the dog at her heels, and she was so golden and light, it was like spring arriving in the middle of winter.

"So, Dogger," said Young Master Tything, "is this another new worker?"

"It is indeed, sir," said the gatekeeper with a nod and a bow. "Another poor soul with no hope of a future, no—"

"Excellent! Well, come in here, young man, and we'll see what you're made of, eh? Thank you, Dogger!"

Young Master Tything ushered Barkbelly into the office and swiftly shut the door.

"Take a seat, young man."

There was a huge wooden desk piled high with papers, a fat velvet chair and a wooden one with a worn leather seat. Barkbelly chose the wooden one and sat down. *Thrrrrp!* A leathery fart-noise sneaked out beneath him. *I hope he didn't hear that.* Barkbelly wriggled uncomfortably.

But the Young Master was too busy trying to clear a space on his desk to notice anything. Five minutes passed before he even looked at Barkbelly, but when he finally did, he leaned across the clutter and peered intensely.

"Well, bless my socks!" he cried. "A wooden boy!" He grinned. "Extraordinary! What's your name, young feller?"

"Barkbelly, sir."

"Indeed!" said Young Master Tything. "Well, Barkbelly, I believe you're looking for work?"

"Yes, sir. I'm newly arrived in town and I saw the sign on your gate—"

"Oh, *excellent* start!" cried the Young Master, clapping his hands together like a seal. "Truly fine observational skills! But—and here's the tricky bit—could you *read* it?"

"*Yes*," said Barkbelly slowly.

"Astonishing! Absolutely first-rate! Oh, you're just the kind of chap we need here! Can you start tomorrow?"

Barkbelly nodded.

"Excellent! Do you need somewhere to sleep?"

Barkbelly nodded again.

"Capital! There's a bunkhouse round the back. You can stay there for a shilling a week, out of your wages. Do you need food? I'll arrange it with the Matron, Missus Maddox. Now, you'll start tomorrow morning at six o'clock sharp and you'll need to report to Mister Mossman, the Overseer. The other chaps will show you where he is. And now all I have to do is to welcome you officially."

Young Master Tything leapt up out of his chair, clasped Barkbelly's hand and shook it vigorously.

"So! *Welcome*, young Barkbelly! Welcome to Tything and Son. Work hard, obey your masters and I see a very bright future ahead of you."

"Do you really, sir?" said Barkbelly.

"Absolutely! Blue sky all the way! Baby blue!"

Barkbelly hadn't smiled in days, but he did now. Baby blue! Not guilty gray or murderous black, but baby blue! Maybe there was hope after all.

Chapter 16

*T*he next morning, at five minutes to six, Barkbelly stood outside the Overseer's office. Around him the factory wheezed and whistled. Flames flickered under vast copper cooking pots. Steam hissed out of pipes. Smoke curled and swirled. The air was sweet with strawberries.

At precisely six o'clock, the office door opened and the Overseer emerged. He was immaculately dressed, with a tie so perfectly straight it must have been aligned with a ruler. There was a badge pinned to his lapel:

MR. CHISEL MOSSMAN
OVERSEER

"So," he said with a reluctant smile. "You are the new boy."

"Yes, sir. Barkbelly, sir."

"Indeed," said Mossman, and in that one word he seemed to dismiss everything Barkbelly had been, was now or would ever be. His polished eyes scanned up and down. "The Young Master was quite charmed by you. But then, he is easily impressed. I will reserve my judgment until I have seen you work. Though I admit, you could be *useful* here. Are you strong?"

"Yes, sir," said Barkbelly. "I'm very tough."

"Mmm," murmured Mossman thoughtfully. "I must decide where to put you. In the meantime, you can have a tour of the factory. *Mallory!*"

"Yessir!" A young man poked his head above a pile of sugar sacks.

"Mallory, take this boy on a short tour and return him when you've finished."

"Yessir!"

The Overseer withdrew into his office and the young man grinned.

"I'm Mop," he said, offering Barkbelly a grimy hand. "What do they call you?"

"Barkbelly," he said, shaking hands.

"Blimey!" said Mop. "You've got a grip on you! What *are* you made of?" He rolled back Barkbelly's sleeve and examined his arm, tracing a finger along the grain.

"Ash, I think," said Barkbelly, "but I can't be sure."

"Handsome!" Mop slapped him on the back but soon regretted it. He winced and rubbed his reddened palm. "Come on, then, new boy!" he said. "You've plenty to see, and Mossman will be clock-watching as usual!"

Together they toured the jam factory. It was a labyrinth of corridors and workrooms packed with pipes and pulleys, belts and boilers, chains, wheels, cogs and kegs. Storerooms were piled high with sugar, lemons and every other fruit imaginable. Workers ran back and forth with barrow loads of ingredients. Wagons waited outside, bringing even more.

The jam was made in Rooms 1 through 6. These were

cavernous spaces, each containing six immense copper pots as tall as townhouses. Below the pots were fires. These were stoked by Fire Feeders—brawny men who endlessly demanded coal from dozens of filthy Coal Boys.

"I'll show you what goes on above," said Mop, shouting above the clamor.

He led Barkbelly up a staircase to a long platform that ran alongside the pots at rim level. Suspended in midair over each pot was a circular track, and on opposite sides of the track there were two bicycles.

Barkbelly noticed that only one was being ridden. He wondered why.

The bicycles had wheels but no tires—the tracks were grooved to fit the exact width of the wheels, and a huge spoon, which dangled beneath the track, counterbalanced the whole contraption.

The bikes were ridden by Stir Boys. They worked in teams of two. While one boy rested, the other rode a bike. As the bike was pedaled, the spoon turned, stirring the jam down below.

The jam bubbled and spurted like hot lava, so the Stir Boys wore thick leather suits to protect them. But the suits made the terrible heat even worse.

As Barkbelly watched, one of the Stir Boys stopped pedaling. Then he climbed shakily off his bike and started to stagger back to the platform. This was a hazardous business. The boy, dizzy with exertion, had to walk along a narrow wooden gangplank. If he fell down into the jam, he would be boiled alive.

Meanwhile, on another platform on the far side of the pot, the second Stir Boy was walking out to the second bike. When he reached it, he climbed on and started pedaling. The changeover was so well timed that the jam was left unstirred for no more than a few seconds.

Beside him, Barkbelly watched the resting boy pull off his goggles and unbutton his suit. He was sweating and steaming. Gasping for breath. His eyes bulged as he leaned on the guardrail.

"This is Wick Ransom," said Mop, putting a comforting hand on the boy's shoulder. "Wick, this is Barkbelly."

The Stir Boy nodded but was too tired to speak. He lumbered over to a nearby pail of water, drank deeply and looked back toward the track. Barkbelly followed his gaze and saw a huge hourglass inside the spindle that held the track to the roof. Red sand was pouring from the top chamber into the bottom; already it was nearly half gone. Wick Ransom sighed and started to button up his suit. Once it was fastened, he had just enough time to pull on his goggles before he had to walk back out along the gangplank. The sand ran out, the other boy stopped pedaling and there was Wick's bike, waiting for him.

Mop tapped Barkbelly on the shoulder. "This way," he said, and he led him down another staircase and into the Bottling Room.

Here the jam was spurted through pipes and squeezed into jars while it was still hot and bubbling. Lids were screwed on and then the jars whooshed overhead on a conveyor belt to the Labeling Ladies, who sat all day with pots of glue and hog's-hair brushes, dipping and sticking. From here, the jars trundled along to the Packers, who swept them up two at a time and packed them neatly into boxes. And finally, the boxes were carried on trolleys into a cool storeroom, ready to be transported to the world outside.

"Are you impressed?" asked Mop.

"Oh, yes," said Barkbelly.

"So you should be!" said Mop with obvious pride. "This is the finest jam factory in the whole of Lindenland."

"Where will I be working?" asked Barkbelly.

"I don't know," said Mop with a shrug. "You'll have to ask Mossman. Which reminds me, I'd better get you back to him. Come on!"

Mossman had decided. "It seems to me, *Barkbelly*," he said, "that a *wooden* boy will not feel pain." He raised a challenging eyebrow. Barkbelly said nothing. "Perfect. You can be a Stir Boy. Since you cannot be scalded by jam splash, you will not have to wear a splatter suit. Therefore, you will not need to take breaks every ten minutes like the other boys—you will be able to work all day. And since you will not need to work with another boy, I can save money. Perfect, see? Start right away. *Mallory!*"

"Yessir?"

"Mallory, the men have just set Pot 3 to boil. Take Barkbelly up there and show him how to work the Stir Bike."

"Yessir. Who will he be working with, Mister Mossman?"

"No one," said the Overseer, straightening his tie in a small mirror on the office wall. "He will be on his own."

"*All day?*" gasped Mop Mallory. "*With no breaks?*"

"He can have lunch. You do need to eat, I presume?"

Barkbelly nodded.

"Fine. You can have lunch at twelve and supper at five-thirty. Work is from six in the morning till nine at night. Off you go."

So Barkbelly went. Back up the spiral staircase to the aerial platform, where Mop showed him how the Stir Bike worked.

Underneath, a pot of gooseberry jam was starting to bubble. Steam swirled in fragrant pink clouds. It was time to begin. Barkbelly stripped down to his underbritches, put his clothes safely out of reach of the jam splash, climbed onto the bike and started pedaling.

Beneath him, the massive silver spoon began to rotate, slowly at first, but swifter as he pedaled harder. And Barkbelly *did* pedal harder as he gained confidence. Wind whistled past his ears. He felt wildly exhilarated. Looking over to his left, he could see a boy struggling to stir a vat of marmalade, hindered by his hefty splatter suit. To his right, another boy was sweating over a black-currant preserve. But he felt good! His strong legs propelled him, round and round through the zesty steam. Down below, the jam was reaching boiling point. It spluttered and erupted, splashed and spurted. Iridescent bubbles rose to the surface and burst like fireworks, shooting fruit and sugar high into the air.

Barkbelly could feel himself getting sticky. Soon he was coated with a fine sugary film. When he licked his lips, he could taste it. The temperature was rising. The air shimmered around him as if it were bending and melting under the immense heat. But still he rode on. He was tireless. He stopped occasionally for a drink of water. He stopped for lunch and supper. But other than that, he worked incessantly, unaffected by the heat or the scalding splashes of jam.

From the factory floor, Mossman watched his new worker like a cat watching a robin. The Overseer was so absorbed that he didn't notice the Young Master was beside him until the factory owner spoke.

"I say, Mossman! What a splendid little chap! Remarkably well suited to this work."

"He is indeed, Master Tything," said the Overseer. "I could use a dozen more like him."

The two men gazed up into the rafters. Barkbelly was thundering round the track as if his life depended on it.

"Extraordinary!" said Young Master Tything. "Quite extraordinary!" He turned to the Overseer and lowered his voice. "We don't want to lose *him*."

"No, sir," replied the Overseer evenly. His gray eyes hardened.

"Guard him well, Mossman. No unnecessary risks."

"No, sir," said Mossman, still looking up. "I will treat him as if he were my own flesh and blood."

"Mmm. See that you do," murmured Young Master Tything. Then he turned on his heel and walked away.

Only then did Mossman lower his gaze. He watched the Young Master wend his way through the machines. "Only he isn't flesh and blood, is he?" he hissed. "And accidents do happen."

Chapter 17

$\mathcal{T}$he factory workers had a rest day once a week and Barkbelly was soon spending his with Wick Ransom. They had plenty in common. They were both Stir Boys. They both slept in the bunkhouse. They both liked Mop Mallory. They both hated Mossman. And they were both orphans. At least, that was what they had told each other. But one afternoon, after he had been at the factory nearly a month, Barkbelly learned the truth about Wick's parents.

The boys were exploring Tythingtown together. It was a sharp winter's day. The back alleys were sulky with frost, but elsewhere glorious sunshine was paving the streets with gold. Barkbelly felt happy for the first time in weeks. He grinned at his new friend and Wick grinned back. They had freedom, sunshine and hot sausage sandwiches. What more could a boy want?

They climbed up on a wall to eat their lunch. From here they had a fine view of a construction site. An immense building was creeping skyward. A gang of men worked at its base, pumping an enormous set of leather bellows that whooshed bricks up a wind tunnel to the builders high above. Dozens of workers banged and hammered, sawed and drilled, shoveled and filled. There were trucks and wagons, endlessly coming and going, with harness rats sweating in their traces. *Just like home*, thought Barkbelly. Only these rats weren't sleek and glossy. They were gray and grim. One had died; two men were dragging it out of a wheelcage by its tail. Barkbelly turned away.

"What are they building?" he asked.

"It's a jail," said Wick, his mouth full of sausage.

"What's a jail?"

"Don't you know?"

"No."

Wick wiped his mouth on his sleeve. "It's a place where they lock people up. People who have broken the law. Thieves. Murderers. People like that."

Barkbelly stopped chewing. He gazed at the thick walls and the barred windows in silence.

"Don't you have a jail? Where you come from?" said Wick.

"No," said Barkbelly quietly. "It's just a village."

"Does no one ever do anything wrong?"

"No." Barkbelly could feel his heart: *thump, thump, thump*.

"My parents are both in jail," said Wick.

Barkbelly turned to his friend in amazement. "Are they? I thought they were dead."

"No," said Wick. "That's just what I tell people. They're in Milltown jail. They were workers at the mill—I was too—but there was trouble." He paused and Barkbelly saw his eyes steeling as the memories returned. "They worked us too hard. I know they work us hard here, but there it was worse. The workers tried to do something about it. There was an uprising and my parents were caught smashing one of the machines. And then when it came to the trial—"

Barkbelly frowned.

"A trial is when you have to stand up in front of people and talk about what happened and why," Wick explained. "And it should be fair. That's the whole point! But this one wasn't. The jury was made up of overseers and mill owners, and they didn't want to hear *why* my parents did what they did. Nor did the judge! He was a mill owner too, and he didn't want the trouble to spread. So he sent them to jail for life. I ran away, in case anyone came looking for me. And here I am."

He fell silent, expecting Barkbelly's life story in return. But it didn't come. Barkbelly sat in silence, screwing up his greasy sandwich bag tighter and tighter.

"You don't have parents, do you?" said Wick encouragingly.

"No," said Barkbelly. He was becoming agitated now, and suddenly, to Wick's surprise, he jumped down from the wall and kicked it hard. "Yes," he said. "I *do* have parents. I don't know why I'm denying them. They're good folk. They took me in as a baby. As an egg."

"You came from an egg?" Wick's jaw dropped.

Barkbelly nodded.

"How big was it?"

"About the size of a goose egg."

"Was it laid by a goose?"

"*No!* It was found in a field."

"So how did it get into the field?"

There was no reply. Barkbelly leaned back heavily against the wall. "I don't know," he said at last. "I didn't think about it for the longest time. When I did, I asked my parents, but they didn't know. I meant to ask my teacher but—" He closed his eyes and slowly rubbed his face. "I don't know what I am or where I've come from. And do you know what? This town is packed with people but I can't find anyone like me. I look all the time. *All the time.* I can't find *anyone.*"

Wick caught the despair in his friend's voice but decided to risk another question. "Why are you here?" he said as gently as he could.

"I ran away."

"Was there trouble?"

Barkbelly said nothing.

"Was it *Pan?*"

Barkbelly stared at him, wild-eyed.

"You talk in your sleep," said Wick hurriedly. "You have bad dreams. You say it over and over."

"Do I?" Barkbelly was breathing so hard, he sounded like the bellows on the building site. "I don't mean to. I'm trying to forget. But I can't."

Wick didn't dare ask anything more. He shivered. "I'm getting cold," he said, "sitting around like this. Come on! I'll show you the river."

They walked on. But the day had become darker somehow, and it was hard to find pleasure with a head full of jails and judges, nightmares and trials.

Chapter 18

Was it the chill of that deceptively wintry day? Or was there something poisonous in the mist that hung heavily over the river? Whatever it was, Barkbelly awoke the next morning with a strange fever. His sleep had been troubled again, and when the bunkhouse bell rang for the morning shift, he could barely lift his head from the pillow.

"Wick," he groaned. "Fetch Missus Maddox."

The Matron swept into the dormitory in a swoosh of taffeta and lace and plumped herself down on Barkbelly's bed. Her skirts settled around her with a sigh.

"Well, tickle my squealers!" she cried. "You're a sick one and no mistake. Haven't seen such a sweat since poor Mister Maddox had the lurgy."

She rummaged in the folds of her skirts and produced a peppermint lozenge. "Here," she said, and she slid it between Barkbelly's parched lips.

"Will that cure me?" whispered Barkbelly.

"Cure you? No, my angel. But it'll stop that dog breath. Don't see we all have to suffer. Now, where's that Wick Ransom gone? Wick! *Wick!*"

Her voice ripped the air like a rusty saw. Spiders fell from their webs.

"Wick, tell Mister Mossman Barkbelly won't be coming in this morning."

When the Overseer heard the news, his eyes narrowed. He called for Mop Mallory.

Within minutes, Barkbelly was being pulled out of his bed. Missus Maddox was flapping like a blackbird, but it was no use.

"I have my orders," said Mop, helping Barkbelly into his jacket. "Mossman wants him to work." Mop's face was as white as a bone.

He carried Barkbelly into the factory and up the stairs to the Stir Bikes. Mossman followed them up and watched as Mop helped Barkbelly put his goggles on.

Barkbelly grunted. The pain in his head was so bad, his eyes were slits, and with the goggles on he was virtually blind. Suddenly he heard Wick's voice.

"Mister Mossman! Mister Mossman!"

"What do you think you're doing? Get back on your bike."

"Mister Mossman! Please! Barkbelly isn't well! He's sick! Really sick!"

"Get back on your bike, Ransom. Now."

"But Mister Mossman, he should be—"

"Don't you tell me what he should be doing, boy! Get back on your bike! Now, boy! Now!"

Barkbelly felt the platform vibrate as Wick stomped away. Then there were hands helping him onto a Stir Bike. He took hold of the handlebars and breathed deeply. He started pedaling, but every push of the pedals was torture. After just one circuit of the track, he had to stop. He was trembling.

"Get on with it, boy."

Mossman was still there! Barkbelly took another deep breath and struggled on, fighting the fever that battered his body. He started to sway in the saddle. The bike was barely moving now. The unstirred jam was beginning to burn. It splashed wildly. Steam billowed, thick as thunderclouds.

Barkbelly gripped the handlebars. He reeled in a fog of sweat and dizziness.

And then he fell.

Flapping like a moth.

Down toward the jam pot.

Down.

Down.

Down.

And—*pdoosh!*—the jam swallowed him whole.

"*No!*" cried Wick, who had seen it happen. "*No!*"

Screams and shouts and feet and fingers, running, pointing, calling, crying: "Water, water, bring water, more, more, more. . . ."

Panic-stricken workers crowded round the pot as the Fire Feeders doused the flames beneath it with buckets of water. "Faster," they urged, "faster." But everyone knew it was too late. No one could survive in a pot of boiling jam.

Finally the fire was extinguished. Mossman called for a ladder. The jam in the pot was still bubbling, so only someone in a splatter suit could climb it. Coat Collins, the eldest Stir Boy, volunteered.

Barely a sound could be heard in the factory. Just the plurping of the jam. The ticking of the office clock. The thudding of boots as Coat climbed the ladder. Then a cry: "*He's alive!*"

Alive? Barkbelly was alive? The workers couldn't believe it. But there he was, clambering out of the pot. Falling into the

arms of the Fire Feeders. Soaked in jam to twice his normal weight. Sticky sweet but smiling.

Wick thought he was looking at a ghost. *How did he do that? He must be indestructible.* Wick was weak with relief. He had to sit down.

As he turned away from the crowd, he saw Mossman standing outside his office. The Overseer was quite still. His face was as gray as his suit. There was a splash of strawberry jam on his jacket and his tie was slightly crooked. Suddenly he took a watch out of his pocket, glanced at it and slipped it away.

"Look at him," said a tired voice at Wick's shoulder. Mop Mallory. "Soon he'll have all this mess cleaned up and everything running on schedule."

And Mop was right. He did.

Chapter 19

*B*arkbelly dreamed he was falling again. Tumbling through a thick, inky blackness that seemed to go on and on without end. But now there *was* an end, and someone was waiting for him there. A tiny figure, down in the darkness, pale as a mushroom. A boy. And the boy lifted his face and smiled, and opened his arms wide in welcome.

"Have you come to play?" said Little Pan Evans.

"*Ohhh!*"

Barkbelly shuddered awake. He clutched the blankets, pulled them closer and stared into the blackness of the bunkhouse. Listened to his ragged breathing and the raw thumping of his heart. Then a new sound—a rustle of taffeta—and in came Missus Maddox, carrying a horn lantern. She neared the bed, put her finger to her lips and beckoned him to follow.

And he did. Between the rows of sleeping boys, through the door and across the courtyard he went, following the guarded glow of her lantern. Through an arch, up a staircase and into a room that sparkled like a magpie's nest.

"You sit yourself down, my sweet," said the Matron. "Make yourself comfy. I'll fix us a nice drop of something, eh?"

Missus Maddox disappeared into an adjoining kitchen. Barkbelly heard the hiss of a stove and the clatter of a milk pan. He looked around the sitting room.

"Flaming foxes!" he said to himself. So many trinkets! Gold and silver and china and glass . . . there wasn't a surface left unadorned. But the room was so clean! How on earth did she find the time to polish it all?

"There you go, my dove," said Missus Maddox as she swept back in. She handed him a steaming mug and eased herself into an armchair. "Bad, was it?" she said. "Your dream?"

Barkbelly nodded.

"Was it Mossman?"

"*No!*" said Barkbelly.

"Oh, you'd be surprised how many times it is," said Missus Maddox. "He bullies by day and night, that one. And after what happened today . . . well, I just thought it might be him."

Barkbelly sipped his hot milk and tasted—rum! It was delicious. He cupped the mug in his hands and breathed in the warm scent. "Mister Mossman doesn't like me," he said.

"He don't like *anyone*, my lovely. It's how he is."

"I know, but he *really* doesn't like me."

Missus Maddox tilted her head thoughtfully. "Well," she said, "I'm not one for gossip, but Mop Mallory did tell me the very same thing. And I can only say this: Mister Mossman is a very simple soul. He don't like what he don't understand."

"Am I the only wooden person in Tythingtown?"

"In the world, I should think! I ain't never seen another. Don't know as Mossman has either. And the thing is, you're strong. Mossman don't like that. He can't wear you down. He likes people tired—they're easier to control. But you, my darling, you don't get tired. So he can shout as much as he likes—

make life a right old misery for you—but he ain't gonna break you. He knows that and it niggles him something rotten."

She smiled mischievously and drank so deeply from her mug, she emerged with a frothy white mustache.

"How did you hear me?" said Barkbelly. "This room is so far away."

"Yes, but I visit in the night, don't I? I listen out for my boys. There's always someone. Muttering. Crying. Having a bad dream. Wetting the bed. You're all so young. So lost. So far from home. Most of you ain't got families—well, none as wants you. You wouldn't be here otherwise. And in the night—when it's dark and it seems like everyone else in the world is sleeping but you—that's when it finds you. The Past. 'Cause it's always in the past but . . . it don't stay there. I wish it did. But it don't. It's always there, in the dark or in your dreams. You hope it gets better in time, but it don't. Not really."

She fell silent. Nothing could be heard except the ticking of a clock and the guttering of a candle.

"Can nothing be done?" said Barkbelly, his voice barely more than a whisper.

"What do you suggest?" said Missus Maddox with a faint smile. "You can't forget the past. You think you can, but suddenly something will remind you and—whoosh!—you're right back where you were, bad as ever. You can run away, as fast and as far as you want, but you'll carry it with you. It clings, like a flea on a dog. I don't know. . . . You can't change things. You can't turn back time. But you can make things better. Well, I hear some people can. It depends what the trouble was."

"I didn't mean to do it," said Barkbelly. "The thing I did . . . in the past . . . it was an accident. It was. But knowing that doesn't make me feel any better. I can't believe what I've done. I can't forgive myself. And I can't forget."

"Could you go back, my plum? Could you explain? Apologize?"

"No," said Barkbelly. "I couldn't go back. It would make things worse. So much worse. If I stay away, perhaps in time they will forget me. I am not worth remembering."

"Neither am I, my sweet," said Missus Maddox. "Neither am I."

But there, in the glow of the firelight, Barkbelly knew he would remember her. Remember this night, this room, this wisdom.

"Don't you ever give up the fight," she said suddenly. "Maybe you've done bad things, but you ain't a bad boy. I can tell. And it ain't wrong to want peace. So you go out there and find it, my angel. Search for it. Fight for it. Win it."

Barkbelly's eyes were shining like two more trinkets. "I will!" he said. "Oh, I will! Thank you, Missus Maddox. Thank you ever so much."

And with that, he returned to his bed and he slept.

Chapter 20

*T*affeta Tything was a sunny soul who brightened up the factory whenever she entered it. Barkbelly saw her most days. Sometimes she was arm in arm with her father, supporting him as he hobbled rheumatically by. Sometimes she was with her brother. But usually she was alone, humming happily to herself as she went about her business. She looked after the stores, making sure that the sugar was always piled high to the ceiling; that lemons always swayed in baskets from the rafters; that the apricots and plums, strawberries and pears, peaches and cherries, grapes and blueberries were always delivered in the best season.

Taffeta always had a kind word for the workers and she was especially fond of Barkbelly. She had been amazed when she first saw him working without a splatter suit. From her vantage point down on the factory floor, she hadn't been able to see he was wooden. All she could see was a boy, purple-splotched with blueberry jam from head to toe, cycling furiously round and round.

In alarm, she had scampered up the ladder to the aerial platform and waved at him to stop. Then, fascinated by his strange skin, she had talked to him for half an hour. And with every passing minute, Barkbelly had fallen deeper under her spell. She was so charming and gracious. So interested in what he had to say. And she was beautiful. Very, very beautiful.

Barkbelly was so obviously smitten, Wick couldn't help but notice, and he teased his friend daily. Barkbelly didn't mind. In a strange way, he welcomed the teasing. As long as Wick thought it was a crush, the truth remained safely hidden. Barkbelly did love Taffeta, with all his heart—but he wanted her to be his *sister*, not his girlfriend.

Barkbelly thought Teak Tything was the luckiest man alive. He had the best sister in the world and she adored him. Some brothers and sisters fought like farm cats, but not these two. Whenever Barkbelly saw them together, they were laughing and smiling. They were the best of friends. No, they were more than friends. With a sharp pang of envy, Barkbelly noticed how Teak instinctively protected his sister. He would guide her away from machinery, steer her round puddles, walk on the outside of the pavement when wagons were passing by.

That was how it worked: Teak cherished his sister and she nurtured him in return. She was there to share his secrets and listen to his dreams—to make things better with a hug or a smile. And she would always, always love him, no matter what.

Wherever she went, Taffeta was shadowed by her dog, Dolly, a wiry little terrier that wore a tartan collar and loved nothing better than flushing out mice in the storerooms. Mice and rats were a serious problem in the factory. Hundreds of them lived there, hidden away under the floorboards or in the walls. There was so much they could eat: dried fruit, fresh fruit, sugar and honeycombs . . . they nibbled everything. But their nibbling wasn't the only problem. Their droppings looked just like berry seeds and could get into the jam without anyone noticing. And whenever they shredded sacks or rags or floorboards, they left behind a mound of debris. Usually the cleaners (a formidable troop of women led by Apron Browning) would sweep it up before it caused any mischief. But one day all that changed.

Chapter 21

*I*t was a miserable morning. Winter was over but the rain persisted, and everybody seemed to be sniffling with a cold. When Apron Browning arrived for work, she found she was missing three cleaners. All of them were at home, tucked up in bed with hot-water bottles and flasks of honey tea.

"Today of *all* days," she moaned, and her "girls" (a gaggle of gray-haired matrons with lumpy legs) nodded sympathetically. They were sitting in the cleaning cupboard, where mops moped in corners and brooms bristled by the door.

Apron sucked on her pipe and went on. "Miss Taffeta is expecting a delivery of vanilla sugar, and you know what that's like. Delicate. Very delicate. It absorbs any smell in the room, and if it ends up smelling of dust and dirt, we all know who'll get the blame, don't we?" The girls nodded solemnly. "So we have to scour Storeroom B, and since there's only four of us in today, we'll have to do the factory floor double-quick and then we can get on with it. The delivery is due at two o'clock and the room will need time to dry, so let's get on."

Apron knocked out her pipe and stood on the embers, smoothed the creases in her overalls, stretched, yawned and led her team out onto the factory floor, armed with brooms and dustpans. Soon they were cleaning and polishing, sweeping and dusting, bagging and binning.

They moved through the rooms like ants. They were relentless, merciless, deadly efficient—but too hasty. At the far end of Boiler Room 1, tucked away beneath a corner cupboard, there was a pile of shredded rags. It was dirty bedding, discarded that very morning by the mouse equivalent of Apron Browning. Normally, it would have been swept away faster than a cat can lick its lips, but not that day. The cleaners bustled by and didn't even see it. And as things turned out, that was deeply unfortunate.

The incoming delivery of vanilla sugar was causing bother throughout the factory. The factory worked on exactly the same principle as its machines. Everything was connected. If a wheel turned, then a belt moved and something shifted. Storeroom B, which was now being scrubbed by Apron's girls, had, until that morning, stored bananas. They had to be moved to make way for the sugar, but where could they go? No other storeroom was free.

This was the problem faced by Overseer Mossman when he arrived for work. His solution was simple: they would make banana jam. But it must be made quickly, because the pot would be needed in the afternoon for raspberry jam, and that definitely couldn't wait. The raspberries were softening by the hour, and if they became too soft, the jam wouldn't set.

Mossman loved days like this, when everyone expected answers and he supplied them. He marshaled his troops without delay. Mop Mallory was ordered to lay a fire beneath Pot 1. The bananas were carried in from the Weighing Room and put into the pot with gallons of water. Soon they were simmering, filling the air with a rich yellow scent. Once they were soft, the Overseer added the sugar, lemon juice and a secret blend of spices, then ordered the Fire Feeders to increase the heat. These Fire Feeders—Dog Doyle and Egg Parrish—were two of the heftiest lads in the factory and they began to work like demons, throwing shovels of coal into the blaze and fanning the flames with an enormous set of wheezy bellows. Barkbelly was given the task of stirring the jam.

Mossman, tiger-eyed, supervised the entire operation. Things were not going smoothly. The Fire Feeders were working at a furious pace and the jam was boiling, but they were falling behind schedule. Mossman blamed the bananas. They had been so hard, they had taken longer than usual to soften. He needed to start a batch of plum jam in Pot 2 soon, but he couldn't have two pots boiling side by side at the same time: it was too dangerous. Perhaps if he increased the heat under the banana jam . . .

"Mallory!" he shouted. "Send a message to the fuel store. Tell them I want more coal in here *now*. Then find the Beckwith twins and bring them to me."

Mop dispatched a boy to the coal store, then disappeared in the direction of the staff canteen. Within minutes he returned with the Beckwith twins, Barn and Bucket. They were massive lads, wide as haystacks, with ruddy faces, piggy eyes and a reputation that traveled far beyond the factory gates. The Beckwith twins were extraordinary. Any Fire Feeder could lay a fire and make it burn, but once it was aflame, he became a slave to it. The fire became a ravenous monster, demanding to be fed, and the Fire Feeder sweated and groveled before it. But with the Beckwith twins, this never happened. Somehow the fire became *their* slave, licking their boots and trying to please. For them, any fire would burn hotter, higher, brighter.

"Ah—the experts," said Mossman, greeting them with a thin slice of a smile. "There is need of you." He led the twins to the problem pot. "This jam needs extra heat. Doyle and Parrish have *tried*"—he leaned conspiratorially closer to the twins—"but this requires *something more*."

Barn Beckwith squatted down like a toad and squinted at the fire. Bucket Beckwith walked slowly around the pot, sniffing.

"Banana?" he grunted.

The Overseer nodded.

"Thought so," he muttered. "Always needs a firm hand, does banana." He started to roll up his sleeves.

"Excellent!" declared Mossman. "Doyle! Parrish! You're done! The twins will take over now."

Doyle and Parrish staggered out from the smoke and stumbled off, overjoyed to be relieved. Behind them, the Beckwith twins started to unload a newly arrived coal wagon. Above, Barkbelly wheeled furiously round and round.

Soon Barkbelly could feel the temperature rising. The fire was howling with renewed vigor. Greedy flames licked the buttery air. When he looked down, he could see the twins working the bellows—and Miss Taffeta approaching them. How could he *not* notice her? She was wearing a red velvet dress, and as she glided between the pots, she looked like a poppy in a field of thistles.

Taffeta briefly watched the twins and then, with her clipboard in her hand, skipped off in the direction of the storerooms. Ten minutes later, when Barkbelly went for his lunch, he saw her counting bags of raisins in Storeroom E. Dolly was snuffling at one of the sacks, her stumpy tail wriggling in excitement as she caught the fresh smell of mice. When Barkbelly passed by again, half an hour later, Miss Taffeta was still there, but she had tired of her counting and was curled up on a pile of sacks, fast asleep. Dolly was dozing beside her, oblivious to the scritching and the scratching of the mice as they continued to feast.

Barkbelly returned to his Stir Bike (which had been worked by two other boys in his absence), climbed on and started pedaling. The jam was nearly set. He could see it clinging to the sides of the pot and the aroma was heavenly. He saw Mossman waving to the twins, telling them to dampen the fire. But the fire was reluctant to die, and as Barn Beckwith sprayed the flames with a fine mist of water, a flicker of flame shot up like a dragon's tongue, spitting defiance, and a fiery snow of sparks flew through the air.

Bucket doused the flame immediately. Soon the fire was nothing but a sullen pile of embers and the twins, congratulating each other, abandoned it like victorious soldiers.

But the fire wasn't beaten yet. A single spark from the dragon's tongue had fallen onto the tiny mound of mouse debris that Apron Browning had missed. And there, beneath the corner cupboard at the far end of the Boiler Room, a new fire began.

It smoldered and smoked, sizzled and burned. The shredded rags were devoured within seconds, and the flames leapt to the cupboard and ate through the wood. Inside they found cans of lubricating oil, fat-soaked rags and greasy ropes. The flames pounced on them and soon the cupboard was engulfed by fire and the wall behind it was alight. Black smoke menaced the air, tainting the buttery scent of the jam. Overseer Mossman smelled it; Barkbelly saw it. He was standing on the platform, drinking water, when the first smoke reached him. Looking down, he saw that the entire far end of the Boiler Room was aflame.

"Fire!" he yelled. "Fire! Fire!" Then he ran down the spiral staircase and started ringing the bell outside the Overseer's office.

"Keep ringing!" shouted Overseer Mossman. "Everybody out! Now! Mallory, fetch the register! Leave it, Collins, and go!"

Barkbelly was swamped by a sea of people, panicking, crying, coughing, shouting. They looked for their workmates, looked for the door. The smoke was thickening like gravy. The fire raged, fueled by the coal set under Pots 2 and 3, the varnished rafters and the burlap sacks piled in the nearest storeroom. Machines exploded. Floorboards buckled. The tin roof started to sag, but still Barkbelly rang the bell. Only when Mop dragged him away did he stop, and even then he took the chain with him. He was holding on so tight that he pulled it right off.

Outside in the factory yard, Mossman was reading out names from the shift register, making sure that every worker was accounted for. But Barkbelly wasn't listening to the roll call. Beneath the roar of the flames and the groan of the timbers, he could hear a dog barking. It was faint, but . . .

"Mister Mossman! Mister Mossman!" Barkbelly cried. "It's Miss Taffeta, sir! She's still in there! I can hear her little dog barking!"

At this, a dozen workers wailed in anguish. Others started crying: Miss Taffeta was well loved. Mossman just stared at the inferno. Now that he faced a real crisis, his ability to make decisions had completely abandoned him.

Apron Browning, standing nearby, suddenly spotted the Masters on the far side of the yard.

"Master Tything!" she shrieked. "Old Master Tything, sir! Over here!"

"Everything all right, Mossman?" asked Old Master Tything, hobbling over.

"No, sir. This young man believes he can hear Miss Taffeta's dog barking inside the building."

The color drained from the old man's face. "Has anyone seen Taffeta since the fire started?" he asked the crowd. No one answered. *"Has anyone seen Taffeta since the fire started?"* Still no one answered. Old Master Tything swayed on his feet. Without his son's arm to steady him, he would have toppled like a tree in a hurricane.

"Teak," he gasped. "We must find her!"

Young Master Tything turned to the Overseer.

"Mossman," he said, "go back inside. See if she's there."

"No."

"What did you say?"

"I said *no*." Mossman turned to Mop Mallory. "Make sure the gates are open for the fire wagons."

Young Master Tything was quivering with emotion. "You will go in there," he snarled, grabbing Mossman roughly by the arm. "You shouldn't have come out until you knew it was clear. It is your fault that she is in there now. So you *will* go back in!"

Mossman didn't flinch. *"I will not,"* he hissed. "I am paid to organize the workforce, not to risk my life for a piece of fluff."

Young Master Tything gasped. Then he clenched his fist, swung it and—*smack!*—Mossman dropped where he stood. Blood streamed from his broken nose.

"You worthless worm," Young Master Tything spat at him.

"If you don't get out of here right now, I will tie you to a plank, throw you into that fire and fan the flames myself."

Mossman staggered to his feet and slowly wiped the blood from his nose. Then he stumbled away, with the shocked crowd clearing before him like mist.

Old Master Tything was utterly distraught. "Taffeta," he moaned. "My beautiful Taffeta. I'm—I'm going in there myself!"

"No!" cried Young Master Tything, pulling him back. "You're not! Stay there, Father. I'm going in."

The Young Master ran toward the factory, ripping off his jacket as he went. But suddenly there was a tearing of timbers and the roof collapsed in a shower of sparks and splinters.

"Teak!" cried Old Master Tything. He began to stumble across the yard. "Teak! Come back!"

Teak Tything was staring at the collapsing factory, his face frozen in horror. "*Taffeta*," he groaned. "*Taffeta.*"

"It's too late, son!" said Old Master Tything, seizing him by the arm. "It's too late!"

"It can't be!" said the Young Master wildly. "It can't be. . . . I *will* go in there!"

"No!" cried his father. "No! I've lost a daughter! I cannot bear to lose a son!" He shook Teak violently, willing him to listen. "Do you think I want to say these things? Do you? *Do you?* Son, we have to let her go. It is too late. No one can go in there now."

"I can," said Barkbelly.

The factory workers were crowding round the Masters, with Barkbelly straining among them.

"You can't!" said Wick, holding him back. "It would be madness. It's too late!"

"It's not!" said Barkbelly, struggling to free himself. "She was in Storeroom E and that block is still standing. See?"

He pointed and everyone saw that he was right. The stockrooms were standing while the inferno raged round them.

"No," said Mop Mallory, joining in the debate. "You can't go. It's too dangerous. Anything could happen in there."

"Not to me!" cried Barkbelly, squirming free. "I'm indestructible!" And with that, he raced toward the flames and disappeared into the smoke.

The workers turned to each other, wide-eyed.

"Has he forgotten he's wooden?" cried Apron Browning.

No one answered, but everyone was thinking exactly the same thing.

Chapter 22

The stockroom wing was still standing, but that didn't mean it was safe. The smoke was unbelievable: a thick black fog that packed the corridors so tightly it seemed almost solid. Fingers of fire snatched at Barkbelly's ankles as he ran by. He choked and retched, coughed and spat. He staggered blindly on, fumbling and stumbling. Fallen timbers littered the floor. Walls spat out their bricks. Everything was bending and twisting in the terrible heat, but still he went on.

Suddenly he saw a ghostly figure waving at him. Taffeta! She was nothing but shadow and smoke: a thin wraith, silver and gray, waving like a windblown willow. Barkbelly could see that she was trying to call out, but the smoke surged down into her lungs. She fell back against a door frame, coughing and gagging. She held her scarf across her mouth with one hand while the other cradled her limp dog.

Barkbelly charged. Every skill he had learned as a Bull Runner came into play now. He swept aside broken pipes and tattered screens. He batted bricks and kicked tiles. He powered his way toward her. He took her in his arms and threw her bodily over one shoulder. He turned and fought his way back through the falling factory. Then he emerged, blinking in the sunlight.

The crowd bellowed and surged forward. They took Taffeta from him and put her down on the ground, where she lay as lifeless as the dog beside her.

"Taffeta!" cried Old Master Tything, cradling her in his arms. "Taffeta!"

"Stand back!" yelled Young Master Tything. "Stand back, for pity's sake! All of you! She needs air! Can't you see that? Stand back! Mallory, get them back!"

Barkbelly was quite forgotten in the fight for Taffeta to breathe. The crowd was moving like a many-headed monster. Everyone was straining to see, to hear, to know. And suddenly, in the dark of the despair, Taffeta coughed. Then she spluttered, and her body folded in upon itself again and again as more coughs racked her body. The dog was coughing too, flapping beside her like a fish.

The crowd howled its relief in a single voice—a deafening roar that brought down the rest of the tiles on the factory roof and drifted over the town into the fields beyond.

Then cheers and hurrahs and screams and shouts. Yells and cries and whistles and hollers. And a chant, rumbling up from the belly of the crowd: "Barkbelly! Barkbelly! BARKBELLY! BARKBELLY!" And the lone voice of Apron Browning screaming above it, "You're on fire! Your little finger is on fire!"

And it was. It was blazing like a torch. Flames feasted on the wooden flesh. Sparks flew like fairies. Coat Collins was shouting for someone to do something. Apron Browning was wailing. The crowd was horrified at this new tragedy thrown upon their young hero.

But Barkbelly just grinned and shook his hand violently in the air, killing the flames. "I'm all right!" he cried. "I'm all right!"

"But you're *not* all right," snorted Apron, taking hold of his hand and examining it. "It's gone!"

People craned their necks for a better look. It was true! The little finger on Barkbelly's left hand was completely burned away. There wasn't even a stump—just a smoldering patch where the finger should be.

"But it's *all right!*" Barkbelly insisted. "Really! This has happened before. Last time it was the whole hand! It will grow back. Believe me! It will. *Watch!*"

He held his hand up in the air and they all watched. And waited. And watched. And waited.

"Nothing's happening," said a disappointed voice somewhere in the crowd.

"Shhh!" hissed Wick. "Be patient! It will start soon."

But it didn't. Barkbelly stared at his hand, willing it to grow, but nothing happened. And there in the factory yard, fear found him, just as surely as it had found him in the playground when Little Pan Evans lay dead at his feet. He felt his belly tightening, his heart fluttering in his chest. He felt hot, then cold. Giddy. Sick. His legs were like tree trunks, rooting him to the ground.

"Grow!" Barkbelly murmured. "Grow."

The crowd was jostling and pushing against him, confused, wanting a happy ending and not getting one.

"Come on!" he growled. He grasped his wrist, urging the finger to renew itself. "*Come on!*"

"It doesn't matter," said Wick, taking him by the arm. "It doesn't matter."

"It matters to *me!*" cried Barkbelly. "*It matters to me! Don't you see? It's not growing back! It's not growing back!* I thought I was indestructible! That's why I ran in to save Miss Taffeta. I thought nothing could ever stop me. Nothing could ever hurt me or kill me. But *look!*" He waved his disfigured hand wildly in Wick's face. "Don't you see what this means? Fire can kill me. *It can kill me.* I thought I could never be destroyed."

Suddenly the crowd cheered ecstatically. The workers hadn't been listening to Barkbelly. They had turned to watch Taffeta, who was being helped to her feet by her proud father. This was better! This was a happy ending! And what's more, the press had arrived! A reporter and an illustrator from the *Daily Truth!* The reporter was firing questions at anyone and everyone. The illustrator was brandishing his pencil and sketchbook, drawing likenesses of Taffeta and her dog faster than a boy could wipe his nose.

Wick could see that his friend was reeling with shock. It was as if the fire, the factory and his heroism meant nothing in the face of this dreadful truth. Wick wanted to take Barkbelly away, back to the bunkhouse, somewhere quiet.

"*There he is! Over there! There's the hero! Barkbelly!*"

The chant started again as the press turned to find the hero of the hour. Questions flew at him like arrows.

"What's your full name, son?" asked the reporter. "What made you decide to go into the fire? Do you know Miss Taffeta well, then?"

Barkbelly ignored him and turned to the illustrator. "What are you doing?" he asked.

"I'm drawing you," said the illustrator. "It's only a sketch."

"I hear you're not originally from this town. So where do

you come from? Somewhere out in the country?" The reporter again. Why was he still there?

Barkbelly grabbed hold of the illustrator. "Why are you drawing me? Why?"

"To put in the paper, of course! You're a hero, Barkbelly! People will want to see you when they hear all about it!"

"What people? How far does this newspaper go?"

"All over the country, lad! All over! You'll be famous!"

Run.

"What did you say the name of your village was, son?"

Run.

"Why did you leave it? Nothing wrong, was there?"

Run.

"We can find out, you know. . . ."

And as Barkbelly felt his past catch up with him, he turned from the crowd and ran.

PART THREE

Chapter 23

*R*ain, rain, endless rain. It fell like footsteps and danced on the rocky ridge outside the cave. Barkbelly silently thanked fortune for it. It had washed away any tracks he had made during his escape. If only it could wash away all memory of him. But it couldn't. In Tythingtown, people would remember. For years to come, they would talk about him—over bread and jam in the factory canteen, over champagne and oysters in the Tything mansion. They would tell the story of the hero who ran away. The boy who had something to hide. The wooden one.

He remembered running through the crowd of factory workers and pushing open the golden gates while Dogger protested. He remembered running through the town. It was market day and he had deliberately turned into the square to confuse his pursuers. He forced his way through the crowd, trying to maintain speed without attracting attention. He slipped on a fish head thrown from a stall. He banged his leg on a trestle as he skidded round a clutter of farmers' wives. He fell over a crate of ducks and knocked a sack of sugar from a baker's hands. The baker bellowed at him and waved a floury fist.

He sprinted along the main road out of town and was amazed at how soon the gray became green. There was a terrace of cottages, one last tavern and then—nothing. Just frowning fields and skeletal trees.

He ran for three days and nights. He barely stopped. He caught a few hours of sleep in a tumbledown barn but it was fitful, soured by the constant animal urge to flee. The miles melted into each other as he ran beyond the farms into the mountains beyond. The rain started on the first night, with a storm that rumbled in from the west. Bruising raindrops, drumming to the rhythm of his running.

He found the cave on the fourth day. A waterlogged dawn was creeping over the mountains. Fingers of light touched trees, boulders, bushes. He was clawing his way over a rocky outcrop when he saw the cave mouth. It was a hard ten minutes' climb away, but it looked promising. At least it would be shelter from the rain.

He scrabbled on, hauling himself upward. When he reached the cave, he sniffed the air suspiciously, alert to any lingering smell of bear or wolf. But there was nothing, and he soon discovered why. The cave was tiny. It didn't tunnel deep into the mountainside, as he had expected. It was no bigger than a room, and a small one at that. A kitchen, say.

And with that thought—*whoosh!*—he was suddenly home. He could see the table laid for breakfast as usual: plates, cups and saucers, knives, forks and spoons. But it looked different somehow, and he couldn't think why. And there was Mama at the stove, stirring the porridge in her worn apron with the blue flowers. And there was Papa, coming in the door with logs under his arm. Rain was dripping off his hat—it was raining there too—and he was saying something to Mama, but Barkbelly couldn't hear the words. And suddenly Mama was turning round, and she had dark rings under her eyes and more wrinkles than he remembered. Papa did too. And as they sat down to breakfast, he saw that the table had been set with only two places. There was no place for him.

He stepped outside again and the vision disappeared. The rain had stopped. Steam was rising in the thin sunlight, curling upward like the breath of a sleeping dragon. He gazed at the horizon and realized that was how far he had come. How much farther did he have to go? He was too tired to think.

Reluctantly he returned to the dry blackness of the cave, curled up and slept. His sleep was thick and dreamless. It eased all the aches and strains that had wormed into his wooden body.

He slept for a full day. When he awoke, it was raining again.

Chapter 24

arkbelly sat on the ridge outside the cave. He took another wild apple from the pile by his side and ate it, crunching the core and swallowing the seeds. His gaze traveled over the valley like a hawk. The rain had gone, leaving a shiny dampness, and there was a flight of geese arrowing across the sky, heading . . . East? West? He had no idea, but he longed to follow them. *Overseas!* That was where he needed to go! Somewhere safe. A new land, where he couldn't be recognized and tried for murder. That was why it had all gone wrong at the factory—he hadn't run far enough. He wouldn't make that mistake again.

If I find the coast and follow it, eventually I'll come to a harbor. Perhaps I can find work as a sailor. Ships always needed crews— he had learned that at school. He was fit and strong, so why not? He wouldn't ask for wages—just free passage across the sea. He wouldn't even ask where the ship was bound.

There was just one problem. Where was the sea? He had seen it on a map once, and it had looked unbelievably distant. Even now, halfway up a mountain, he couldn't see it on the horizon. So when he started walking, which direction should he choose?

Follow the geese! They would be flying to the coast! Or

would they? Geese flew to water, that was true, but any water seemed to suit them. They were always flying into Otterdown Mere back home and that was little more than a marsh. They might lead him in completely the wrong direction. But what other choice did he have?

Barkbelly slid down the mountain and found a road. It was empty and desolate, but it looked safe enough. And surely it would lead to a village? A farm? With hope in his heart and hunger in his belly, he started down it.

For the first few hours, his step was jaunty. He whistled as he walked. But as the day lengthened, he began to falter. The road was longer than he had imagined. It went on and on, with no end in sight, twisting and turning between two unbroken mountain ranges. Gaunt sheep gazed at him from the crags, their yellow eyes as bleak as the landscape. Sometimes he passed the remains of those that had lost the fight for survival. Broken-mouthed, they had fallen where they stood, watched by ravens that gathered like mourners at a funeral. When Barkbelly approached, the fleece-rippers didn't fly away. They stared at him with boot-black eyes and raucously demanded that he walk on. He did.

On his third day of walking through the pass, Barkbelly realized that the mountain ranges on either side of the road were closing together like crab's claws. His stomach lurched.

"I don't believe it!" he said, though no one was listening. "I've come so far and there's no way through!"

Yet still he trudged on, wanting to believe there would be some kind of track ahead. And there was. Suddenly he saw it: a rough path, spiraling up into the mist. With luck, the mist would clear as he climbed. When he reached the peak, he would have a view of the horizon—and the sea.

He started climbing with renewed vigor. He scuttled up the path like a spider. Stones clattered down the mountain behind him. His arms powered him on. His breath steamed like a genie. He was getting there.

Finally the road leveled out and the mist started to clear. He caught his breath and strained to see something. But there was nothing. Nothing but bitter disappointment. He was on a plateau: a vast arena, ringed by stone, totally barren and desperately cold. No trees, no bushes—no hint of a horizon. For that, he would have to cross the plateau; judging the distance, he thought it would be a full day's trek.

And that was when Barkbelly cried. For the first time in his life, he wept like the child he was. He sank to the ground, his shoulders started to heave and fat blue tears rolled down his wooden cheeks. He made no attempt to wipe them away. He simply let them fall. There was no one here to see them. And with that thought, the tears fell faster. He had never felt so alone. So lost. So small. So friendless.

Cold despair covered him like snow, freezing him to the ground, blotting out any hope of a bright future. What more could he do? He had walked for days, without food, without company, without help of any kind. No one had been there to encourage him, to tell him he was doing the right thing, to hold him and say it would be all right in the end. No one had sung him to sleep at night or greeted him with a smile in the morning. He had seen no one for days—weeks? How long was it? He had no idea.

He took a deep breath, clambered to his feet and tried to calm himself. *There must be something here. There must be someone.* He stood up, wiped his eyes on his sleeve and looked around. But still there was nothing. And suddenly he had a terrifying thought. *What if I am the only person left alive in the world? What if there has been a terrible disaster and everyone's gone?*

He felt giddy just imagining it. He started to sway unsteadily. His mind groped for answers but found more questions instead. *What if this is a different world? What if my world is back on the other side of the mountains? It could happen, some shift in time or space. What if I can't find the way back?*

His legs gave way underneath him. He sank to the ground again and curled up on the hard rock. He wrapped his arms tight round his knees and whimpered like a wounded animal. He had struggled on for days, but now it was over. He could do no more.

He must have slept, because when he awoke it was dark. Not a clear, sharp darkness but a fuzzy, foggy blackness. The mist was so thick he couldn't see his own body. Now he couldn't move even if he wanted to. He was helpless. The terrors of the night could be all round him and he wouldn't even know.

He sat completely still, listening for any sound of danger. Nothing. Minutes went by. He could feel the damp mist sinking into his wooden limbs. He listened on. Nothing. But then . . . He tensed. It wasn't a sound exactly. It was a movement. *There were tremors in the earth.* He could feel them. He listened hard. He could hear dull thuds somewhere in the distance. They were regular, like footfalls. And they were coming closer. Definitely coming closer.

And now there was a new sound: the thump of his own terrified heart as it sensed something closing in. *The terrors had found him.* Long gray arms reached out toward him. They had no hands—just wet stumps. They prodded and probed. Slick and slimy, they nudged and nuzzled, spitting steam into the darkness. And then came a head. An enormous head with one eye loomed out of the mist. The eye examined him, while below, a dripping tongue tasted the air.

I'm going to die, he thought. *I'm going to die. Oh, Mama, let it be quick. Painless. Please.*

But death never came. The great gray elephant harrumphed her recognition, lifted her massive head and trumpeted into the night. The other elephants joined her, and the plateau echoed with the bellow of their welcome and the clanking of their ankle rings.

Barkbelly opened his eyes and saw a light. A single light was swaying through the fog: a lantern on the side of a wagon. And suddenly he could hear the muffled rumble of wheels and the wagon emerged from the gloom. It had flowers painted on the front. Wet tassels dripped at each corner. There was a wagoner in a wide-brimmed hat and a coat with the collar turned up against the drizzle. Beside him was a young girl, swathed in a long black cloak, with a worn leather hat pulled down low over her face. Two silver braids were hanging damply beneath it.

It was Candy Pie.

Chapter 25

*A*nd so Barkbelly was saved by the circus. The wagoner (who turned out to be the strong man, Anvil Allsop) reached down and in a single movement lifted Barkbelly high onto the seat beside him. And there Barkbelly sat for the rest of the night, draped in a blanket, while Carmenero's Circus trundled on.

As dawn broke, the circus finally descended the mountains. Ahead, Barkbelly could see Appleforth, the next village on the tour, still asleep on the plain. But as the circus rolled up the main street, curtains twitched, bleary faces were pressed against windows and unwashed children came running like rabbits to gaze at the new arrivals.

The circus meandered to the village green. Soon the campfires were lit and the kettles were singing. Barkbelly sat with Candy and her mother, Peaches. Everyone seemed to remember him. The men slapped him on his back and said it was good to see him again. The women kissed him and handed him cinnamon buns, syrup pancakes, hot chocolate. Jewel the storyteller gave him dry clothes. Gossamer the wire-walker winked at him. Even the great Carmenero shook his hand and asked if there was anything he needed. Barkbelly told him there wasn't. He had absolutely everything he needed and so much more.

No one asked him why he had been wandering so far from home. Not even Candy. She had learned that the circus was not a place where questions were asked. But she did want to hear about the village.

"Bark," she said, pawing his arm excitedly. "Tell me what's been going on."

And suddenly—*whoosh!*—Barkbelly was back in the playground.

"Don't you know?" he said, though he wondered how he'd managed to speak.

"No! Of course I don't! I haven't been back," she said. "And I am *dying* for news. So tell me!"

So Barkbelly told her. Not about Little Pan Evans. Not that. But he did tell her about the babies born and the coffins carried. He told her about the summer fête and the village picnic. He told her about the drama at the harvest fair, when one of the fireworks had shot down the chimney into Freckle Flannagan's house and exploded, shattering all the windows. He told her how Farmer Bunkum had caught Fish Patterson stealing apples in his orchard and given him such a thrashing that Fish had sworn revenge. And later that night, Fish had crept into the farmer's cider house, opened up the cider flagons and peed into every one. The very next week, Farmer Bunkum had entered them in the county fair and won the cup for Best Cider in Show.

Candy laughed and gasped and questioned and nodded as he told his tales. She enjoyed every little detail, and Barkbelly enjoyed telling her. And when she suddenly hugged him and told him how lovely it was to see him, he believed her. Candy had changed.

This wasn't the spiteful little madam who had prowled the playground, spitting out insults. This was a new Candy: warm, welcoming and surprisingly modest. The fancy hair ribbons had gone and she was wearing a hand-me-down dress that looked faded and shabby, despite the sequins on its bodice. But Candy clearly loved it. When she was listening to the saga of Fish and the flagons, she took hold of the skirt and crumpled it up between her hands. When the tale was over, she carefully smoothed the creases out.

"Thank you!" she said, beaming. "That was *wonderful!*"

"I haven't told you the best bit." Barkbelly grinned. "You have a new name."

"No!" squealed Candy. "What do they call me?"

"Cotton Candy!"

"*Oh!* Who came up with that? Moth Williams?"

Barkbelly nodded.

"I thought so. I can just imagine him saying it." She smiled wistfully. "I liked Moth."

"Did you? Wow. We never knew. Do you miss the village?"

"I suppose I do," said Candy. "I've never really thought about it until now. But hearing all your stories . . . Yes, I do miss it a bit. I'd miss it a lot more if my mother were still there, but she's not. I don't want to go back, though. Oh, no! Bark— you won't *believe* what I am now!"

She gathered armfuls of her skirt into her hands again and started rocking back and forth in her excitement.

"I am . . . *a trapeze artist!*"

Chapter 26

*N*ewcomers to the circus were always welcome, but they had to work for their keep. No one was allowed to laze in the sun while others toiled.

As soon as breakfast was over on that first morning, Barkbelly was told to help the men erect the Stardust Palace. Once that was done, he was given an enormous brush and ordered to clean the elephants. Their trainer, Oat Ormsby (or Emeraldez, as he was known professionally), had taken them down to the river to be scrubbed. When Barkbelly arrived, he found the dapper little man already soaked to the skin. His long black mustache was dangling like a rat's tail, while his hair was curling riotously on his head and dripping suspiciously black drops.

"It's nobbut a bit o' high spirits," said Emeraldez apologetically, shaking Barkbelly's hand. "They do this to me every time. You're *naughty* girls, ain'tcha? Naughty! *Naughty!*" He tugged at a huge flappy ear and its owner lifted her trunk and squirted him full in the face.

Barkbelly spent the whole morning scrubbing the elephants. They were grimy after the long trek over the mountains. The dust had settled into every fold and wrinkle. But

Emeraldez was insisting on perfect cleanliness for the opening show. It meant hours of backbreaking work, but Barkbelly labored on. He could feel his legs growing heavier as the river water soaked into his wood. When the job was finally over, he lumbered back up to camp. But he felt like dancing. He was truly part of the circus now.

Barkbelly's first week passed by in a flurry of sawdust and spangles. Every morning he hummed through his chores. Every evening he wallowed in the magic of circus. And every night he slept. The bad dreams had gone. Sometimes he would think about Little Pan Evans and Taffeta Tything, and wonder why the joy of saving one life did nothing to heal the pain of taking another. It made no sense. But mostly he was too busy to think. He learned how to polish saddles and groom animals. How to paint wagons and mend nets. How to tie knots and pack canvas. He heard himself muttering, "This is fantastic!" all day long. Every new experience was sheer pleasure.

Then he worked with the skunks.

Barkbelly found the skunk trainer at the water pump. He was a bear of a man with grizzled gray hair and eyes like marbles. His name was Samovar Rubek and he came from a distant country with an unpronounceable name. And in that country, according to Rubek, everything was massive. Enormous trees. Vast plains. Skyscraping mountains. Big people—and he was no exception. Everything about Rubek was big. His wagon was bigger than all the others. His boots were big enough to use as dog kennels. His hands were as big as buckets. He claimed the space around him and filled it with a thick stew of language and laughter. When he spoke, his voice rumbled up from his belly with such a hum that Barkbelly fancied he had a swarm of bees nesting in his rib cage.

"You are helper today? That's good! Good!" He smacked Barkbelly hard on the back in welcome and Barkbelly felt the tremor ripple down his legs. "My babies are in tent. I fill bucket, then we go to them."

Rubek pumped furiously and a torrent of water sploshed into the bucket below. What a bucket! It was enormous: at least twice the size of an ordinary bucket. But in Rubek's hands it looked positively small. Then he picked up a second bucket, already full, and led Barkbelly across the campsite to his wagon. There was a fancy tent pitched alongside it, striped black and white, just like the creatures it housed. Barkbelly dashed forward and lifted up the tent flap. Rubek carried the buckets inside and Barkbelly followed.

The smell was the first thing that Barkbelly noticed. The musky-rose scent of the skunks, mingled with the sweetness of the bedding, produced a warm, welcoming aroma. It was heavenly. There were ten skunks. Two were snuffling around the pen, but the others were asleep, curled up on little loft beds. There was a low constant hum: the sleeping skunks were purring like cats. And with the purring and the heady scent, Barkbelly felt overwhelmed by a sudden urge to sleep. He could feel his eyelids drooping. He yawned, and seconds later he yawned again.

Rubek prodded him with a fat finger. "You are tired?"

"No," replied Barkbelly. "Well—perhaps a bit. I can't stop yawning."

"You will get used to it. Open up tent flap. Air will help."

Barkbelly tied back the canvas flap and started to feel brighter. He looked admiringly at the animals. They all had long, glistening black coats with a distinctive white stripe running down their backs, from nose to tail.

"My babies," crooned Rubek. "Have you ever seen such beautiful creatures? No! Of course you have not! They are most beautiful creatures in the world. This is Honeysuckle." He pointed at a sleeping bundle of fur. "And this is Rose . . . Lavender . . . Lily . . . Violet . . . Magnolia . . . Daphne . . . Lilac . . . Camellia . . . and Jasmine. And they must be brushed. Every day!"

He picked up a skunk and stroked it lovingly. "This coat must shine. Like white moon coming out from black cloud, see? Beautiful."

He kissed the skunk's nose and the little animal giggled. Rubek returned the skunk to the pen and strode over to a fine wooden chest at the far end of the tent. He lifted the lid.

"Come!" he said, and he beckoned Barkbelly nearer. "Look! Best brushes! Made from—"

"Urchin bristle!" cried Barkbelly, and he picked out a brush and started examining it. "Brown-Eared Marsh Hog," he said. "Fine quality."

"You are expert!" cried Rubek, slapping him hard on the back again. "How come you know this?"

Barkbelly didn't answer. His head was suddenly full of memories. He could see the farm and all the men standing in the yard. Old Pot Williamson, Brick Pullman, Farmer Muckledown—they were all there. Then he saw the sheds and the urchins in their pens. And Bramble. Not in a pen but in the forest, as he had seen her last.

"Hello?" said Rubek, waving his hand in front of Barkbelly's face. "Are you still in there?"

Barkbelly gazed dreamily at the skunk trainer. He didn't

speak, but he didn't need to. His face told Rubek all he needed to know.

Rubek smiled, revealing a generous helping of teeth. "You have memories of these things, yes? They are good memories—I see. Keep them. Hold them close to your heart. They are precious things." He fell silent. "I have *many* memories," he said at last, and his eyes brimmed with tears. He was quiet again, but it wasn't an awkward silence. It was a comradely one and Barkbelly felt strangely comforted by it.

"My babies," said Rubek with a great sigh. "Brushing. They like it, but use brush that is not hard. And do not lift tails. This they do not like." He took another brush from the chest and gave it to Barkbelly. "Try this with Lily." He indicated a small skunk that was wide awake and scratching. "I must see Carmenero to talk things. But I will return. Not too hard, remember?"

Barkbelly nodded.

"Good man," said Rubek, and he strode heavily out of the tent.

Chapter 27

Barkbelly waited till he was sure Rubek had gone, then he carefully lifted Lily out of her pen, settled her on his lap and began brushing. She seemed happy enough and he had her coat gleaming within minutes. He returned her to the pen and picked up Lilac. She was adorable. She nuzzled him as he cradled her in his arms. Soon she was silky soft and shining. Camellia was next, then Lavender and Magnolia. Rose. Jasmine. Honeysuckle. Then Daphne. *Just one more to do! Rubek will be so impressed. I'll have them finished by the time he gets back!*

Violet next. Barkbelly couldn't find her at first. She was rolling around in the chalky dust underneath one of the loft beds, and by the time he coaxed her out, she was almost completely white. Barkbelly groaned and put her on his knee. He started brushing her with the same soft brush he had used on the others, but her fur was so matted, the bristles just bounced over it. He would have to use something harder.

He rummaged in the chest until he found a stiffer brush. Violet sat patiently while he straightened out her knotted fur. But it was taking so long. He wanted to be finished before Rubek returned. He started to brush harder. He pulled. He tugged. He dragged the brush along her tangled back. Violet was unnervingly quiet. She had flattened herself against his lap, but Barkbelly hadn't noticed because he was so intent on finishing the job.

With a grunt and a grimace, Barkbelly cleared the last of the snarls on Violet's back. Next—her tail. *What a mess!* It was like a ball of wool a kitten had been playing with. He didn't know where to begin. Perhaps it was smoother underneath.

Barkbelly lifted Violet's tail and—*pssss!*—a hot shower of scent shot from her back end and hit him full in the face. And this wasn't the clear, rose-scented perfume that sprayed the audience nightly. This was hot brown goo with a smell bad enough to peel paint. It was an *unbelievable* stench. Positively evil. It made his stomach churn and his eyes water.

I've got to get out. I've got to get out.

He put Violet back into the pen, and as he did, the little devil giggled. Then, as he stumbled toward the tent opening, with the goo dripping from his hair into his eyes, all the other skunks turned their bottoms toward him, lifted their gorgeous tails and—*pssss!*—the whole tent was rainbowed with arcs of steaming stink. Barkbelly's clothes were soaked and, worse, his wood was starting to suck up the stink like a sponge.

And just when he thought things couldn't get any worse, the tent opening was suddenly filled with Rubek *and* Carmenero.

"*No!*" Barkbelly wailed, and he barged past them, ran across the campsite, leapt the fence, raced through the meadow and slithered down to the riverbank. Then he hurled himself into the river and lay down in the shallows, praying he could rinse away the stink. But he couldn't. After an hour, the stench was stronger than before. Barkbelly whimpered. Fat tears rolled down his cheeks.

"Stink is bad, yes?"

Barkbelly looked up. Rubek was sitting on the riverbank. A hint of a smile flickered at the corners of his mouth. His marble eyes shone mischievously, and for all his great bulk, he suddenly looked no older than Fish Patterson.

"Will it ever go away?" Barkbelly asked.

"Of course," replied Rubek. "In time."

"How much time?"

Rubek shrugged. "Two weeks. Maybe three."

Barkbelly's face crumbled like cheese.

"Unless . . ." Rubek reached inside his waistcoat pocket and pulled out a bottle of purple liquid. "Unless we use this!" He grinned and threw his arms out wide. "Come!" he cried. "Come! You must rub this into your—your—*skin*! Your wooden skin! Now! Right now!"

Barkbelly dragged himself up the bank, stripped off his clothes and started rubbing palmfuls of the purple liquid onto his body. It had a strange, sweet smell. He thought he had smelled it somewhere before, but he couldn't remember where. It certainly worked. Within minutes, all trace of the stink had disappeared. He dressed himself in the fresh clothes that Rubek had brought for him and sat down in a pool of sunshine beside the skunk trainer. He felt clean and calm and wonderfully fragrant.

"I know this smell," Barkbelly said at last. "But I can't remember what it is."

"Is magic recipe," said Rubek. "Good for all kinds of things. Is made from herbs and flowers. Sage. Rosemary. Chamomile. Wood rose."

"Yes, I can smell all those things," said Barkbelly. "But there's something else." He breathed in deeply. "It's a sweet smell. Really quite strong. What's that?"

"Oh, that?" said Rubek with a smile. "That, my friend, is scent of very small woodland flower. You know it well, I think. It is *violet*."

Chapter 28

*B*arkbelly was polishing the lion cage when Candy came toward him, walking on her hands. She had a crumpled piece of paper between her teeth.

"It's for you!" she gasped, righting herself and passing it to him. "Carmenero handed it to me himself. He wants to see you at two o'clock in his wagon. You are *so* lucky!"

Barkbelly read the note but was disappointed to find that it didn't contain anything more than what Candy had already told him.

"What's lucky about it?" he asked.

"Well, for starters, you get to see inside his fantastic wagon. And when he serves you tea, he has the best cakes in the world. And—" She paused dramatically. "If he has decided to offer you a job, you will be rich!"

"Rich?"

"Yes! Well, no. Not really. I made that bit up. No one gets paid very much around here. But you will get something."

"But what if he doesn't want to offer me a job?" said Barkbelly. "What if he just wants me to leave?"

"I don't think that's likely," said Candy. "You're not exactly *ordinary,* are you?" She smiled, and Barkbelly noticed for the very first time that her mouth curved up like a harp. Then, without warning, she somersaulted backward and skipped away. "Don't be late!" she called over her shoulder.

Barkbelly watched her go. As she passed the ticket booth, he saw Gossamer pounce on her from behind and she squealed. Then she giggled and they strolled on together, arm in arm, flitting like damselflies between the busy circus folk.

"Please let it be a job," said Barkbelly, and he put the note carefully into his pocket.

Like all the showmen's wagons, Carmenero's was wooden, with intricate carving round the windows and the door. It was painted a deep midnight blue and the domed roof was silvered with stars. Outside, an enormous black dog dozed in the bright spring sunshine, her head resting on the bottom step.

Barkbelly carefully mounted the wagon steps, trying not to disturb the dog. But instantly she was awake and sniffing at his legs while he knocked. Wooden knuckles on a wooden door. . . . The sound ricocheted like gunshots and the wagon quivered up and down its length as the force rippled its timbers. Barkbelly cursed. This was a worrying start.

But when the door opened, Carmenero was grinning behind it.

"Come in!" he said. "While I still have a door to close behind you! Stay, Lady."

The dog wagged her tail and Barkbelly stepped inside. Candy was right! The interior was fantastic. The paneling for the seats and cupboards was rich oak, lovingly polished. The seat bolsters were moss-green velvet, embroidered with tiny primroses. The carpet was green too: thick and lush as a

meadow bank. And the ceiling . . . *Ah!* Just for a moment, he thought the wagon didn't have one. It was painted so cunningly, he thought he was looking straight up into the sky. But inside the wagon it was sunset, and the sky was a wonderful pink-orange, veiled with wisps of cloud.

Even the ceiling seemed ordinary, though, when Barkbelly saw the walls. Just as he had thought the wagon hadn't any roof, now he thought it hadn't any sides. The campsite had vanished. He was looking out into the heart of an emerald forest. Sunlight filtered through the leaf canopy. Tigers eyed him from the undergrowth. Snakes hung from the branches. Gaudy butterflies festooned the flowers. Hummingbirds hovered, sipping sweet nectar. It was so unbelievably lifelike, Barkbelly swore he could smell the damp earthiness of the forest floor.

With a jolt, he suddenly remembered where he was. He was standing in Carmenero's wagon, gaping like a goldfish and totally ignoring the most important man in the world. He had been so utterly entranced by the mural that he had forgotten his manners just when he needed them most.

"Oh! I'm . . . Ohh! I—I am sorry, er, Mister Carmenero," he stammered. "Just for a moment, I completely forgot where I was. I thought it was all real."

"Are you sure it isn't?" said Carmenero with an enigmatic smile. "Look closer."

Barkbelly looked at the walls again. This time he noticed a parrot sitting in one of the trees. It was looking right at him. And as Barkbelly watched, it winked.

Barkbelly was stunned. *What on earth . . .* Then the parrot winked again. And again. Always the same lazy, knowing wink. Barkbelly was totally bewildered. He thought it was just a painting, but now . . .

There was something not quite right, though. Carmenero was standing behind him, and now and then, out of the corner of his eye, Barkbelly saw him lean ever so slightly to one side. And whenever he did that, the parrot winked.

"It's a trick!" he cried out, spinning round. "You're making it wink!"

"Of course!" laughed Carmenero. "It's a trick of the light. See?"

He stood aside, revealing a lantern hanging on the wall behind him. "If I lean in like this, I cover the lantern—and when I lean back out, the parrot seems to wink. It's very easy, but it fools people every time. You were quick! Some people take ages to realize, but then, Truth is a snail."

Barkbelly frowned. "A snail?"

Carmenero nodded. "Have you never heard the story 'Truth and the Dragon'?"

Barkbelly shook his head.

"Ask Jewel," said Carmenero. "She's the best storyteller round here."

He sat down on one of the plush seats and indicated that Barkbelly should do the same. Now, sitting opposite the great man, Barkbelly realized that this was the first time he had really looked at his face. Until this moment, he had just had a head full of impressions. Carmenero the ringmaster, with his showman's flair and booming voice. Carmenero the leader, rolling up his sleeves and sweating with the men as they raised the Stardust Palace. Carmenero the charmer, flirting with the circus girls as they blushed with pleasure. Carmenero the carer, giving quiet reassurance to anyone who needed it. Carmenero the boss, roaring his disapproval at anyone who offered less than his or her best, in or out of the ring. Carmenero the loner, walking through the misty morning fields with his dog. Carmenero, the beating heart of the circus, loved by the circus folk and adored by audiences.

Carmenero was truly revered. The circus girls talked about him as if he were a god. So Barkbelly was surprised to discover that the circus owner wasn't blessed with the looks of one. He was handsome, yes, but not perfect. And he wasn't as tall or as brawny as some of the other men in the circus. But he had something else. And it was this something else that made Barkbelly decide that if he could choose to look like anyone else in the world, he would choose to look like Carmenero. Quite simply, Carmenero was such a good man, it showed in his face. Carmenero was handsome on the inside.

"You're probably wondering why I've called you here today," Carmenero began.

Barkbelly just nodded. His mouth felt too dry for words.

"Tell me, Barkbelly, are you happy here?"

Barkbelly nodded again, but more vigorously this time.

Carmenero smiled. "That's good," he said, "because I'd like to offer you a job."

"*Oh!*" cried Barkbelly, and he slumped with relief. "Thank you, Mister Carmenero," he said. "I've been so worried, I can't begin to tell you. I won't let you down, sir. I'm ever so strong and I'm really good with animals. I don't mind mucking out or what have you."

"Excellent, because we need an assistant skunk keeper."

Thick silence flooded the wagon. Barkbelly could hear nothing except his own heart thumping in dismay. Carmenero watched him with curious eyes.

"Thank you, Mister Carmenero," repeated Barkbelly in a tiny voice. "I won't let you down, sir." He stood up and headed for the door, but Carmenero was there before him, blocking the way.

"You really do want to stay here, don't you?" he asked. Barkbelly looked straight into the circus owner's eyes, and Carmenero thought he had never seen such bleak despair on a face as he saw then on Barkbelly's. "That's good," he continued, "because I have great plans for you. And they don't involve skunks." Carmenero grinned impishly and grabbed Barkbelly warmly by the shoulders. "Sit down!" he said. "We still need to talk."

Barkbelly sat down again. His head was spinning.

"Now," said Carmenero as he gathered his thoughts, "you are far too special to work backstage. That would be a complete waste of your talent. You are unique. When you first saw the show at Pumbleditch—do you remember Meteor Man?"

Barkbelly thought. "Was he the human cannonball?"

"He was! But he's not with us anymore, so *that's* the job I'm offering you. I want you to be the Cannonball Kid! We need a new act. Something to bring the crowds in. I'll start a big publicity campaign. Lots of posters, that sort of thing. Your face will be everywhere! You'll be a star! You'll need a little time to work up the act, of course, and we'll have to strengthen the net. We can't have you ripping through it every night. Think of the splinters! You'd kill half the front row!" He beamed reassuringly. "Peaches will have to make you a costume, but I think we could have you in the show in, say, two weeks' time. What do you think?"

Barkbelly sat very still. He thought. "If you don't mind, Mister Carmenero," he said carefully, "I would rather work backstage."

Carmenero breathed in. Those five little words told him

more about Barkbelly than others would learn in hours of con-versation. *Barkbelly was in hiding.* And he wasn't the only one; Carmenero could think of half a dozen others who had sat in his wagon and said the same words. They were in the circus right now, mending canvas and sweeping up sawdust. None of them performed. Sometimes, in certain towns, they wouldn't deal directly with the public at all. They would slip into the shadows until the circus moved on.

If Barkbelly had been just another runaway, Carmenero would happily have agreed to backstage work. There was al-ways plenty to do. But Barkbelly was different. He was special, and the circus did need a new act. He thought hard, while Barkbelly shifted uncomfortably in his seat and stared at the grassy carpet.

"You could wear a mask."

Barkbelly looked up. "A mask?"

"A mask! Not just across your eyes—a fully fitted hood that completely covers your head. With holes for your eyes. No one would ever see you."

Barkbelly considered the idea. It seemed to make sense. And he would be a performer. A *performer!* Just like Candy. He would be out there under the lights, with the band playing and the people loving him. It would be a dream come true.

"What do you say?" said Carmenero with the easy charm that made everyone love him. "Will you do it?"

Barkbelly grinned. "Yes," he said. "I will."

Chapter 29

*B*arkbelly's costume was fantastic. Everyone said so. Peaches was delighted with the response. From the moment she drew the design, she knew it was special. When she cut out the white leather, gangs of children gathered round the open door of her wagon to watch. When she sewed on the rhinestones, Candy and Gossamer drooled with envy. When she hung up the finished suit, Barkbelly gazed at it with tears in his eyes.

And now, with Barkbelly wearing it for the first time, everyone was telling her it was the best work she had ever done. She was thrilled. That was something she had secretly believed all along.

Carmenero was especially pleased. He turned Barkbelly this way and that, noting every detail.

"This is glorious," he said. "Just glorious."

Barkbelly beamed at him, and Carmenero could see the joy in his eyes. But that was about all he could see. Barkbelly was covered from head to toe. A tight leather hood masked his face. A jumpsuit covered his body. Matching gloves concealed his hands. Smart leather boots covered his feet. Peaches had followed Carmenero's instructions perfectly.

Two weeks had passed since Barkbelly's meeting with Carmenero. In that time he had been rehearsing his new act, but he was far from confident. He had been so busy. Some days they had been traveling, and when they reached a new town, there was rigging to be done. He had chores, whether they were on the road or not. He couldn't practice in the Stardust Palace when there was a show in progress. He couldn't practice when the animals were in the ring—the noise of the cannon terrified them. So he had made just two test flights.

But he had spent time with Gossamer. She was teaching him how to present himself to the audience. *Showmanship*, she called it. She drew a line in the sawdust with a stick and told him to imagine it was the curtains at the back of the ring. Then she made him walk over it again and again and again while she made improvements.

"Stand up straight!" she scolded. "Head back! Eyes forward. No, you're slouching! Again!"

Barkbelly tried again.

"That's better!" she praised. "But don't forget to smile."

Barkbelly stopped dead. "Don't forget to smile? I'll be wearing a mask. The audience won't know whether I'm smiling or not, you pudding."

"*You* will know," snapped Gossamer, putting her hands on her hips. "And *they* will *feel*. So don't argue with me. Just do it."

Barkbelly walked over the line again. This time he smiled, and he was amazed at the difference it made. Suddenly he felt confident. Truly in control.

"It works!" he cried. "It really works."

"Of course it does, brittlebrain! I do know what I'm talking about, you know. I'm a professional!" She threw him her best smile and somersaulted across the ring in a breathtaking series of flips and tumbles. "And remember," she said, returning to him, "you're not a clown. You're a daredevil act. You must be regal. Like a king. Like Carmenero. Showmanship, Bark, *showmanship*. Like this."

She disappeared behind the velvet stage curtains as a girl. But she reemerged as an empress. With her hand held high in the air, she acknowledged the cheers from the audience on her left . . . on her right . . . to the front . . . and as she did, Carmenero slipped through the curtains behind her. He winked at Barkbelly, put a finger to his lips and watched Gossamer's performance.

"That is how it should be done," said Gossamer. "You must be commanding."

"Like Carmenero," said Barkbelly.

Gossamer nodded. "Like Carmenero. Proud but not haughty. Strong but not intimidating. And it helps if you're handsome. That's why *you* will be wearing a bag over your head."

"You think Carmenero is handsome?"

"Of course he's handsome. He's . . . heartbreakingly handsome. He's . . ." Her voice trailed off and she gazed up toward the trapeze, as if she would find the words there. "He's . . . perfect," she said, looking at Barkbelly again. "Just the most . . . *gorgeous* man ever." She smiled like a pansy and bit her bottom lip.

"I'm sure he's pleased to hear it," said Barkbelly, and he nodded in the direction of the curtains.

Gossamer turned and saw and gasped and turned back and covered her mouth and flushed, all in the space of a second. Barkbelly was impressed.

"You skunk butt!" she hissed, and ran out of the tent.

Carmenero strolled over, smiling. He sat down beside Barkbelly.

"Are you ready for tonight?" he asked.

Barkbelly nodded.

"You'll be fine. Especially with all the help you've had from my, er . . . admirer." He grinned. "If there's anything you're worried about—anything at all—you come to me. You know where I am."

He put his arm round Barkbelly's shoulders and hugged him close. Just for a second or so. Then he stood up and strolled away.

Barkbelly watched him go. He was in a daze. It had all happened so suddenly. So unexpectedly. It was just a hug, for goodness' sake. But for that moment, while it had lasted, he had felt *safe*. Suddenly tears were welling in his eyes.

Carmenero reached the entrance and lifted the tent flap. Sunlight poured in and he vanished into it. The flap fell back. He was gone.

Chapter 30

$\mathcal{T}$he circus was camped in the small market town of Withybank. It was one of those places where nothing much ever happened. If a runaway bull charged down the main street or someone grew an especially large squash, the townsfolk would talk about it for months afterward. So the arrival of the circus caused a sensation. People were quivering with anticipation. At the market stalls traders were so befuddled that they weighed out carrots instead of parsnips and the customers didn't care. They were too busy talking to their neighbors about Carmenero's new attraction. Shiny posters were pinned up everywhere:

THE CANNONBALL KID!
COME AND BE AMAZED!

They were impossible to ignore; Carmenero had made sure of that. They had caused chaos in the box office. The demand for tickets was overwhelming. The opening night was fully sold out, and Carmenero was considering an additional night's stay. Barkbelly was a success before he even entered the ring.

Now he stood backstage, waiting for his big moment, while the other performers bustled around him. Gossamer and her sisters were at the dressing tables, fastening on their head-dresses and cloaks, brushing sawdust off their tights, fiddling with ribbons while the elephant keeper shuffled by them with a bucket of muck.

Barkbelly heard the roar of the crowd: Anvil Allsop was bending an iron bar with his teeth. Slippers was over by the tent flap. Peaches was sewing a huge button back onto his coat, and when the clown saw Barkbelly watching, he pointed at the button. Then he started to mime: *Panic! Despair! Relief!* Barkbelly giggled and forgot the tension in his stomach for a good ten seconds.

Suddenly the crowd was clapping and cheering . . . the band was bouncing on its platform . . . the girls were pulling the curtains back . . . Anvil Allsop was running out of the ring . . . Gossamer and her sisters were skipping in. And Barkbelly realized he was next.

Slippers joined Barkbelly by the curtains.

"Not long now," he whispered. It was his job to entertain the crowd while the circus gang dragged the cannon into the ring.

Barkbelly smiled grimly. The crowd was gasping as Gossamer and her sisters flew like falcons. He could hear the girls' calls and the slap of hands as their father caught them in midair. Then there was a huge burst of applause and the curtains were swept aside and Slippers went out as the girls came in.

"Walk tall!" whispered Gossamer as she ran past. "I'll be watching!"

Barkbelly could hear the muffled roar of the cannon wheels

as the great piece of iron was moved into the center of the ring. Next, a metallic clang as the ladder was attached. His mouth felt dry. His stomach was a knot of nerves. He pulled the leather hood over his head. With it on, he could hear his own breathing, quick and shallow.

Then he felt a hand on his shoulder. Barkbelly couldn't see whose it was—the hood blocked out his side vision. The hand gave a reassuring squeeze and then it was gone.

Carmenero swept through the curtains into the ring. Barkbelly heard the band clatter into silence as he raised his hands.

"Ladies and gentlemen, boys and girls. You have seen the posters. You have heard the rumors. And tonight, people of Withybank, you will witness the birth of a brilliant new star. He's bold. He's daring. He's the one and only . . . Cannonball Kid!"

Barkbelly strode through the curtains like a king. He waved to the crowd. He bowed. He strutted. He smiled inside his hood. Then, as he heard the band begin the launch music, he climbed up the silver ladder and, with a final wave, slid down the barrel of the cannon. There he lay in the dark while one of the circus hands lit the fuse. Carmenero led the count-down: "Ten—nine—eight—seven—" Barkbelly closed his eyes and—*thuud!*—the world exploded around him as an invisible fist thumped him skyward.

He opened his eyes and saw he was flying higher, higher, higher toward the roof. The rainbow lanterns were flashing by. The darkness was beckoning—reaching out—grabbing him with black fingers. But Barkbelly arced into a daredevil descent. He dived down like a hunting hawk. Then he relaxed his muscles, closed his eyes and let the net embrace him.

The people of Withybank leapt from their seats. They stamped their feet and threw their hats in the air. The noise was deafening, even through the thick hood. As Barkbelly tumbled expertly from the net, Carmenero seized hold of his wrist and lifted his arm triumphantly high.

"Ladies and gentlemen!" bellowed Carmenero. "I give you the Cannonball Kid!" Then he stepped back into the shadows.

Gossamer watched proudly from the rear of the tent. She could feel what nobody could see. Inside his hood, Barkbelly was beaming.

Chapter 31

*A*fter his great debut, Barkbelly's life settled into the daily routine of a performer: chores in the morning, a nap in the afternoon and a show in the evening. Then, when the crowds had wandered happily homeward, he would sit beside the campfires and listen to stories under the stars.

There were several good storytellers. Anvil Allsop was the most entertaining. He could talk for hours, throwing words into the air like magicians' doves. Tall tales, true tales, jokes, riddles—he knew them all, and he always drew the largest crowd. Rubek told the most exotic tales. He had traveled all over the world and seen extraordinary things. To listen to Rubek was to enter strange and fabulous lands. Surprisingly, Slippers was the scariest storyteller. He told the goriest ghost tales imaginable. On dark nights Barkbelly would listen for hours while fear crawled up his back like a beetle.

But of all the storytellers, Barkbelly still loved Jewel best. She told every kind of story: folk tales, fairy tales, circus tales. . . . And whatever the tale, whatever its age, Jewel could breathe new life into it. Sometimes she didn't tell stories at all—she just talked about the people she had known in her long, long life.

Barkbelly especially loved to hear about Jewel's family. She could trace her family line back through generation after generation. Dozens of aerial artists, knife throwers, jugglers and acrobats passed before his eyes as she described them. Sometimes her descriptions were so vivid that Barkbelly believed she had actually brought her ancestors back to life. He could see them standing in the shadows behind her, listening to their own lives, nodding and smiling.

It was late autumn. There was a chill in the air and the stars were hanging as low as lanterns. Barkbelly was sitting with Jewel outside her wagon. A fire was blazing before them, and Jewel was knitting a bonnet for her new grandchild and telling a tale about her great-great-grandfather Falcon Lavelle. When she had finished, Barkbelly sighed and said, "It must be nice to have a family."

"Oh, yes, it is," said Jewel. Suddenly she stopped knitting. "You *have* a family!" she exclaimed. "I remember you telling me about them when we were back in your village. And there was that lovely girl too."

"Freckle Flannagan."

"That's right. So what do you mean?"

"I don't have a *real* family," said Barkbelly. "I'm adopted. I don't have brothers or sisters, or aunties and uncles. I don't have grandparents. There's only me. I'm just thinking it must be nice to have a whole lot of you. All the same, like a gang. But I'm one on my own."

"Yes, but you did have a mother and a father at one time," said Jewel.

Barkbelly looked at her in amazement. "Did I?" he asked.

"Of course you did! Where do you think you came from? You weren't made in one of those new factories, you know! Oh, bless the badgers, Barkbelly! You do have some funny ideas!"

"But if I had a mother and a father *at one time*, where are they now?"

"I don't know, my lovely," said Jewel. She swung the kettle over the fire to boil. "They must still be on the island, I suppose. Do you want tea?"

There was no reply. Jewel glanced up. Barkbelly was staring at her as if he had seen one of Slippers's ghosts.

"Whatever's the matter?" she said.

"What island?"

"The island you come from," said Jewel in some confusion. "Ashenpeake. But you must know this?"

Barkbelly shook his head.

"Has no one ever told you? Did you never ask?"

The kettle began to boil. It bubbled and steamed, spitting water onto the flames below.

"Did you think you were the only one?"

Barkbelly nodded. Jewel took the kettle off the boil and filled the teapot, glad to have something to do while she made sense of it all.

She put a mug into Barkbelly's hands but he barely noticed. He was motionless, staring into the dark night. Any movement seemed beyond him. She had to wrap his fingers round the mug to stop it from sliding.

"Drink it," she coaxed. "It'll do you good. I've put lots of sugar in. You've had a bit of a shock."

"I had no idea," said Barkbelly at last. "I know I came from an egg. I know Papa found it in a field. But you're right—I thought I was the only one. And everyone else did too. Back home, I mean. No one ever said different. Even in Tything-town there was no one like me. I asked Missus Maddox, the Matron in the factory, and she thought I was the only one. She had never seen any wooden people, and she was old. Not as old as you, though."

"No," said Jewel, trying to hide a smile.

"I'm sure she was telling me the truth," said Barkbelly.

"I'm sure she was too," said Jewel. "Ashenpeakers are sel-dom seen in this land, and that's a fact. I've only ever seen one other in all my traveling round. That was at Pebbleport. On the quayside he was, unloading a sailing ship. Course, I might have seen more without knowing—as might Missus Maddox. You don't look any different from a distance, after all. It's only close up that you see the grain."

"This island," said Barkbelly. "Ashenpeake. Where is it?"

"Now, that I don't know," said Jewel. "But Rubek probably will. Ask him."

"*I will!*" cried Barkbelly, and he leapt to his feet and sped away.

Rubek was sitting outside his wagon when Barkbelly found him.

"Hello, my friend!" he said. "You have come to join me, yes? Is beautiful night to sit and look at stars. You want beer? Of course you do!" He reached inside the wagon for a second glass, filled it with frothy beer from the flagon by his side and handed it to Barkbelly. "Drink!" he cried. "And enjoy!"

Barkbelly drank. The beer was strong and malty. He could feel it surging toward his head. He sat down quickly.

"Rubek," he began, "have you ever heard of an island called Ashenpeake?"

"Of course," said Rubek, sucking on a long clay pipe. "I have been there."

Barkbelly gaped. "You've been there? What's it like?"

"Is wonderful!" said Rubek, waving his pipe around. "Is land of forest. Is dark. So many trees. I did not see all country, you understand. I was on ship. We pulled in for water and supplies. We did not stay long. But I saw."

"Did you see any people?"

"Of course! Many people! They are like you. Pale. Not tall, but strong. Very strong. Like you! That is what they are famous for."

"What do they do—my people?" asked Barkbelly eagerly. "Are they woodsmen? Or fishermen? Are they farmers?"

"Some of them, yes, but . . ." Rubek paused and looked long at Barkbelly. He frowned. "My friend," he said at last, "do you not know these things?"

"No," said Barkbelly. "I know nothing. I have spent the whole of my life believing I was alone in the world. And now I hear there is an island with people like me! It's so exciting! I want to know everything you can tell me about them."

"Oh, my friend," said Rubek heavily, "then I have to tell you this. Barkbelly—most of your people are *slaves*."

Chapter 32

*B*arkbelly leaned heavily on his pitchfork and thought about his people. In truth, he had thought of little else all night, but now, bringing breakfast to the elephants, their slavery became sickeningly real. The elephants were chained. Thick golden chains ran from their ankles to wooden posts that had been hammered into the ground. Yes, the fetters were burnished gold, engraved and adorned with bells, but they were still fetters. These glorious beasts—for all their strength and majesty, for all their wisdom and dignity, for all the wonder and admiration they provoked nightly from the crowds— were still slaves.

The night before, Rubek had told him all he knew. Yes, Ashenpeakers were sold as slaves around the world, but they were not usually shipped alive. The slave traders dealt in eggs. This curious phase in the life cycle of Ashenpeakers, combined with their extraordinary strength and stamina, had sealed their fate.

The solid wooden eggs made perfect cargo. They could be packed tightly into crates and transported unattended. Once the eggs were sold, the slave owners could store them indefinitely, and when fresh slaves were needed, they simply threw the eggs into a fire. New workers were born within minutes and, with their incredible growth rate, could be working a month later.

And the most wonderful thing of all, from the slave owners' point of view, was this: the slaves had no memories. They had been born into slavery. They had no recollection of home or family. They had no experience of capture or transportation. They had never known any other way of life. As long as they were kept reasonably comfortable and well fed, they had nothing to worry about. They weren't troubled by dark dreams at night. They had no desire to return home. *This* was home. Everyone was happy.

Barkbelly had been appalled. He knew this cozy picture wasn't true and had forcefully said so.

"I would agree with you there, my friend," said Rubek. "But this is story as slave traders tell it."

"Just because they have no memory, it doesn't mean those slaves can't feel," said Barkbelly, bristling like a brush. "I had no memory, but I felt . . . whenever I was in a forest, or a wood, I *felt* something. Like I belonged there. And now I know: I do belong there. That is my home. Ashenpeake. And Bramble and Thorn . . . they had no memories either, but they felt that pull. That's why they had to go. That's why I had to help. Somewhere deep inside, we all know where we belong. And once you know where that place is, you have to go there. You have to."

"You have lost me now!" said Rubek.

"I want to go there."

"To Ashenpeake?"

"Yes," said Barkbelly. "I must. Not just for my sake, but for the sake of all those slaves. I have to see it for them. If I can do it, perhaps one day they can do it too."

"Perhaps," said Rubek, "but I think not. They are slaves. They are not free to travel as they choose. You cannot change world, my friend. Is big place, full of bad things. I know—I have seen them with my own eyes. Barkbelly, this is life! This is not story. This is not book. It will not end happily ever after for some people. Maybe not even for you."

"Do you think I will be in danger if I go?"

"No! You will not be caught with net and sold as slave, if that is what you think! No! I told you—slave traders like eggs: *they* do not put up fight! My friend, no sane man will pick fight with Ashenpeaker! You are so strong! He would be mad! No, you will be safe. But you will be alone. You understand? You will be alone. Carmenero's Circus will not go with you."

Chapter 33

*B*arkbelly had decided. He was going to Ashenpeake. There he would find his roots and his home. And most importantly, he might find his family. What was it Missus Maddox had said? *It ain't wrong to want peace. So you go out there and find it.* Well, if he found his family, he might find peace at last.

It would break his heart to leave the circus, but he had to go. He would leave it at Pebbleport, the last town on the tour. After that, the circus would begin the long journey back to its winter quarters in Greenglade.

Pebbleport. That was where it would all begin! It had one of the busiest harbors in the country. Ships sailed from there to every part of the known world. Rubek said that its quays were packed with sailors of every shape, size, color and tongue imaginable. It was where Jewel had seen an Ashenpeaker. Perhaps he would see one too.

He didn't tell anyone about his plan. He guarded his thoughts as if they could be stolen. Whenever the circus moved, he traveled on the lead wagon, wedged between Anvil and Candy. His eyes were fixed on each new horizon. Every hill held the promise of the sea behind it. As the wagon strained up each new incline, he felt quivers of excitement all over his body. Now he would see it! But he didn't. The same vista always lay before him: fields and forests, rivers and streams and still more hills to climb.

But one dark day, as the rain clouds gathered and the wagon slithered through leaf-layered lanes, he heard a familiar honking sound behind him. When he turned, he saw a flight of geese coming up the valley. Soon they were passing overhead, and he heard himself saying, "So many of them."

"Aye," said Anvil. "Going to the salt marshes at Pebbleport, most likely. Not far."

Barkbelly stared at the strong man. He took a deep breath and tried to sound calm. "Not far?"

"No," said Anvil. "There's the sea—look."

He looked. And he saw it: a thin gray smudge on the skyline. Nothing you would especially notice. It was just a line of darker color beneath the heavy mass of clouds. But it was the sea. He would be there by nightfall.

Barkbelly's last few days with the circus were over too soon. He wanted to cherish them. He wanted to capture as many memories as he could so that he could hold them in his heart and carry them always. But the days skipped by as usual, dipped in dirt and glitter, and soon they were gone.

The final performance was over. The men were hauling down the Stardust Palace, singing as they heaved. Barkbelly picked his way through a snake pit of ropes and turned toward the costume wagon. Peaches was there, as he had hoped. He told her he was leaving and why. She hugged him close and said to be careful, but she didn't try to stop him from going.

Candy arrived halfway through the hug and demanded to know what was going on. When she heard, she sat down on the wagon steps and cried. Really cried. Barkbelly was shocked. He hadn't expected that. He hadn't known she cared, but clearly she did. Soon he was sitting with his arms round her, rocking them both, whispering, "I have to go, I have to go," over and over again into her hot ear while she sobbed, "I know, I know."

By the time he left her, he was weak with grief, and he stumbled off into the dark like a drunkard. It was nothing like the farewell he had imagined, with Candy and Gossamer waving prettily at him as he departed on his Big Adventure. It was awful. He felt peeled, as if a layer of something had been stripped away. He was raw and sore. It was awful.

As he staggered on, he saw Gossamer. Unfortunately, she saw him too. He stopped her questions with a wave of his hand. "Ask Candy," he said bleakly, and walked on.

Jewel's wagon beckoned with candles and the scent of chocolate. For the third time, he revealed what he was about to do and why, all the time thinking, *How many more times do I have to say this? I can't bear it,* while Jewel listened, diamond-eyed. Then she gave him a mug of hot chocolate and said simply:

> "May the sun warm your day
> And the moon guard your night.
> May hope be your lantern
> And love be your shield
> And dreams be the boots that carry you home."

Barkbelly closed his eyes and savored the chocolate, the warmth of the wagon and the presence of Jewel. There would be nights to come when he would long for such things.

He stole a few precious minutes more, then slowly opened his eyes. Jewel was looking at him fondly. Her head was tilted, and with her bright eyes and sharp nose, she looked like an old parrot, with wrinkles for feathers. Barkbelly smiled in spite of his sadness.

"You must tell Carmenero," she said.

The door to his wagon was closed, but Carmenero was inside. Barkbelly could see him in the galley, pouring a glass of wine.

Barkbelly tapped gently on the door and Carmenero opened it.

"I'm sorry to bother you—"

"You're not bothering me," said Carmenero. "Come in."

Barkbelly climbed up the steps and went in. The black dog was asleep on the carpet. She opened a tired eye as Barkbelly stepped over her, but she was soon asleep again, her paws twitching as she dreamed.

Barkbelly didn't know where to begin. He stared at the carpet but could feel Carmenero watching him. He took a deep breath and looked up. Yes, Carmenero was watching him. Barkbelly noticed his eyes were brown. Rich, warm, nut brown. And they were so full of compassion, Barkbelly had to look away.

"I'm leaving the circus," said Barkbelly, and his eyes were filling before the words left his lips.

"I know," said Carmenero. "I passed by Peaches's wagon earlier. There were three of them in there, crying like kittens. But between you and me, I think they were rather enjoying it."

Barkbelly smiled and wiped his nose with his hand. Carmenero pulled a silk handkerchief out of his pocket with a flourish and handed it to him.

"They told me you're headed for Ashenpeake."

"Yes," said Barkbelly as he dabbed his eyes. "I want to see the island. The forests. And Jewel . . ." He paused and thought for a few seconds. "Jewel said that I must have had parents at one time. I can't stop thinking that they might still be there. I want to find my family."

"How will you identify your parents?"

"I don't know. I hadn't thought of that."

"Do you have a family name?"

"No."

They sat in silence. Lady sighed in the space between them.

"I won't try to stop you," said Carmenero at last. "Though I will be saddened to see you go. When do you plan to leave?"

"Um . . . now," said Barkbelly. "While it's dark."

"No," said Carmenero, shaking his head. "I won't let you do that. You're not running away. You don't have to creep around in the dark like a thief. Stay here tonight. Sleep on the sofa. Wait until dawn. You must always leave in the light. It's important."

"I don't want to see anyone."

"You won't. Not even me."

Barkbelly looked at Carmenero. He could hear a voice inside his own head saying, *Ask him to be there when you leave.* But he said nothing.

So when he left the circus the next morning, he did so on his own. He walked across a campsite chilled with the first frost of winter. Silver morning mist coiled about his feet like serpents. His breath steamed.

No one saw him go. Except Carmenero. He stood at the window of his wagon and watched until the small figure had disappeared into the lemony dawn. "May he find what he seeks," he said, "and may he like what he finds."

Barkbelly strode on. The circus was camped on a headland at the southern end of town. He found the cliff path and followed it down as it twisted through a copse. When he finally emerged into the light again, dawn was in full glory. Bands of yellow light rimmed the sky and illuminated the forest of masts down in the harbor. And suddenly Barkbelly felt his spirit soar like a blackbird, and whistling like one, he descended into Pebbleport.

PART FOUR

Chapter 34

The shouts of the sailors, the scent of the spices, the
jostling of the people . . . Pebbleport harbor was so dazzling, Barkbelly struggled to absorb it all. It was so loud, so
brash, so exotic. He wondered why anyone in this town bothered to go to the circus when they had all this for free. Here in
the harbor, he could see sailors shinning up masts higher than
anything in the Stardust Palace. They dangled from ropes,
clambered up rigging and inched along the yardarms sideways
like crabs.

And the clothes! They were gaudier than anything
Peaches would make. Stripes, spots, checks, diamonds . . . the
sailors wore them all, side by side in an explosion of color.
There were bows and buckles and belts and braces. Huge white
shirts that billowed like sails. Tight britches that ended at the
knee. Hats with long tassels. Boots with curled-up toes. Bare
feet. Hairy feet. *Black feet!* Barkbelly had never seen black skin
before, but Jewel had told him about the Midnight Princes—a
fabulous troupe of black acrobats who used to be with the circus. They came from an island called Balaa, and Carmenero
had sacked them because they were too handsome. Runaway

girls were following the circus wherever it went, just to be near them. Too many to handle, Jewel had said. Carmenero was tired of dealing with angry fathers.

And now, here in Pebbleport, he was surely looking at a Balaan. A long-limbed sailor with skin as rich as licorice was strolling into town with money to spend. He paused at a fruit stall. He gazed at the peaches. His hand slid into his pocket. Out came a fat moneybag. He flashed a coin. He took a peach and sank his teeth into it. Ah! The sweet taste of land.

The Balaan walked on and was soon lost in the crowd. So many people! Merchants in plumed hats, nodding and smiling, counting their wealth in boxes and crates. Traders with handcarts, juggling their wares, calling to the first mates on board as the ships were loading. Girls looking for sweethearts, flouncing and flirting. Tavern-bound sailors, swaggering in gangs. Tearful wives with sticky babies, heading home to empty houses. An ocean of people, married to the sea.

Barkbelly ate a pot of pickled herring and wondered how sailors found work. Did they ask the merchants who owned the ships or the sea captains who sailed them? Did they ask in the taverns? He couldn't go into a tavern—he was too young. But even if he weren't, he wouldn't go in. Rubek had told terrible tales about cutthroat murderers, and the stories always began in taverns.

I'll have to ask someone, he thought. There was a lad running errands—would he know? He had passed by three or four times and he had a friendly face. Barkbelly decided to ask him.

"You'd want the first mate for that," said the lad. "He does the hiring and firing."

"Where would I find him?"

"On board, if the ship's loading. You wanna go today?

'Cause I know one that's sailing on the next tide. The *Hope*, she's called. First mate goes by the name of Flynn. I'll take you to him, if you like. Cost you sixpence, mind."

Barkbelly wavered.

"Well? Do you want to go or not?"

"Yes," said Barkbelly, "I do. But I was hoping to go to Ashenpeake. I don't suppose—"

"No. It ain't. You've got bad timing, matey. There was a ship sailed for Ashenpeake yesterday. Won't be another one for two or three weeks now, and Pebbleport ain't the kinda place to hang around in, if you know what I mean. No, if I were you I'd go with the *Hope* to Farrago."

Barkbelly gasped. Farrago was famous: a sprawling new town on the borders of the known world. "Is that where it's going?"

"Sure is, an' I'll tell you this for nothing: Farrago is one *wild* place. Been there meself. You wouldn't believe the kinda things I got up to, an' me a gentleman an' all! Listen, matey, you wanna see a bit o' the world! You can see Ashenpeake anytime. The *Hope*'s not a bad ship. Flynn's a bit sharp, but he's bound to be, ain't he? He's the mate. Captain's fair, though. So what do you say? Are you gonna give me that sixpence or not?"

Five minutes later, Barkbelly was staring at the most magnificent ship he had ever seen. The *Hope* was a three-masted galleon with dark, shining timbers and a golden figurehead of a goddess gleaming on its bow. The lad pointed out Flynn, the first mate. He was standing on the quarterdeck, barking out orders.

Barkbelly took a deep breath.

"Good luck," said the lad.

"Thanks," said Barkbelly, and he walked up the gangplank.

Flynn was a sinewy man with silver earrings and salt-washed hair. His eyes had scanned so many horizons, they were permanently narrow. Now they scanned Barkbelly, from the tip of his tousled hair to the toes of his dirty boots.

"What do you want, boy?" he growled. "A job, is it?"

Barkbelly nodded.

"Been to sea before, have you? No? Well, there's a first time for us all. And a last." A sly smile puckered his mouth. "You're very young."

"I'm old enough, sir. And I'm very strong—strong as a man."

"I don't doubt it. I've worked with your kind before. I want no trouble, though, see? No fighting. Agreed? Good. *Baxter!*"

A crusty-looking sailor joined them on the deck.

"Take this lad below. Find him a berth, then show him the galley. *Ferdinand!* Watch those chickens, boy! We want them alive, not dead!" And without another word, Flynn strode away.

"Is that it?" said Barkbelly.

"Aye, that's it," said the sailor, hitching up his trousers to reveal tattooed toes. "Welcome to the *Hope*."

Chapter 35

*T*he galley was in the belly of the ship and during the day
Barkbelly barely saw beyond it. He wanted to climb the
rigging and haul on ropes, swab the decks and repair sails. Instead, he found himself peeling potatoes and scrubbing dirty
pots. *It's not fair. I'm wasted here.* He knew he wasn't the
cleverest boy in the world. He couldn't play a musical instru-
ment or paint pictures. He couldn't run especially fast. But he
was strong. And he was fearless. He would happily do the jobs
no one wanted. He knew the sailors hated climbing the masts
in bad weather. Miles up in the air, with the ship rolling beneath them and the wind whistling past their ears—it was so
terrifying, Flynn used it as a punishment. But Barkbelly longed
to do it. The height didn't worry him—why should it? A fall
wouldn't kill him. But it would damage the ship. He had to admit that. He would hit the deck so hard, he would tear through
the timbers like a cannonball. And if he went right through to
the keel and tore a hole in it, the ship would sink and everyone
would drown. Perhaps that was why Mister Flynn never sent
him up the rigging.

Barkbelly's world was the galley and his hammock and

nothing much in between. The only time he could experience the sea was late at night, when he would creep above deck and sit under the stars, listening to the sounds of the ship. It was never, ever quiet. Ropes creaked. Timbers groaned. Sails flapped. Sometimes there were footsteps: the ship's captain often promenaded at that time. Barkbelly, sitting on his favored tarpaulin, would hear the strike of a match as the captain lit his pipe. The light would flare in the dark like a firefly, and then the captain's walk would begin.

Captain Kempe was an immaculately dressed, impossibly handsome man. But for one so blessed with good looks, he was never haughty. On the contrary, he was utterly charming.

The captain had discovered Barkbelly's secret place just two nights into the voyage. Barkbelly had been sitting on the deck, thinking, when he was horrified to see an unmistakable pair of boots coming toward him. He cowered, waiting for the tongue-lashing to begin. But instead, the captain smiled and introduced himself. He asked Barkbelly's name. Asked him if he was enjoying his first voyage. Remarked about the beauty of the sky and bade him good night.

Now the captain nodded a greeting whenever their nocturnal paths crossed. Sometimes he would even make conversation. Barkbelly liked that. It was civilized. The captain was so clean and polite—quite unlike his crew. Barkbelly hated leaving the deck to return to the mess. Down there, the timbers echoed with the snores and grunts of sleeping men, and the air was thick with sailor smell.

The stink was caused by diet. At the start of the voyage, the men were given fresh fruit and vegetables every day. But as the weeks went by, the stores dwindled until there was little left but onions, salt beef and biscuits. The beef had to be soaked for hours to get rid of the salt, and even then it was tough as leather. The biscuits were even worse—so hard that the sailors broke their teeth on them. Barkbelly wondered how long the crew could live like this. How long was the voyage? He didn't know. He had never asked. And were they really going to Farrago? No one had said so, except the errand lad. He decided to ask the cook.

The cook's name was Griddle, and as long as he was in his galley, he was happy. He didn't care where the ship was heading or how long it would take to get there.

"It's not my business to know where we're going," he replied when Barkbelly asked. "I concern myself with the provisioning of hot dinners for the working men. 'Leave the navigating to Captain Kempe, Griddle,' that's what I tell myself. 'Leave the navigating to Captain Kempe. That's what he's paid for. Let him do his job and I'll do mine.'"

"But you must know how long the voyage is," Barkbelly persisted, "otherwise you wouldn't know how many provisions to take on board at the start."

"Quite right, young man! I do need to know how long the voyage is, but that's not what you asked me. You asked if I knew our final destination and I don't. What I do know is this: it's a three-month voyage, with a provisioning stop at six weeks. We're putting in at Sharkteeth Island to take on fresh water, fruit, vegetables and such fresh food as we're likely to need to complete the voyage. And Sharkteeth Island, by my reckoning, should be appearing on the horizon any day now."

Griddle was right. The very next morning, Barkbelly awoke to cries of "Land ho!" and the din of running feet as all the sailors dashed up on deck for a welcome glimpse of land. Barkbelly joined them, but there was nothing much to see.

Just a disappointing smudge on the horizon: a line of dark gray where the sea met the sky. But the next time he sneaked out from the galley to look, it was a different story. The island rose majestically out of the ocean: a tantalizing vista of palm trees, beaches and blue bays, crowned with a trio of jagged mountains. It looked so calm. So peaceful. Quite unlike the ship, which was a nightmare of noise. Gulls were screaming. Flynn was shouting. Swarms of sailors were swinging from the yardarms, furling the sails. Others were hauling on ropes or readying the longboats. And in the middle of the frenzy stood Captain Kempe, calmly looking through his telescope and smiling.

Barkbelly felt deliriously happy. After weeks at sea, he longed to walk on firm land again, and Sharkteeth Island looked such a beautiful place. *By tonight, I will be sitting on that beach with a coconut drink in one hand and a barbecued steak in the other, wriggling my toes in the sand and listening to the waves lapping on the shore. Lovely!*

But he was disappointed again. The ship was anchored just long enough to fetch the supplies. Admittedly, that took the best part of the day, with the longboats going back and forth from the ship, but nobody went ashore. Barkbelly found himself in the galley as usual, peeling onions and stirring soup. And when evening tide came, he heard Flynn stomping on the deck above, shouting, "Prepare to weigh anchor," and the chain rattled and they were sailing again.

He was still feeling glum when he sat on the deck later that night. He was so lost in thought, he didn't hear the captain's approach. But suddenly the long, glistening black boots were there beside him. Barkbelly scrabbled to his feet and mumbled a good evening.

"Good evening to you, Barkbelly. Taking the air, are you? Good to feel the sea breeze after the heat we've had today."

Barkbelly nodded miserably. The captain glanced at him.

"I suppose you were hoping to go ashore," he said. He sucked his pipe and blew the spicy smoke out into the darkness. "Maybe another time. Certainly when we reach Farrago."

"Where does the ship go after that, sir?" asked Barkbelly timidly.

"Up the coast to Barrenta Bay," said the captain, tracing an imaginary map in the sky with his pipe. "Then across to the Rimba Islands. And from there a long voyage east to Maaloo. But you might not be with us then."

Barkbelly frowned. "Why?"

"Because Farrago will steal your heart and you'll never want to leave!" The captain smiled. "Seriously, it is a fine place. It has such energy; you can feel it on the streets. It's . . . *intoxicating*. So you might decide to stay. Many do."

Barkbelly thought for a moment. "I don't think so," he said at last. "I want to go somewhere else. Ashenpeake."

The captain slowly exhaled. The smoke climbed up the rigging like a gray lizard.

"I want to find my family. My real family," said Barkbelly, filling the sudden silence.

The captain laughed. "Forget that idea," he said. "Your family is in the past—the best place for them. Leave them there." And with that, he thrust his hands into his pockets and walked off into the shadows.

Chapter 36

*G*riddle was not in a good mood. It was one of those mornings when everything had gone wrong. Now he was making pastry for three dozen apple pies, he was up to his elbows in flour—and a whole barrel of apples had gone rotten.

"Patience, Griddle, patience," he said, taking a deep breath. "These things are sent to challenge us. Apples is apples and they will go off, I don't deny it. But having said that, when I next see that Pebbleport fruit and veg man, there will be words. Oh, yes. There will be words. I'm trying to run a healthy ship here and he is not helping. The carrots aren't too clever either."

"What shall I do with these?" asked Barkbelly, still holding the apple barrel.

"Give them to the goats. That's all they're fit for. I hope the goats will be all right, mind. The apples are fermenting a bit, and there's nothing worse than tipsy goats, especially when they've got horns."

Barkbelly bumped the barrel out of the galley.

"And when you've done that," Griddle called after him,

"go down into the store and bring up another. See if you can find one that's better."

But each of the barrels was as bad as the next. Barkbelly opened every one in the store and found nothing but moldy brown fruit. *What shall I do?* he thought. *Griddle's got to have apples. He's halfway through making the pastry.*

Would there be more barrels in the hold? He didn't know. He had never been in the hold. It was packed with cargo. No one went down there except Flynn.

Barkbelly climbed back up on the deck and approached the hatch. There was no one around. He lifted it and peered down. It was dark. He would need a lantern. There was one hanging from the rail, but it needed lighting. He remembered that the one in the store was already lit; he went back to fetch it. Then he returned to the hatch, lifted it and climbed down the steps into the dark.

He could hear rats scratching in the far corners. He held the lantern higher and crept forward. He peered around, searching for barrels, and found half a dozen lined up by the steps. But they weren't apple barrels—they had wooden bungs. They would be wine or rum. Barkbelly explored further.

The hold was packed high with wooden crates. All of them were exactly the same shape and size. Row upon row, tower upon tower. Something was stamped on them in red paint. He held the lantern closer and saw a single word: ASHENPEAKE.

Barkbelly felt his heart lurch in his chest. *No. It can't be.*

He had to know. He walked between the aisles until he found a place where the timbers sloped. There the crates weren't stacked so high. He put down the lantern and lifted a crate from the top of the pile. It was sealed. Barkbelly banged his fists on the lid. Wood on wood, harder and harder he hammered. The crate shattered under his blows and he ripped away the splinters. Eggs. It was full of wooden eggs. He pulled down another crate and pummeled it to pieces. More eggs. Dozens of them, spilling out onto the floor, rolling away in all directions, and every one of them carrying a life. A life that would begin and end in slavery.

So this was the cargo the *Hope* carried. Not wine or wool but people. His people.

He had to set them free. He wanted to smash open every crate. Throw every egg into the sea. Let them drift away to who knows where. Anywhere was better than where they were going now. He grabbed hold of a crate and started to carry it toward the hatch. Then he stopped. Was he mad? He couldn't do this now, in the middle of the day! He had to wait until it was dark.

He fetched the lantern and climbed back up the steps. He peered out of the hatch. Still there was no one around. He climbed out into the sunlight and closed the hatch behind him.

"Tonight," he said to himself. "I will do it tonight."

Chapter 37

Barkbelly lay in his hammock, floating on a sea of snores. Everyone was asleep. It was time to go.

He eased himself to the floor, wound his way between the swaying hammocks and climbed the companionway to the deck. It was deserted. Only the night watch would be around, and he was at the other end of the ship. The moon was cloaked in cloud. The stars were sleeping. It was perfect.

Barkbelly slowly lifted the hatch and felt his way down the steps into the hold. He hadn't brought a lantern this time. But he had brought an iron bar and soon he was hard at work.

Crrrp! The sound of splintering wood ripped through the darkness. Surely someone would hear. Barkbelly waited, his heart pounding, listening for footsteps. But none came.

He carried the opened crate out of the hold and set it down on the deck. He reached inside, took an egg in each hand and drew them to his lips. "Good luck," he whispered. Then he kissed them and threw them over the side. The splashes were lost in the sound of the waves breaking against the ship; they wouldn't give him away. He took two more from the crate and then two more. But it was too slow, bending up and down. So

he picked up the crate and wedged it between the ship's rail and his belly. Then he started throwing eggs one after another, faster and faster, as if he were scattering corn. They flew like swallows and disappeared into the night.

Soon the crate was empty. Barkbelly threw it over the side and returned to the hold for a second. Then a third. And a fourth. There were hundreds of eggs floating on the sea now. He fetched a fifth. And a sixth. And he was just emptying the seventh crate when he was grabbed roughly by the shoulder and a voice hissed out of the blackness: "What do you think you're doing?"

"What does it look like I'm doing?" said Barkbelly.

"Don't you get cocky with me, boy," growled Flynn, and he shook Barkbelly like an old carpet.

"I'm doing what's right," cried Barkbelly.

"No," sneered the first mate, "you're robbin', that's what you're doin'—robbin'."

"I'm setting my people free," said Barkbelly, wriggling out of Flynn's grip. "I won't have them slaves."

"And I won't have my wages thrown overboard," said Flynn, and he pushed Barkbelly up against the rigging. "I told you I wanted no trouble. You're all the same. Just can't help it, can you? I should throw you over the side right now."

"Go on, then!" shouted Barkbelly. "I'd rather drown out there than sail on a slave ship with scum like you!"

Flynn exploded. He grabbed Barkbelly by the legs and tried to shove him over the side. Barkbelly clung to the rigging and kicked hard. Flynn swore and held on. Barkbelly twisted and turned like a fish on a line. Curses, cuts, bruises, blows . . . Flynn was suffering more than Barkbelly ever would. *Serves him right. He's nothing but a—*

"Flynn!" The voice cut through the fight like a blade. "What is going on here?"

Flynn released Barkbelly and stood back. Barkbelly dangled like a puppet from the rigging. Captain Kempe looked from one to the other, then down at the broken crate on the deck.

"I caught him," said Flynn, wiping the blood that trickled from a cut lip. "Robbin' cargo. Throwing it overboard." He took a deep breath as the pain kicked in.

"So you thought you would throw him overboard too?" said the captain. "I'm surprised at you, Flynn. You normally know the value of things." He ran a hand through his hair. "Cage him."

"Sir?" Flynn was still dazed.

"Cage him. Leave him in the hold. We'll sell him at the market in Barrenta Bay. I know they prefer eggs, but they buy live ones too." He pulled out his pipe and lit it.

In the sudden flare of light, Barkbelly saw three more sailors standing behind the captain. Too many to fight. They seized him and carried him down into the hold, and there, in the farthest corner, he saw a cage. They threw him into it and banged the door closed. Flynn had a lock. He fastened it through the bars.

"Sweet dreams," he said, leaning close.

The sailors laughed and, taking their lantern with them, climbed up the steps and closed the hatch.

Barkbelly was alone, with neither light to see nor water to drink. There was nothing. Just the blackness of the hold, the creaking of the timbers and the scratching of the rats.

Chapter 38

$\mathcal{D}$ays passed. How many, Barkbelly didn't know. It was impossible to tally them from the slivers of light that crept through the gaps in the hull planks. Every day a sailor came to give him water and a handful of biscuits, and every day Barkbelly hoped he would leave his lantern too. But he didn't, and as the sailor climbed back up the steps, Barkbelly would feel his hope receding with the light. He wouldn't see sunshine until Barrenta Bay, that was certain, and even then it would be filtered through the bars of a holding pen in a slave market.

Why do these things keep happening to me? he asked himself over and over again. *I am not a bad person. I took a life, that's true, but I saved another. I try to do my best. I was only doing what was right. Why can't they see that? Damn Flynn! I'd like to see him and Kempe and the whole blessed lot of them eaten by sharks. From their toes to their knees, slowly, slowly. Then up to their bits . . . slowly, slowly! Then—*

"*Pirates!*"

The lookout's yell was so loud, it smashed through the deck and flooded the hold.

"*Pirates!*"

Chaos and confusion! A bell ring, foot stomp, Flynn fly, do-or-die, panic-stricken sailor cry, chaos and confusion! Barkbelly could almost feel the ship listing to the left as everyone gathered portside to see the terrible truth.

Next came Kempe's voice, firing a volley of commands. A flurry of footsteps as sailors ran to obey. A rumble of cannon wheels as the guns were rolled into position. Barkbelly braced himself, waiting for the fighting to begin. But it didn't. A strange silence had settled on the ship. Suddenly he realized why: the lookout had seen the pirate ship while it was still distant and the *Hope* was trying to outrace it. Listening carefully, he could hear the waves breaking more urgently across the bows. They were fleeing.

But the pirates were clearly gaining, because as time went by the murmuring above became a babble, then a frenzied chorus of shouts and screams and oaths and orders and—*boom!*—the *Hope* lurched violently to starboard and the firing began.

Barkbelly was flung against the bars as the ship heeled. The hold echoed with thuds and bangs as the *Hope* returned fire, pounding the pirate ship with grapeshot and cannonballs. And then it happened. A flash of light, a monstrous roar, a terrifying wind and—*pdoooom!*—the world exploded as an eighteen-pounder tore through the hull planks and smashed into the cargo.

Barkbelly was thrown to the floor. The hold was a cauldron of dust and debris. Splinters flew like arrows from shattered crates. Eggs ricocheted off the cage. He covered his head with his arms and kept his eyes closed against the onslaught. But then he smelled it. *Fire*. He peered through the dust cloud and saw a flicker of flame just spitting distance away. The fire was tonguing one of the crates. The dry wood smoked, then flared into orange flame. And inside the crate, the eggs started to move. Slowly at first, then—*bang!*—the crate exploded and the eggs burst out.

They smashed against the hull; bounced back off the roof beams; rolled along the floor. They started to grow. The leathery sacs strained and bulged. An arm poked out here; a leg poked out there. The hold was alive with babies, gnashing their teeth and crying for food.

But now Barkbelly had eyes for only one thing: the fire. It was creeping closer and closer. Crate after crate was being devoured. It was unstoppable. And he was trapped. The cage was iron. The lock was iron. There was no escape.

"*Help!*" he yelled. "*Help! Someone! Please! Help!*" But he knew it was hopeless. The crew would be engaged in hand-to-hand fighting by now, and even if they weren't, they wouldn't hear him above the bawling babies. And why would they save him anyway? He wasn't crew—he was cargo, and that was expendable.

But then he saw a chink of light. The hatch was opening. Someone was coming down. Through the dust and the smoke he saw the silhouette of a tall man holding a bunch of keys.

"I'm over here!" cried Barkbelly. "Over here!"

"I can see that," said Griddle. "It's just a question of finding the right key." He started to fumble with the lock. "It doesn't seem to be here."

"*It must be!*"

"Aye, you'd think so, but it's not."

"It *must* be!"

"Well, I can't find it. And don't rush me."

"*Don't rush you!* Griddle, the place is on fire, I'm trapped in a cage and I'm made of wood! *Ohhhh!*" The fire was licking at the bars.

"Don't fret. If it's here, I'll find it. Oh, bother!" The keys fell to the floor.

"*Griddle!*" The fire was burning the boards under Barkbelly's feet.

"I've got them."

"The big one! The big one!"

"Right." And the key slid into the lock and turned.

Griddle pulled off the padlock, Barkbelly pushed open the cage door, they both scrambled up the steps—and fell into the belly of the battle.

A two-masted brigantine, the *Mermaid*, lay alongside the *Hope* and her crew was slaughtering Kempe's men. The pirates fought joyously, slicing the air with silver cutlasses. They swung their swords, parried and lunged, danced like demons. They crawled up the rigging with knives between their teeth, grinning at the sailors who clung to the main yard. Trapped and terrified, they had nowhere to go but down. Down, down, down to the drowning sea and the rip and tear of the killing spree. Sharks had gathered, lured by the tantalizing trail of blood. The water churned crimson; the air was cut with cries. And loudest among them were Flynn's. Barkbelly heard him, and when he looked over the rail, he saw him: he was in the water, fighting a shark. Grimly gripping his dagger, Flynn brought it down, again and again between the glassy eyes. But the shark opened his jaws in a cold smile and the first mate stabbed no more. And Barkbelly felt his heart move with something more than horror.

Captain Kempe was dead too. Barkbelly could see him on

the main deck, lying in a pool of blood. His fine white shirt was soaking it up. Barkbelly remembered that long afterward.

Finally it was over. The *Hope*'s crew had been reduced to barely a dozen prisoners. Two pirates guarded them while the others tackled the blaze in the hold. But the firefighting was hampered by wooden babies. Some were crawling underfoot. Some were toddling. Some were still shooting around like bullets. The most troublesome of all was a tiny toddler who was so pale she looked almost white. She had attached herself by her teeth to the leg of one of the pirates and wouldn't let go. When anyone tried to pull her off, she growled and gripped harder. The pirate was in agony, but his pleas made no difference.

Barkbelly and Griddle were watching from the quarterdeck. Griddle held up a finger. "An idea," he said, and he disappeared in the direction of the galley. Soon he reappeared with an extra-large pork pie. He offered it to the pale toddler. She sniffed at it suspiciously. Then her eyes widened and she dropped from the pirate's leg like a ripe apple. Soon she was climbing up the main mast, holding the pie in her mouth, and the pirate was seeking a dressing for his tooth-marked leg.

"She's a little monkey, that one," said Griddle when he returned. "You mark my words! I'm not often wrong."

Barkbelly was about to say something when he saw a peacock-blue velvet hat coming up the companionway. Below that, a golden neckerchief . . . a gorgeous velvet frock coat . . . matching britches . . . and two shiny blue boots. The pirate eased himself up onto the deck, then stretched and yawned as gracefully as a cat.

"If I don't find something to eat soon," said the pirate, "I swear I will kill someone. Oh—too late." He teased a lace handkerchief from his pocket and wiped the blood-smeared dagger that dangled from his fingers. "Griddle, be a hero. Fix me my favorite."

The cook grinned. "Aye, aye, Cap'n!" he said. And then he saluted, put his hand firmly on Barkbelly's shoulder and marched him away.

Chapter 39

"*G*riddle," said Barkbelly, "do you know the pirate captain?" They were in the galley, frying fish for the captain's table.

"Oh, yes!" said the cook. "We go back years, Lord Fox and me."

"Is that his name? Is he really a lord?"

"True as I'm standing here. Lord Foxwell of Fenland. He's from a very distinguished family."

"Then why is he a pirate?"

"Well, he likes the dressing up and that's a fact," said Griddle, "but it's more than that. Truth is he's hungry. Hungry for gold. It gnaws away at him inside, like a big fat worm. It gives him no peace. He always wants more and he'll do anything for it. Anything! He'd sell his own family—in fact, I think he *did* sell a sister or two. . . . Aye, he did. He told me. The family's not spoken to him since."

"Why would he sell his own sister?"

"Debts. He's a terrible gambler. And a very bad loser. I once saw him slice open a man, straight down the middle, all over a game of dice. Not very pleasant. . . . Right, we're done here! Let's get this to the captain's cabin."

Balancing platters on both arms, they made their way aft to Captain Kempe's old cabin. Barkbelly had never seen it before, and when he stepped inside . . . oh, it was so opulent! So light and airy! Compared to the squalor of the mess deck, it was heaven. Golden sunlight poured in through a high glass window. There was even a fireplace!

Lord Fox was sitting at the table, eager to eat. Griddle set the platters down before him and said, "I was just telling Barkbelly here, we go back a long way."

"Oh, we do," said Lord Fox. "We do. Ten years or more. Must be five or six ships I've raided that have had Griddle as cook." He pointed to an empty chair. "Sit down, young sir."

Barkbelly froze. Sit down? In the captain's cabin? He was a galley boy! But to his amazement, he saw Griddle was already seated—and was helping himself to a portion of fish.

"Sit," said the pirate captain again, and with Griddle nodding encouragingly, Barkbelly sat down.

"So," said Lord Fox, turning to the cook, "what have you been up to, you old devil?"

Griddle grinned and the stories began. Times and places, ships and faces . . . it was a feast of friendship. Barkbelly was welcome to join in, but he had nothing to say and no space to say it. Griddle and the captain had mouths that were never empty of words or fish or wine—and they were unexpectedly generous with that. After one glass, Barkbelly's legs staggered off without him. After two glasses, he was floating somewhere near the ceiling while the conversation swirled beneath him. He was vaguely aware that Griddle was asking Lord Fox what he planned to do with the *Hope*.

"Scuttle her," said the pirate captain. "The ocean's deep

just here. She'll cause no problems. The chaps will strip her to-morrow and purloin the cargo. Then we'll move on."

"She's in a sorry state," said Griddle.

"Yes, she is," said Lord Fox. "But even if she weren't, we wouldn't take her. She's too big."

"Aye, and slow with it," said Griddle. "What you gain in timber, you lose in time."

"Exactly," said Lord Fox, and he reached for another bottle of wine, pulled out the cork and turned to Barkbelly. "So, you're an Ashenpeaker?"

Barkbelly sank down from the ceiling and stared glassy-eyed at the captain. "Yes," he said, pleasantly surprised that his mouth had managed it.

"Freeborn?"

"Aye," said Griddle, noting Barkbelly's puzzlement.

"Have you ever been to Ashenpeake?" said Lord Fox.

"No," said Barkbelly. "No, I haven't. . . . But I hope to get there one day."

"Oh, it's wonderful," said the captain. "The view from the sea is amazing. The sun rising over Ashenpeake Mountain, with the forest shadowed below . . . oh, it's fabulous. But the sea can be naughty sometimes. Dreadfully misty. So, much as I would like to promise you a good view of it, I can't." He slipped another forkful of fish into his mouth. "But perhaps you'll see something."

Barkbelly frowned. "I'm sorry, sir. . . . I don't understand."

"No?"

"No."

"I will explain," said the captain with a smile. He buttered a piece of bread and cut it into fingers. "Ashenpeake, as you know, is an island. But it is surrounded by smaller islands, and we have a hideaway on one of them. That's where we're heading tomorrow."

Barkbelly's befuddlement disappeared instantly. "How long will it take to get there?" he said, trying to sound casual.

"With a fair wind, we should arrive by this time next week."

This time next week! Barkbelly went wobbly all over.

"Seven days? They'll pass in no time," said Griddle. "You mark my words."

It was dark by the time the meal was over. When Barkbelly went up on deck, he found the rigging festooned with lanterns. Someone was playing an accordion; the notes flirted in the air, sweetening the smoke of a dozen pipes. The pirates lounged in the golden glow of the lamps, drinking rum and laughing. A silver moon curled like a fingernail in the great dome of sky above. Soft waves kissed the ship in the blue below.

Barkbelly leaned against the ship's rail and thought about what Griddle had said. Seven days would pass in no time, wouldn't they? He hoped so. He was already counting.

Chapter 40

*L*ord Fox's men began stripping the *Hope* at first light. Shrouds, ropes, ironware, provisions . . . everything was taken. As the sun journeyed across the sky, the plundering went on. Endless booty disappeared into the *Mermaid's* hold. Finally there was little left to take except the cargo.

Barkbelly was swinging from the rigging when he saw the first crate being carried out of the hold by the man they called Tanglebeard. Instantly he scrabbled down and blocked the pirate's way.

"Where are you going with that?" he said.

Tanglebeard spat out a glob of tobacco juice. "That's none of your business."

"I'm making it my business."

The pirate saw Barkbelly's clenched fists and wavered. "It's going onto the *Mermaid*," he said. "Along with all the rest o' the stuff."

"Oh, no, it isn't," said Barkbelly, and he wrestled the crate from him.

"Oh, yes, it is," said Tanglebeard, and he wrestled it back.

"Oh, no, it isn't," said Barkbelly, seizing it again. "This isn't cargo. This is mine."

The pirate snorted. "Take it, then, and go. I can't be bothered to argue with you." He turned back toward the hold.

"Where are you going?" said Barkbelly.

"There's plenty more down there," said Tanglebeard over his shoulder.

"You can't! They're mine too."

Tanglebeard stopped, stiffened, swiveled his head and looked hard at Barkbelly. "Now you're being greedy," he said. "I was prepared to let you have *one*—a lad needs something in life to get him going—but now . . . Do you know how much those crates are worth?"

"You're not having them," said Barkbelly. "I will fight you for every one."

"Then you will die!" cried the pirate, and he roared with laughter. "You don't know who you're dealing with."

"I am strong."

"But we are many. You fight alone."

"No, he doesn't," said a voice.

Tanglebeard looked down. There was the pale toddler, standing no taller than his knee, staring up at him with goose-gray eyes. "I will fight with him," she said, and she smiled, displaying her sharp wooden teeth. "And so will my friends." Then she whistled, and from nowhere came an army. They dropped down from the rigging. Crawled out of the hold. Wriggled out of boxes. Slid down the masts. Dozens of fat wooden babies, armed with teeth and fingers.

Tanglebeard was surrounded. He shifted uneasily. "What do you want, missy?"

"I want you to fetch the captain," said the pale toddler.

213

"And my name is not 'missy.' It is Snowbone. Remember that."

Tanglebeard disappeared, cursing under his breath. When he returned with the captain, they had to force their way through an ugly crowd: the entire crew of the *Mermaid* had surrounded the babies and they were all squabbling like chickens.

Lord Fox struck an elegant pose in the middle of the rabble and waited for silence. "Now," he said when it finally came, "would someone care to tell me what this is all about?"

"It's about the eggs," said Barkbelly. "I want them."

"But they're ours," said Lord Fox. "We don't attack ships for the fun of it, you know. We do it for the booty. We're robbers."

"I understand that," said Barkbelly. "And if the *Hope* was carrying wine or wool, I wouldn't argue. But she's not. Those eggs . . . to you they're cargo, plunder, booty—call it what you will. But to me they are so much more."

The captain leaned closer. "Do you know how much those eggs are worth?" he said. "They are worth *thousands*. Slaves don't come as cheap as you might think."

"It's not about money!" cried Barkbelly. "It's about freedom." He ripped a hole in the crate at his feet, pulled out an egg, clambered up on the crate and held the egg high in the air for every pirate to see. "This is a life. And what you decide, here and now, will determine how that life is lived. You can sell it into slavery. You can set it free. *It's your choice.* And you have that choice because you are free men. You are not slaves. You can turn your ship into the wind and sail wherever you want. You can sleep when you want. You can eat when you want. And if you tire of the sea, you can find a house and a wife, and you can have children and you can send them to

school. And they will not have to work all day, every day, to make a rich man richer. They will not have to live alone, in a strange land, with no real family—no *memory* of family.

"I don't know who is inside this egg. It could be my brother or my sister. My niece or my nephew. I don't know. But I *do* know there is a little part of me inside this egg. This egg holds the past and the future of my people. It is worth more to me than any amount of money. That is why I will fight for it. But I hope I don't have to."

He climbed down from the crate. It had gone horribly quiet. The pirates were sneaking glances at each other but no one dared speak.

"Give me the egg," said Lord Fox.

Barkbelly handed it over. The pirate captain gazed at it and traced the wood grain with a jeweled finger. He tossed it into the air and caught it. He nuzzled it. And then he threw it. Higher and higher it flew, over the heads of the pirates, over the side of the ship and—*pdoosh!*—everyone heard the sound of freedom. Lord Fox punched his fist in the air and picked up the opened crate. He carried it to the rail and emptied the eggs overboard.

"Bring me another!" he cried.

But no one did, because no one was listening. They were too busy barging their way into the hold. Every man wanted a crate of his own to empty and he was prepared to fight for it. With a pull and a punch and a kick and a tear and a spit and a shove and a handful of hair, they all claimed their prizes and carried them up into the sunshine. Then the egg hurling began. Some threw them like stones, hard and accurate. Some held them awhile, then dropped them gently into the foam. Some placed bets on who could throw the farthest. But all of them watched the eggs float away to freedom, and no one returned to work until they had disappeared.

When that moment came, Barkbelly suddenly felt a tugging on his britches. It was Snowbone.

"Tell me 'bout our people," she said.

"What do you want to know?" said Barkbelly.

"*Everything.*"

Chapter 41

*T*he sun was nearing the horizon when Lord Fox gave the order to abandon ship. The pirates scrambled over the rails and dropped onto the *Mermaid*'s decks. With a push on the capstan, the anchor rose, the shrouds were unfurled and the pirate ship pulled away. Once a safe distance had been reached, the captain ordered the cannon to fire. The first volley took the *Hope* amidships, ripping an enormous hole in her timbers. The sea poured in through the wound. She started to list. A bell on her masthead began to toll all by itself.

As Barkbelly watched the galleon disappear, his emotions churned like the water around her. She had given him so many memories and not all were bad.

"She was a grand old dame," said Griddle. "Bit poky in places, but grand nonetheless."

"What will you do now?" said Barkbelly.

"Oh, I'll stay with Lord Fox for a while yet. He's always good company. And then, in time, I'll find a new ship."

"Will you return to Lindenland? To Pebbleport?"

"Oh, yes! I'm Pebbleport to my bones. It's where I was born and where I'll be buried, if the waves don't claim me first. In the meadow, looking out to sea, with a gentle breeze playing around my headstone and a view of the sun going down. Aye, that'll do for me. And incidentally, if ever *you* need me, Pebbleport's the place to look. Ask at the Dog and Puddle, down on the quay. They'll know where I am. And what about you?"

"Well, I want to go to Ashenpeake," said Barkbelly. "As soon as I can. I think I'll ask the captain for a boat."

"I don't think you'll need to ask him, what with Snowbone and all them other babies underfoot. He won't want them on his island, you mark my words! No, I think he'll put as many as will go into a boat and send it on to Ashenpeake. North end of the island, I should think. No one lives up there, so they'll not be bothered. Oh, look—she's going."

Nothing remained of the *Hope* now except her masts, silhouetted against the sunset, and as Barkbelly watched, they too disappeared beneath the waves. The water churned briefly, then settled into ripples of burnished gold.

"They do say," said Griddle, "that all the shipwrecks in the ocean move across the seabed. They travel many miles until they reach the Silverana Sea. And there they stay: a great graveyard of ships, surrounded by a forest of seaweed, circling endlessly, round and round, for all eternity."

"Is that a true story?"

The cook nodded.

"Wow," said Barkbelly. "I would like to see that."

"Happen you would! But you have things to do. Places to go. People to find. Have you forgotten?"

Forgotten? No. How could he? Ashenpeake had filled

219

Barkbelly's thoughts from the moment he first heard about it. Whether he was asleep or awake or somewhere in between, Ashenpeake dominated his dreams. And now it lay just over the horizon, watching and waiting in the dark like a great bear. So close, he could almost hear it breathing.

Chapter 42

The seven-day voyage to Ashenpeake was surprisingly swift and enjoyable. Griddle took up residence in the *Mermaid's* galley but declined Barkbelly's reluctant offer of help.

"It's not that I'm ungrateful," he said, "but I have a new assistant. And, in truth, he's considerably more able and infinitely more willing. So you can forget the dirty pots and do what you want for the rest of the voyage."

And so Barkbelly became a true sailor, working between the sea and the sky. Surprisingly, Tanglebeard became his mentor. He taught him how to mend sails, tie knots and swab decks. Swabbing was backbreaking work, but Barkbelly loved it. He was given a brush, a bucket, a long rope, an endless supply of water—the sea—and told to get scrubbing. Tanglebeard explained to him that it must be done every day to prevent disease. This was something all sailors feared, along with fire and drowning—most of them couldn't swim. He also taught him the danger of ropes and cables. If a man was caught in a coiling rope, it would cut him in two.

"No!" said Barkbelly.

"Yes!" said Tanglebeard. "I've seen it myself. Arms and legs cut off, like slices of cheese."

"No!"

"Yes! I don't know whether a rope would cut through you, as it would a flesh-and-blood man. Perhaps it would, perhaps it wouldn't. Either way, I don't care to see. Do you?"

Barkbelly gulped. "No, sir."

"Then you just be careful. I've lost too many mates over the years. I don't want to lose another."

Barkbelly stared at the pirate. At his beard, braided with blue ribbon. At his golden earrings, glinting through a tumble of hair. At his arms, more tattoo than skin. This man was an adventurer. There was nothing he hadn't seen. Nothing he wouldn't do. He was Danger and Daring.

"Am I really your mate?" said Barkbelly.

Tanglebeard nodded. "Until you beat me at cards. Then I'll slit your stomach and throw your gizzards to the gulls." But he winked, and Barkbelly breathed again.

When Barkbelly wasn't working with Tanglebeard, he studied the wooden babies. Hundreds had been born during the pirate attack, but very few remained—no more than thirty. All the others had jumped overboard, to float away in search of adventure.

The babies were the first wooden people Barkbelly had seen and he was fascinated by their rapid growth. The Gantrys had told him the story of his birth, but until now that was exactly what he had thought it was—a story. He hadn't believed it was real.

But now he knew it was true and he tried desperately to remember exactly what he had seen during the pirate attack. It wasn't easy. The hold had been full of smoke at the time and he had been frantically trying to escape from the cage. But he could remember one thing: the horror he had felt when he saw the leathery sacs straining and bulging. They were so . . . *reptilian*. Horrible, nightmarish things. And to think he had started life like that . . . *Urgh!*

But the babies were most agreeable. They were bold and inquisitive, strong and sturdy. They never cried; they felt no pain. Barkbelly was astonished to see one toddler nose-dive from the rigging, hit the deck, bounce, pick himself up, giggle—and then begin the long climb back up the rigging to do it all again. This was Blackeye—the most adventurous of the babies. Like Snowbone, he was easy to identify. With Snowbone, it was her pallor. With Blackeye, it was just that: a striking black eye paired with a common brown one.

Unlike Barkbelly, the pirates found the babies troublesome. There was nowhere they wouldn't explore, nothing they wouldn't chew, and they were always underfoot. They howled when they were hungry and ate such huge quantities of food, Griddle was worried that their supplies wouldn't last till land. But quite unexpectedly the problem was solved by a dead shark. The pirates had noticed the shark tailing the ship, speared it and hauled it up on deck. When they returned to it later, they found nothing but bare bones and a pile of snoring babies, their breath rusty with blood and their teeth tagged with flesh.

Griddle was delighted. "Saves me cooking for 'em," he said. "They're greedy little beggars and they don't appreciate my subtle use of spices. Raw it is from now on."

And so the supplies were saved for those who needed them. And the barefoot pirates never kicked the babies out of their way again.

Chapter 43

$\mathcal{L}$ord Fox was right. The view from the sea was amazing. On the morning of the seventh day, Barkbelly rose at dawn and climbed to the main top. There he sat, cursing the mist that refused to rise, preferring to filter the first rays of sun: lemon, gold, orange. But then, miraculously, the mist cleared and he saw it: a breathtakingly beautiful, snow-capped mountain, mantled in forest. *Ashenpeake.*

It completely dominated the island that bore its name. At this distance, the harbor town that nestled at its base was no bigger than Barkbelly's thumbnail, while the peak was two hands high. And Barkbelly knew: that harbor town, Fessel, was a thriving port, with thousands of inhabitants. It wasn't a fishing village. It only appeared so because of the immensity behind it.

As the *Mermaid* sailed north, skirting the island—as the sun rose higher behind the ashen peak—Barkbelly found that he was shaking. His whole body was aquiver; he ached with yearning. There was a whisper on the wind: his heart could hear it, as clearly as he could hear the gulls screaming overhead. The island was calling him home.

                    *   *   *

The pirates' hideaway was on a tiny island northwest of
Ashenpeake. As the *Mermaid* drew close, puffins raced from
the rocks and sped alongside. Gulls wheeled above, waiting for
the scraps that would soon be thrown. And to Barkbelly's
amazement, women and children appeared on the jetty that
jutted out into the bay. Wives! Families! No one had mentioned them.

The *Mermaid* dropped anchor, the longboats were lowered,
the pirates rowed ashore and the homecoming celebrations began. The men shaved and bathed, while the women prepared
food and carried it to the beach. The children built bonfires
and polished lanterns. By nightfall everything was ready. Then
came the singing and dancing, the feasting and foolery, the
stories and kisses . . . all under a sky peppered with stars.

Barkbelly was lazing on the jetty when Lord Fox found
him.

"I know you want to be getting along," he said, "but the
chaps will need a day to unload the ship. So if you would like
the longboats, you can have them the day after tomorrow. The
chaps will take you and Snowbone and all the other little pop-
pets to the north end of Ashenpeake, and then they'll come
back here. How does that sound?"

"It sounds perfect," said Barkbelly. "Just . . . perfect!"

Chapter 44

The departure day arrived with driving rain and a bitter wind. Barkbelly went to see Tanglebeard and Griddle for one last time and felt the old familiar pain. *Is this what growing up is all about? Letting go and saying goodbye? Does it always have to be like this?*

Then he returned to the beach, clambered into one of the longboats and wedged himself between Blackeye and another baby. At just ten days old, they were as big as five-year-olds, and they jostled him for space like cuckoos in a nest.

Snowbone was in the next boat. He could see her eyes shining, pale as pearls. She waved and grinned when she saw him.

Suddenly the boat was being pushed out into the waves. The pirates were heaving on the oars. The beach was receding. Tanglebeard and Griddle were standing there, waving. He was going.

He gave one last wave and turned away. *Better to think about what's ahead than what's behind.* But what was ahead? He had no idea.

He was so lost in thought, the journey was over before he

realized. Suddenly he was looking at a beach. A long, narrow beach with black sand and beyond that—forest. Endless forest.

The boat scraped against the sand. The pirates leapt out and hauled it ashore. The passengers climbed out. Only Barkbelly remained. He had traveled so far, waited so long for this moment. Now it was here. . . .

One of the pirates offered him his hand. Barkbelly took a deep breath and accepted it. Then he stepped out of the boat onto the black sand.

He had done it. He was home.

PART FIVE

Chapter 45

"*H*ow long do you think it would take me to walk from one end of this island to the other?"

"Don't know."

"Guess."

Barkbelly and Snowbone were sitting on the black beach, throwing pebbles into the breaking surf. The rain had stopped; a timid sun had appeared from behind the clouds. Everything was freshly washed and warming.

Snowbone thought for a moment. "If you walked in a straight line, right down the middle, I'd say . . . two weeks."

"Yes. That's what I'd say," said Barkbelly.

"Is that what you're planning to do?" asked Snowbone. "Walk the whole island?"

"No. Well, maybe. I don't really know. I want to find my family—my real, birth family—but I don't know where they are. And I don't know *who* they are. I don't even know my family name."

Snowbone shrugged. "Why is it important? Finding your family?"

"I want to make things right," said Barkbelly. "I was stolen.

The slave traders came and took me away from my parents. I want them to know I survived. And I want to know what they're like. They're part of me. A part that's missing. I want to feel whole. Complete. At peace."

"I don't feel like I have a bit missing," said Snowbone, "and I'm the same as you."

"No, you're still young. This feeling grows on you. You see families. Your friends have brothers and sisters. You start to wonder. Anyway—what are you going to do?"

"Stay here," said Snowbone. "Make camp. Grow up. Then I'll know what we have to do."

"We? You mean the others? Will they stay here with you?"

"Yes."

"Are you sure about that?"

"Yes."

Barkbelly looked at her face and knew she was right.

"Look after yourself," he said, standing up.

"And you," said Snowbone. Then she smiled: a warm, baby smile. But her eyes were older and colder than the pebbles on the beach, and at that moment Barkbelly would sooner have kissed a wild dog than this strange, pale, wooden girl.

And so he walked away, up the beach to the forest edge, and there he turned for one last look. Snowbone was still sitting on the shoreline where he had left her, lost to the wind and the waves. He turned away. Back to face the forest: a silent world of sunlight and shadows, moss and fern.

"Let the search begin," he said, and stepped inside.

Chapter 46

As Barkbelly plunged deeper into the forest, he wondered why it felt so familiar to him. He had grown up beneath the cover of Ferny Wood, of course, but this feeling went beyond that. And Ferny Wood was different. It teemed with life. Every leaf held an insect; every tree held a bird. There were flowers to pick and fruit to find. This forest was a wasteland in comparison. Yet something about its very emptiness was curiously comforting.

For the first few hours, he bounded between the trees. After so long at sea, he had forgotten how wonderful it was to walk. To feel the earth beneath his feet. But as the day wore on, he began to worry. Exactly how big was this forest? Was he walking out of it or still walking in? Was he lost? How would he survive? There was nothing to eat. No nuts or berries. Nothing.

He walked on, but it was growing murkier by the minute. Night was falling, and without light, he would lose the path altogether. It was time to stop.

He curled up at the foot of a pine and stared into the trees. Darkness came silently, like a herd of deer. Soon he could see nothing—not even his boots. But strangely, with the darkness came sounds. The forest had seemed utterly lifeless during the day, but now . . . Unseen hoofs trampled the forest floor. Snouts upturned the earth. Owls flew so low he could feel the downbeat of their wings. Cries cut through the night as talons found fur.

Rain began to fall. Barkbelly could hear it rattling on the forest canopy. Soon the drips fell through, *drip—drip—drip*, like the ticking of a clock. And with this lullaby, he drifted into sleep.

By morning, the rain had passed. He awoke to find that a ring of mushrooms had grown around him and he feasted happily. Then he drank from a nearby spring and ambled on.

In time, he saw the sunlight turning from freckles into pools. The forest was thinning. And suddenly he found a glade, with a cloudless sky above and a house in the middle. A rickety timber house with a tin roof, a squat chimney and dozens of pots and pans dangling from the eaves. And in front of it was a tinker man, cleaning knives.

The tinker looked up and waved. "Hello there!" He beckoned Barkbelly closer. "It's a grand day, isn't it?"

"It is," said Barkbelly, staying where he was.

"I'm just about to put the kettle on. Do you fancy a cup of tea?" The tinker put down his knife. "I've had breakfast. I won't eat you. I have cake! Come on. You know you want to." He cocked his head to one side like a robin and smiled roguishly.

"Thank you," said Barkbelly after some deliberation. "That would be nice."

The tinker disappeared into his house. Barkbelly followed

him in. There was just one room, with an earth floor, a table, two upright chairs, an armchair, a cupboard, a rumpled bed and a small stove.

"Sit down," said the tinker. "Make yourself at home." He filled the kettle from a pail by the door and took it to the stove. "The name's Figgis. What do they call you?"

"Barkbelly."

"Do they, now? That's a grand name!" He opened the cupboard and brought out a large berry cake. "Made it myself."

The tinker started to cut thick slices, and as he did, Barkbelly caught hold of his arm.

"You're wooden!"

"I am," said Figgis. "But so are you. So what are you saying?"

"You're a man!"

"I was the last time I looked, yes. And you're worrying me now."

"I've never seen a wooden man before."

Figgis sat down and stared hard at Barkbelly. "And how can that be? On an island full of wooden people?"

"It's a long story," said Barkbelly.

"I have long ears," said Figgis.

"You wouldn't want to hear it."

"I would. But only with a pot of tea on the table before me, so wait there while I fetch it."

He made the tea and brought two cups. Buttered the cake and found two plates. Pulled up his chair and settled himself comfortably on it.

"Now," he said, "begin."

So Barkbelly told his story. Pumbleditch, Tythingtown, the

circus, the *Hope* . . . Figgis listened like a child. When it was over, he could barely speak.

"Ah . . . well!" he said. "So! That's . . . That's a fine old tale! It is! And do you know what I like best about it? It's not over yet. There's still your family to find."

"That's true," said Barkbelly. "But I don't know how I'll find them. I don't know who they are."

"Give me your hand."

"Eh?"

"Give me your hand. No, not like that." He held his hand up in the air, with its palm facing Barkbelly. "Like this."

Barkbelly copied him and Figgis brought his hand forward till their fingers touched. Barkbelly gasped. His fingers were tingling. It was a strange sensation: neither pleasant nor unpleasant, but both at once. A bit like he imagined nettle stings to be.

Suddenly Figgis broke contact and peered at Barkbelly's hand. "You're not a Figgis," he said.

"What do you mean?"

"Look at your hand," said Figgis.

Barkbelly looked. The wood-grain patterns on his palm were glowing. The faint tracery of lines had become an unmistakable map, bold with swirls and flourishes.

"Now look at mine. What do you see?"

"The same," said Barkbelly. "All the lines and markings are standing out, like someone's just painted them on."

"And what color has the painter used?"

Barkbelly peered closer. "Golden brown."

"Exactly," said Figgis. "But if you were a Figgis, like me, it would be green."

"So I'm not one of your family?"

237

"More than that. You're not one of my clan."

"I don't understand," said Barkbelly.

"I wouldn't expect you to," said Figgis, "you being a stranger an' all! It takes a bit of explaining. Would you like me to try?"

Barkbelly nodded.

"Well now," said Figgis, "let's see. . . . Long, long ago, the Ancients were born. They came out of the earth and they grew tall and then they mated. Now, because there were nine Ancients, one of them was left out when it came to pairing up, and that caused all kinds of complications, as you can imagine! But they sorted it out in the end, to everyone's relief. Anyway, what I'm saying is this: every Ashenpeaker is descended from one of those nine Ancients. So there are nine clans. Everyone who is descended from Fig—like me—is in the Figgis clan. Everyone who is descended from Pel is in the Pellan clan and so on. Now, we know you're not a Figgis, so you must belong to one of the other eight."

"And you can tell what clan someone is in by the pattern on their hand?"

"Yes," said Figgis. "There are nine different patterns, one for each clan."

"I have a question," said Barkbelly. "You say that everyone is descended from *one* Ancient, but surely everyone is descended from *two*, mother and father. So why is there just one pattern on your hand, when there should be two?"

"That is a *brilliant* question," said Figgis, "and a tricky one to answer. Think of it like this. Imagine the sky. Imagine the sun is shining in the sky. You can see it. But then, a cloud comes along and covers it. Where is the sun now?"

"It's still there," said Barkbelly. "Behind the cloud."

"Exactly. It's still there. Strong as ever. You just can't see it. Well, it's the same with the patterns. The mark of one Ancient will cover the mark of another, just like the cloud covering the sun. So even though the descendants had the markings of two Ancients, only *one* showed on their hands. And it was all fairly done. Fig's pattern covered Pel's, but Pel's covered Kip's. Do you see what I mean? That's how all nine patterns survived."

Barkbelly thought for a moment. "So if a . . . Figgis marries a . . . Pellan . . . and they have a baby . . . the baby is a . . . Figgis! Right?"

"No."

"*No?* But it must be! Fig covers Pel—you said so!"

Figgis shook his head. "You're right, in theory, but . . . Ah, this is where it gets complicated! The Ancients had children. And those children had children. For hundreds—no—*thousands* of years, people were marrying between the clans and having children. But then a strange thing happened: eggs stopped hatching. Funnily enough, it wasn't every egg. If an egg had parents from the same clan, it was fine. It hatched. But if an egg had a father from one clan and a mother from another, it wouldn't hatch. No one knew why. It was like a plague. It came in the night, it spread across the land and it's never gone away. So now, if you want to have children, you must marry someone from your own clan."

"That's terrible," said Barkbelly.

"Yes, it is," said Figgis. "But it makes your job so much easier."

"Why?"

"Because you will only have to consider people from one

clan. Think about it! If you're, say, a Kippan, then your mother and your father will both be Kippans. Your grandparents will be Kippans. Your brothers and sisters will be Kippans. So already, you can forget about—"

"Everyone from the other eight clans!"

Figgis grinned. "You've got it!" he said. "Now, will you put that kettle on again? I've got to go." And with that, he disappeared into the garden.

Barkbelly refilled the kettle and set it to boil. Figgis had given him so much to think about! There was just one thing. . . .

"Figgis," he said when the tinker returned, buttoning his britches, "how can I find my family when I don't know their name?"

"You can't."

Barkbelly froze. Suddenly the roof was lifting off the house . . . a huge hand was hovering in the sky above, holding a hammer . . . the hammer came down, smashing him to the ground.

"I can't find my family?"

"No," said Figgis, making a second pot of tea. "But you can find your mother. And if you're lucky, she'll still be with the rest of your family."

Barkbelly slumped back into his chair. Figgis seemed to be talking in riddles.

"I gave you a bit of a fright there, didn't I?" said the tinker. "Come on. Take a drop of tea."

Barkbelly picked up his cup and drank deeply. "How can I find my mother?" he said at last.

"With your hand," said Figgis. "You remember: if the pattern turns golden brown, it's someone from another clan. If it turns green, it's someone from the *same* clan. If it turns *black*, it's your mother."

"It's that simple?"

Figgis nodded.

"Blimey."

Chapter 47

*B*arkbelly awoke to the clatter of pans and the smell of porridge.

"Breakfast's ready!" said Figgis, ladling great dollops of porridge into two bowls. "Honey or sugar?"

"Honey, please."

Figgis fetched an earthenware pot from the cupboard. "From my own bees," he said, holding it like a trophy. "You won't taste finer." He opened the pot and a rich clover scent filled the room. "Did you sleep well?"

"I don't know," said Barkbelly, joining him at the table. "I had strange dreams and I still feel tired. But I'll wake up when I start walking, I'm sure."

"So you're traveling on?"

"Yes, I am. Do you mind? I'd love to stay, really I would. There's so much more I'd like to know. But I have to go."

"Of course you do," said Figgis. "You're a born adventurer, I can tell. Not like me! I go into town to sell my pots and pans and that's far enough! I like a chair and a kettle and a comfy bed."

"There's just one more thing I'd like to know," said Barkbelly, "before I go."

"Oh, don't start me off again! I will talk till my tongue wears out if you let me."

"No—it's just a little thing. Is everyone in your clan called Figgis?"

"No. That would be too confusing! I am called Figgis because at school I was the only Figgis. So that was what they called me and it stuck."

"Ah, I see," said Barkbelly. "I was just wondering."

"Of course you were. And that's what I like about you. You have a sense of wonder. Some people look, but they don't see. And they listen, but they don't hear. And they accept everything without question. But for you there will always be a why. And a when and a where and a what and a who! But it's the why that is special. When you're tired, it will carry you on its back. When you're hungry, it will sit in your stomach. When you're lost, it will shine in the dark like a lamp. It will take you as far as you need to go. . . . Would you like some sandwiches to take with you?"

"Yes, I would. Thank you."

And so, armed with cheese and chutney sandwiches, Barkbelly continued on his way. Figgis waved him off and wished him well, and when Barkbelly promised to return, he truly hoped he would.

"If all Ashenpeakers are as fine as Figgis, this will be easy," he said to himself as he returned to the dark of the forest.

But they weren't. And it wasn't.

Chapter 48

$\mathcal{T}$he first thing that Barkbelly noticed when he finally cleared the forest wasn't the river or the road or the whispering fields of corn. It was the farmhouse. The low, red-roofed farmhouse with the coughing chimney. Just the sight of it refreshed him, and with a smile on his face, he headed straight for it.

But he didn't reach it. A man came out into the yard and shouted something he couldn't hear, and three enormous dogs sprang out of nowhere and started running toward him. Barkbelly froze. He had no idea what to do. They were covering the ground faster than he could think. Surely they weren't going to—

"Ai-eee!"

The dogs sprang at him like a three-headed monster and knocked him clean off his feet. Suddenly he was writhing on the ground with the beasts on top of him: a frenzy of fur and flesh and belly and paw and tongue and breath and snout and jaw. They snapped and snarled. Shook him like a sheep. Sank their teeth into him. He had a dog on each arm and one on his leg, clinging like leeches. Yet there was no pain, just shock and

disbelief. Why had the man set them on him? Why? He was doing nothing wrong.

And with that thought, shock turned to anger. He filled his lungs. Clenched his fists. Gathered his strength. Tensed his muscles. Kicked as hard as he had ever kicked anything. *Boof!* The first dog flew through the air and landed like a sack of potatoes. Barkbelly scrabbled to his feet. *Oof!* He punched out his arm—the second dog arced across the sky and thumped down with a terrified yelp. *Oof!* He punched again and the third dog skimmed the grass, hit a fence and fell in a crumpled heap.

"Come on!" he shouted, beckoning the dogs closer. "Come on, ya scabby mutts. What ya waitin' for?"

The dogs stared at him, their mouths gaping like wounds as they panted through their pain. He took a step toward one; it lowered its head and slowly backed away to a safe distance, watching Barkbelly out of the corner of its yellow eye. Then it ran off with its tail between its legs and the other two followed.

"Scaredy cats," snorted Barkbelly, and he walked on.

Barkbelly fared no better at the next farm. The farmer didn't set dogs on him, but he did threaten him. At the third farm, the farmer's wife threw stones and encouraged her children to do likewise.

But just when he was giving up hope of ever finding a warm welcome, he met Tansy Furlow.

When Barkbelly first saw her, she was in her garden, unfolding an enormous piece of blue cloth. She noticed him passing by and smiled. The cloth had a golden crab sewn on it: a mighty creature, with pincers big enough to catch a boy. And as Barkbelly watched, the woman opened a box, took out a silver star and pinned it between the crab's claws.

"There," she said. "I think that's straight." She reached for her sewing box. "There's fresh lemonade on the porch if you'd like some," she said, threading a needle. "You can keep me company while I sew."

Barkbelly poured himself a glass and joined her in the garden. Soon they were chatting like old friends, and when Tansy discovered he was a stranger to the island, she explained her work.

"Ashenpeakers like flags," she said. "The clans have flags, families have flags . . . towns, villages . . . they all have them! And they can be quite fancy. People don't want stripes, they want symbols. Suns, moons, half-moons, leaves, shells, stars . . . I do them all. Finished!" She cut the end of the thread, put her needle back into the sewing box and started to fold the flag. "I make a living. Not a *good* one, but it's enough. No one's rich on Ashenpeake. Even the farmers are struggling to survive. You wouldn't believe it, but . . ."

Tansy talked on. Barkbelly wasn't really listening. He was happy just to hear the sound of her voice. It cuddled him. Comforted him. He had no desire to leave. This felt like home.

No. She couldn't be.

He stared at her. She looked old enough. Her skin was exactly the same shade. He looked at Tansy's hair . . . eyes . . . how tall she was. He was getting light-headed; he was forgetting to breathe. That voice . . . that smile . . .

"What clan are you?" he said suddenly.

Tansy paused in midfold and looked at him. "Eddar," she said. "Why do you ask?"

"I don't know what clan I belong to."

"Oh, you poor lost thing!" cried Tansy, and she dropped the flag, hurried over and hugged him. "Let's find out." She held up her hand.

Barkbelly took a deep breath and held out his own.

The tingles rippled up his arm. He looked at Tansy. She had closed her eyes. She was smiling. But then she pulled her hand away and said, "You're not an Eddar."

"No," said Barkbelly, staring at his brown palm. Suddenly he could hear Rubek's voice in his head: *This is not story. This is not book. It will not end happily ever after for some people. Maybe not even for you.*

And now it seemed that Rubek was right.

Chapter 49

$\mathcal{T}$ansy was worried about her visitor. Barkbelly had barely spoken since the business with the hands. She had taken him inside and made him supper. She had offered him a bed for the night and he had accepted. But he was quiet. Too quiet for a boy his age.

"It doesn't matter, you know—not being an Eddar," she said. "Each of the clans is as good as any other."

"I know," said Barkbelly, and he screwed up his face to dam the tears. But it didn't work. His shoulders started to heave and with a great snort they came: fat, salty tears that ran off the end of his nose and splashed onto the table. "I'm sorry," he said. "I hate doing this. I'm such a cry-baby!"

"Don't you worry about that," said Tansy. "You just let it all out. And when you're finished, you can tell me what's the matter. If you want to, that is."

Barkbelly did want to. He told her everything and felt a lot better for it.

"It's going to be so hard," he said, "finding my family, when people are so hostile. I can't even say hello."

"They're not hostile—they're frightened," said Tansy. "Slave traders were sniffing around last week."

"No!"

"Oh, yes. My neighbor saw them. A whole gang of them, heading east. She said they had a cart laden with crates."

"But I was on my own," said Barkbelly. "And look at me: do I really look like a slaver? I'm just a boy. And I'm wooden!"

"Well, the slavers do use boys as scouts. And as for being wooden . . . I'm ashamed to say that some of the slavers are wooden too. People are scared. You can understand that, can't you? They're not trusting anyone at the moment."

"*You* trusted me."

"I don't have any eggs."

A terrible silence crept into the room. Tansy started fiddling with a teaspoon. Her face was as bleak as the fields in winter.

"I married a Kippan," she said at last. "So there were no children."

"Where is he?"

"Dead."

Barkbelly wished he hadn't asked.

"He died in a house fire."

"*Really?*"

Tansy gave him a strange look and he wished he hadn't sounded quite so interested. But he longed to know more. This was something he had meant to ask Figgis. How do Ashenpeakers die? And when? Well, now he knew something—fire *was* deadly, just as he had suspected. Oh, he wished he could ask Tansy more! But, looking at her stricken face, he couldn't. He changed the subject.

"What really worries me is the size of the island," he said. "I

don't know where to begin looking. My family could be anywhere."

"That's true. But they are most likely to be on the southern
peninsula."

To Barkbelly's relief, she seemed to be brightening. She
pulled open a drawer in the kitchen table, brought out a pencil
and paper and started to draw.

"This is the island," she said. "We are here." She made a
mark in the middle of the island, toward the top. "Here is
Ashenpeake itself." She marked the mountain, midway up the
west coast. "And here is Kessel."

"I saw Kessel! On the way in!"

"You would. It's the biggest town on the island. You can't
miss it. You remember the flag I was sewing earlier—the crab
and the star? That's a Kessel flag. It's for the harbor. They always have one at the end of the quay, but the wind gives them
such a battering, they need replacing every year or so. Anyway,
here's Kessel, and that is the main port. But the slavers use another place: Spittel Point. That is right down here"—she
pointed to the southernmost tip of the island—"on the southern peninsula. And this bit of the island—this southeast
corner—is where they do most of their trading. So that's where
I would look."

"But there must be thousands of women living down there.
Even if the people are friendly—"

"They are! Believe me!" said Tansy. "This fear is just a passing thing."

"How can I touch hands with thousands of women? Complete strangers? They'll think I'm mad."

"You'll have to be charming! Chat to them. Ashenpeakers
love to talk. Tell them you're visiting the island and you want

to find members of your clan. That's reasonable enough. Once you know what clan you are, you can say, 'I'm a Kippan'—or whatever—'what are you?' If they don't match, you can bid them good day. If they *do* match, keep them talking and then, being friendly, take their hand in both your own and start shaking it, like you're saying goodbye. 'It's been lovely talking to you'—that kind of thing. Keep on talking till you've made good contact—that's important. Then let go and glance at your hand. It won't be as bright as the pattern you get from a formal touch, but it'll be enough. And if she's not your mother, you just go on to the next."

"And the next. And the next. It could take months."

"It could take years," said Tansy. "You might never find her at all."

"No—I will find her," said Barkbelly. "If she is out there, I will find her. That's a promise."

$\mathcal{B}$arkbelly walked on through the midday sun. Two days had passed since his meeting with Tansy and in that time he had barely seen anyone. There were few farms and he was wary of approaching them, despite Tansy's promise that Ashenpeakers were friendly at heart.

The road was leading him toward a copse. He would welcome the shade. But there was a cottage chimney rising above the canopy of leaves. He would have to be careful.

He entered the cool of the copse and heard the sound of running water. The road was meandering over a small stone bridge, with a stream clattering beneath.

Barkbelly went down to the water's edge and drank deeply. Then he washed his hands and his face, and was just about to pull off his boots when he heard giggling. Two children—a boy and a girl—were sitting in the shadow of the bridge. The boy was younger than he was. Only a few months old, he guessed. The girl was younger still. A baby. But Barkbelly had an idea.

"Do you want to play a game?" he said.

The boy nodded.

"Great!" said Barkbelly, clambering over the pebbles

toward them. "Let's play touch!" And he wiggled his fingers in the air. The boy mirrored him, smiling. Barkbelly held his hand still and the boy made contact.

"It's tingling," said the boy, and he laughed.

Barkbelly nodded, then he took a deep breath and pulled his hand away.

"Brown!" said the boy, and he laughed again.

"What clan are you?" said Barkbelly.

But the boy wasn't listening. He was holding up the little girl's hand and touching her fingers.

"What clan are you?"

Still no answer.

"Tingle!" cried the little girl. "Tingle!"

Barkbelly turned away in despair.

"Brown!" cried the boy.

Brown?

"It should be green," said Barkbelly, turning round. "She's your sister."

"No!" squealed the boy. "You're silly! She's not my sister. She's my friend."

Barkbelly's heart lurched inside him. "Give me your hand," he said to the little girl. "Like this." He touched her fingers.

"Tingle!" cried the little girl. "Tingle! Tingle! Tingle!"

Barkbelly broke contact and looked at his palm. It was green. Bright leaf green. The pattern was unbelievably clear. Every line was glowing. Every swirl. Every whorl. Every flourish.

"What clan are you?"

"Tingle!" said the little girl. "Again! Again!"

"What clan is she?" he asked the boy.

The boy frowned. "Don't know."

"You *must* know!"

The boy shook his head. Barkbelly seized the little girl by her arms. "What's your clan?" he said. He started to shake her. "What is it?"

The little girl stared at him like a rabbit.

"What's your clan?"

Her tiny face crumpled. She sucked in all the air around her and cried, "Dada!"

"I'm sorry, I'm sorry," said Barkbelly, desperately trying to calm her. "I just want to know."

"Dada!"

Suddenly Barkbelly was grabbed from behind and thrown into the stream. At first he floundered, but then he spun himself over. Spat out a mouthful of mud. Glared at the man towering above him.

"What do you think you're doing, lad?"

"I was just trying to ask her something."

"She is three days old! She knows nothing!"

"But I just want—"

"I know what you want! We've heard the rumors. The slavers can't get enough eggs, so they're stealing little 'uns. You're working for them, aren't you? Coming on ahead. Sniffing round. Asking questions. Well, you won't get my daughter! I will die first! So get out of here!" And he picked up a handful of pebbles and threw them right into Barkbelly's face. "Go on, before you get my boot up your bony backside!"

Barkbelly staggered to his feet. His eye was watering; one of the pebbles had bruised it.

"Go on! Or I swear I will smack you in the face. And your nose won't argue with prime Pellan fist."

Barkbelly stumbled out of the stream, staggered over the

bridge and started running. His eye was watering now. He wanted to bathe it but he couldn't stop. Not yet.

He ran until he reached another bridge, then he came off the road and threw himself down in the shadows beneath it.

"That was dirty fighting," he said to himself as he bathed his eye. "Chucking pebbles. If he had thrown a punch, I wouldn't have seen it coming."

He decided to rest awhile. He knew he was in shock. He was starting to laugh about it all and it wasn't funny.

"'You'll get my boot up your bony backside!'" he said, mimicking the man's gruff accent. "'Your nose won't argue with prime Pellan fist!'"

He caught his breath. *Pellan fist?* His heart started to thump in his chest. *Think carefully, now.* The man said the little girl was his daughter . . . so they would be the same clan. Pellan. And he had clan-matched the daughter.

Barkbelly sank back against the bridge.

"Blessed moons," he said. "I'm a Pellan."

Chapter 51

*B*arkbelly traveled and talked his way south. Now that he knew his clan, he could follow Tansy's advice. In every village, in every hamlet, at every lonely farmhouse and cottage, to every wayfaring woman he met, he said the same thing: *Hello! Can you help me? I'm a visitor to the island and I'm ever so keen to meet fellow clan members. Are you a Pellan by any chance?* And usually it worked. Tansy was right: Ashenpeakers were friendly folk. The northerners had just been scared. Farther south, where traders were commonplace, the islanders were incredibly warm. The women chattered like parrots, wanting to know all kinds of things about the world beyond. If they weren't Pellan, they would direct him to a home that was. If they were, they warmly shook his offered hand and frequently invited him in for tea.

But as the days became weeks, Barkbelly started to lose heart. His conversations became longer as he delayed contact, dreading the disappointment of another green palm. Sometimes he couldn't bear to look at his hand afterward. His pain was painted there in a pattern of failure. But still he traveled on.

But one day, quite unexpectedly, his spirits were lifted.

He was wandering aimlessly along, head down, hands in pockets, when he glanced up and said, "Great. Just great. I'm hungry, I'm tired, I have a hole in my boot and now I have a hill to climb. The day just keeps getting better."

He walked on, cursing his misfortune as he went. But when he reached the top of the hill, he forgot his troubles in an instant. Because there, stretched out before him like a treasure map, was the southern peninsula. It was long—so long, he couldn't see an end to it. But he could see both coasts and ships far out to sea; a scattering of villages and wildwoods; lots of windmills and straight roads latticing the land.

He was so captivated by the sight, he sat on the hill until it was dark. He wanted to watch the shadows creep over the land. He wanted to see the lights shimmer around the coastline like a necklace. And when they did, he felt close to happiness.

In the glow of one of those lamps sat his family.

Chapter 52

"*T*his is a diamond day!" said Barkbelly to himself. "Sparkling. Bright. Clear with a hint of blue round the edges. Perfect!"

He had been searching on the peninsula for five days. One disappointment had followed another, but the fine weather had buoyed his spirits. Now, bouncing along a cliff-top path, he felt deliriously happy. He grinned at the cows in the adjoining field. He knocked the heads off the thistles. But one thing was niggling him. That ship sailing toward the horizon—what was it carrying? Spittel Point was close. . . . He tried not to think about it and turned his attention to the path ahead. There was a woman approaching with a huge wicker basket hooked over one arm.

Could it be a slaver? He looked at the ship again. It was a clipper. *Three-masted, fast . . . she would be perfect for a quick run to Farrago. She could outrace anything.*

He was so lost in thought, he didn't see the bull breaking through the fence behind him. But he did hear the farmer shout, "Look out there!" and suddenly the beast ran by him in a flurry of hoof and horn and careered down the path toward the Basket Woman and she didn't see it because she'd stopped to pick flowers and it smacked her on her backside and her basket went one way and she went the other and she flew through the air like a puffin and disappeared over the edge of the cliff.

"Whoa!" said Barkbelly, and he ran to where she had fallen and peered over.

He saw a storm of gulls—shouting, wheeling, dive-bombing gulls—and waves, far, far below, foaming and snarling against the rocks. But, miraculously, the woman was still there, desperately dangling from a windblown tree. And when she saw him, hope fluttered in her eyes like a moth in a jam jar.

"Help me," she said. "Please. Help me."

Barkbelly flattened himself against the ground and wriggled forward. He reached down as far as he could, stretched out his hand—and drew it back. *I can't help her. She'll pull me over.*

"Help me!" said the woman again, and she held out her hand to him.

He was just about to say *I can't*, when he felt his legs being gripped and a man's voice said, "I've got you, boy!"

So he reached down again, stretched out his fingers and seized the woman's hand. "*Pull!*" he shouted to the man up top, and the man did pull, harder and harder, until both bodies were safely back, lying in a tangled mess of limbs.

"Thank you," said the woman. "Thank you."

"You're welcome," said Barkbelly, and gingerly he picked himself up. *Oh!* He ached all over. He'd stretched so far, he could swear he was taller, and he had terrible tingles up and down his right arm.

"Look at the state of your clothes!" said the farmer. "Your mama will have somethin' to say to you!"

"If she does," said Barkbelly quietly, "she can say it now."

He was staring at the palm of his hand. It had turned black.

Chapter 53

"*M* ama?"
The woman said nothing. She wasn't listening. She was fretting over a rip in her skirt.

"Mama?" Barkbelly caught her by the arm. "Are you my mama?"

"No," said the woman. "I've never seen you before in my life."

Barkbelly took hold of her hand. The pattern on her palm was black as treacle.

"Then how do you explain this?" he said, holding her hand up in front of her face. "And this." He showed his own blackened palm.

"Who are you?" said the woman, seeming nervous now. "How did you get here?"

"By ship. I've come to find you. I'm your son, Barkbelly."

The woman pulled her hand away and cradled it. She turned away and looked out to sea, trawling for answers but finding none. "I don't know what to say," she said at last. "This has never happened before. I don't know what to do."

Barkbelly wanted to give her time to think, but his head was full of questions.

"Do you have a family?" he said.

The woman nodded.

"Do I have brothers? Sisters?"

She nodded again.

"I'll be off!" said the farmer, shattering the moment. "Got to find that bull o' mine."

"Thanks," said Barkbelly. "For your help, I mean."

The farmer slapped him on his back and strode away.

"You'd best come home," said the woman. "Have some dinner."

Barkbelly's heart melted like chocolate. He wanted to shout, scream, jump in the air, grab hold of his mother, kiss her, hug her, shake her. But he didn't. Somehow he didn't feel she would welcome such things.

"My basket," said his mother, looking around.

"I'll find it for you," said Barkbelly, and he did. It was caught up in a tangle of brambles and all around were strange creatures he had never seen before. Bright red balls, bigger than his fist and covered in spikes. And except for the fact that they didn't have heads or legs, he would swear they were hedgehogs.

"Thank you," said his mother, taking the basket from him. She tossed the spiky bundles into it.

"What are these things called?" said Barkbelly.

"Sea urchins."

"Really? Are they alive?"

"Yes," said his mother, "but not for long. These are your dinner."

Chapter 54

arkbelly's mother led him back along the path the way he had come, but suddenly she turned down a track between two fields. Then they went over a hillock and Barkbelly saw a handful of houses below.

"That's my house," said his mother, and she pointed to a lopsided cottage on the edge of the village. "It's small but it's home."

As they drew near, Barkbelly saw that the cottage was made of pebbles bound together with cement and built up like a sandcastle. It was square and sturdy, with a well-tended garden behind.

His mother opened the front door and they went inside. There was no hall: they stepped straight into a kitchen–cum–living room, sparsely furnished but comfortable enough. Rows of socks, big and small, dangled from a line over the stove. A vase of wildflowers brightened the window ledge. Someone had been shelling peas at the kitchen table. Someone had left boots in the middle of the floor. Someone had forgotten to put the butter away after breakfast. And seeing these things, so familiar and yet so different, gave Barkbelly the strangest of sensations. This was his home, but he felt he was intruding. It was all so real. So personal and intimate. So vulnerable. These people knew nothing of him, the stolen son, and he might change their lives forever.

His mother was bustling around the kitchen, tidying up. "Can you—I'm sorry, I've forgotten your name—can you bring in some water from the well at the back?"

"Yes, Mama," said Barkbelly.

"And—what is your name? Right. Barkbelly. Can you call me something else? It feels . . . weird, you calling me Mama. Call me Rue. That's my name—Rue Bufton."

Barkbelly fetched the water and Rue made him tea. Then he sat in a chair by the stove while she prepared dinner. He soon realized that Rue was more comfortable when she had something to do. Her tongue was looser if she didn't look at him. She answered his questions. She told him he had two sisters and one brother, though she had to ask him how old he was before she could say whether his sisters were older or younger. Barkbelly found that curious but he didn't say so, and he didn't ask about the night he was stolen. That could wait until the right time. Instead, he talked about his life and his journey. But Rue didn't seem particularly interested—until he described the circus. She actually stopped what she was doing when he talked about Candy.

"Just fancy that," she said, misty-eyed. "She made her dreams come true. Just fancy that."

Barkbelly talked on, happy to have found something that interested her. He was still talking when the door opened and his father came in.

It *had* to be his father: he had Barkbelly's face. Not just his features but his expression and the tilt of his head—it was like seeing the future. And behind him came Barkbelly's sisters, one of them carrying a toddler.

"Who's this?" said his father.

"It's Barkbelly," said Rue. "Come from overseas. He's your son."

"You're sitting in my chair," said the man, and he stood over Barkbelly, waiting for him to move. As soon as he did, the man sat down, stretched and closed his eyes.

"He's called Dill," said Rue, "and this"—she took hold of the toddler—"is Bay. And these are your sisters, Hyssop and Comfrey. Girls—this is your brother, Barkbelly."

"I don't have a big brother!" said Comfrey, the smaller girl.

"You do now," said Rue. "Go and get cleaned up. Dinner's nearly ready."

Ten minutes later, the whole family sat down together to eat and Barkbelly thought he would burst with happiness. This was it: the homecoming dinner he had dreamed about for so many months. He had found peace. He was complete. He was back where he belonged. His new life was beginning right here, in this moment. So why was no one else excited? Why was no one interested in what he had to say? He had traveled halfway around the world to find these people, but they were discussing carrots. Should they grow them this year? Would parsnips be better?

He tried to tell them about Papa Gantry, but the conversation turned to Papa Hemming, a man in the village whose house needed a new roof. Barkbelly was stunned. They didn't seem to realize what they were doing. They were polite, but that was all. They certainly couldn't be described as welcoming.

There was no improvement after dinner. The girls retired to their room. Dill pottered in the garden until it was dark. Rue went to visit her sister down the road and when she returned it was bedtime. Except there wasn't a bed for Barkbelly. Rue gave him a blanket to lie on and suggested he sleep on the floor by the stove. So that was what he did, although it took him an eternity to fall asleep. The homecoming dinner was lying heavy on his stomach and his breath was sour with the bitter tang of disappointment.

But these were small troubles. If he had known about the shock he would receive the next morning, he wouldn't have slept at all.

Chapter 55

*B*arkbelly awoke soon after dawn. Rue was already busy, kneading bread at the table.

"I'll need to get to that stove in a minute," she said.

Barkbelly moved out of the way and sat on a settle by the window. He watched the kitchen fill with his family and suddenly thought of the jam factory. These people worked like a well-oiled machine, effortlessly moving around each other, finding a space here, a bit of bread there. Everything was fluid and easy. He didn't dare join them in case he upset the balance.

But Rue invited him to the table, and as he listened to the breakfast babble, he thought he had never enjoyed a bowl of porridge more. Afterward, he did the washing up while Rue worked around him. He told her about Pumbleditch and the Gantrys, and she seemed a little more interested. But when he had finished the dishes, he was surprised to see a packed lunch on the table.

"There are ham sandwiches," said Rue, "a bit of cheese, a couple of sausage rolls and a bag of scones. I hope that will be enough." Suddenly she looked him straight in the eyes. "It's been nice meeting you," she said. Then she kissed him on the cheek and opened the door.

"I don't understand," said Barkbelly. "Am I going somewhere?"

Rue frowned. "You're going home, aren't you?"

"No!" said Barkbelly. "I've come to stay!"

"Here? But we've got no room! How long were you planning to stop? A few days? A week?"

"No," said Barkbelly. "Forever. I've come home."

"This isn't your home."

"It is! You're my mother."

"Yes, but—you can't stay."

"Why not?"

"We don't want you here."

Her words flew like arrows. Barkbelly reeled under their impact.

"I'm sorry," said Rue. "I didn't mean it to come out like that. You *are* welcome. Really, you are. But you can only stay for a few days. We don't have the room or the money to feed you. And we're happy, you know, just as we are."

"I've come so far," said Barkbelly.

"I know you have," said Rue. "But it doesn't change things."

"Could I stay in the village? I could build a house."

"I don't know," said Rue. "Maybe. Look, let's not talk about this now. Stay for a week and we'll talk then. You might change your mind after seven days with us!"

And Barkbelly smiled with her, but he knew he wouldn't. This was his home. He was staying and that was final.

Chapter 56

*H*yssop was two years older than Barkbelly and she clearly knew a thing or two about life. More importantly, she loved to show off her knowledge. And since Barkbelly had been pondering the question of life and death for as long as he could remember, he decided that she was the perfect one to ask.

They were sitting in the back garden. Hyssop was stringing onions, expertly twisting the twine between her fingers. Barkbelly introduced the subject by showing her the stump of his little finger and telling her about the factory fire.

"Will it ever grow back?" he asked her.

"No," said Hyssop. "Fire is final. There's no coming back."

"It's strange being wooden," said Barkbelly. "At least, it's been strange for me. I've had no one to ask. I know how we're born, but I don't know how we die or how long we have. Can you tell me, from beginning to end?"

Hyssop beamed at him, put down her onions and began.

"Now, you have to remember," she said, "that we are a very old race of people—perhaps the oldest in the world. And the way we live and grow seems odd to some, but that's how we

271

are. We begin as an egg—you know that. But you probably don't know this: for six months, that egg can't hatch. It must lie dormant. And during that time, it's very vulnerable. It can easily be stolen, and that's why people worry about the slavers. But after six months, it can be thrown on a fire and a baby will be born.

"So we grow very rapidly in the first month, but then we stop until we're ten years old. Then there's a second spurt of growth and that takes us up to adult size.

"People start pairing up around the age of fifteen. If we want children, we have to pair with someone of the same clan. Oh—do you know about clans?"

Barkbelly nodded.

"And then we just get older. Our skin starts to wrinkle. It looks a bit like bark, but it doesn't hurt. As for how long we live, well . . . We don't get serious illnesses like the flesh-and-blood people do—just an odd fever now and then—but we do sicken toward the end. There's no pain. It's more like a weakening. A feeling that it's time to go. And that can happen anytime. Some people will sicken before they're ten. Some will go on until they're a hundred or more. But whenever that time comes, we Move On."

"Move on? You mean we die?"

"No, it's not dying. Moving On is a transformation process. You know when it's time to Move On. You feel the time is right. And then you walk to somewhere nice and stand there, and slowly you are transformed into a tree. Roots will grow out of your feet. Your arms will become branches. Your head will be in the middle of the tree trunk. For a few weeks, you will be able to see and talk, but then you will Move On completely and your face will gradually disappear."

Barkbelly stared at her. "Does this hurt?"

"No. It's natural. It's just the way of things. It comes to all of us in time. In fact, you've just missed Grandpa. He Moved On last week. He's down there."

"Where? In those trees?" Barkbelly pointed to a wildwood at the end of the garden.

"Yes. But they're not trees! They're Ancestors!"

"All of them?"

"Yes! Half of the trees on this island are Ancestors. We call them ashen trees. It's confusing, I know, because they *look* like trees. And they *are* trees now—but they didn't start off that way. Do you want to see Grandpa?"

"No!" said Barkbelly. "He'll still have a face, won't he? Oh, no. I couldn't handle that. I had no idea this would happen. It's grotesque. I feel sick."

Hyssop laughed. "You'll get used to the idea! It's wonderful— you have a whole new life ahead of you."

Barkbelly sat in silence, struggling to make sense of what he had heard.

"Does everyone Move On?" he said at last. "Does no one die?"

Hyssop picked up her onions again. "If you're lucky, you Move On. Some people do die, but it's rare. You see, it's very hard to kill an Ashenpeaker. We're strong. We can survive falls and blows. If we have a bit cut off, it grows back. We float, so we're not going to drown. We can't be shot or stabbed to death. Poison doesn't really work—it acts like a trigger. It starts the Moving On process. There's only one thing that can kill us and that's fire. Like I said before, fire is final. There's no coming back. It's a terrible, *terrible* way to go."

Barkbelly stared at the stump of his missing finger. "I had

no idea," he said. "When I ran into the factory to rescue Taffeta Tything—I had no idea."

"If you had known," said Hyssop, "would it have made any difference?"

Barkbelly thought for a moment. "No. It wouldn't. I would still have gone in there."

"Then you're very brave."

"Or very mad!"

Hyssop smiled at her brother. "Or both."

Chapter 57

*B*arkbelly lay in front of the stove, curled up like an urchin. He couldn't sleep. He was halfway through the week and his mother was still talking of him leaving at the end of it. He needed a plan.

It was the quietest of nights. Everyone was asleep. All he could hear was the ticking of the clock and the occasional grunt from his father as he turned over in bed. But then he heard a new sound: the rumble of cart wheels on the street outside. In the middle of the night? That was odd. Then he heard the door softly opening and his mother crept into the kitchen. She glanced in Barkbelly's direction; he pretended to be asleep. But he watched her open the back door and step into the garden.

Barkbelly went to the window and looked outside. Everything was blue: cool, lunar blue, with shadows behind every tree, sharp as comet tails. It was so bright, he could see his mother clearly. She was standing by the garden shed. Two men were with her. They were talking and nodding. Then Rue opened the shed door and disappeared inside. The men waited. Rue came back out, carrying a tray of something. Barkbelly couldn't see what.

One of the men fished in his coat pocket and pulled out a small bag. He opened it. Silver coins flashed in the moonlight. Rue turned and Barkbelly saw what she was holding. Eggs. Fat wooden eggs. A dozen or more. She smiled and took the moneybag. The men took the eggs and disappeared into the shadows.

The back door opened again and Rue crept in.

"Don't tiptoe on my account," said Barkbelly, blocking her way. He ripped the moneybag out of her hands. "What's this?"

"That's none of your business."

"Who were those men?"

"What men? There's no one out there."

"They're slavers, aren't they?"

"No."

"I saw you. You gave them eggs. They gave you this!" He shook the bag in her face.

"So?"

"So! Is that all you can say? You have just given away a dozen of your children!"

"I didn't give them away. I sold them."

"And that makes it better? Getting money for them? You've sold them into slavery!"

"You don't know that!" said Rue. "You don't know where they're going! They could have a life of luxury. Four meals a day and a comfortable bed. That's more than I ever had as a child! If they have to work for it, so what? We all have to work. That's life."

"No," said Barkbelly. "You're forgetting—I was taken by those men."

"Yes, and look at you! You've hardly suffered, have you? All those tales of Pumbleditch and the blessed Gantrys. You've done more, *seen* more than I ever will! So don't complain to me."

"You just don't understand, do you?" said Barkbelly. "What they are doing is wrong. They are taking people's lives. I thought you of all people would see that. You lost your son to those men. They stole me from you."

"They didn't."

Barkbelly stared at her. "What did you say?"

"They didn't steal you. I sold you."

Barkbelly staggered back against the table and gripped its edges for support. The world was falling away beneath his feet. "No," he said. *"No."*

"Yes. You and a hundred others. How do you think we live? There's no work round here. A bit of fishing, a bit of farming, but that's all. I'm not the only one, you know. You go to every house in the village—they'll tell you the same story."

"I can't believe I've come back to this," said Barkbelly.

"No one asked you to."

"No, but—I came because I wanted to find you. I wanted to love you, but . . . I hate you. *I hate you.* More than I thought I could ever hate anyone."

"Then go!" cried Rue. "If you hate me so much—go! I won't stop you!" She flung open the back door and stood there defiantly.

"I will go in the morning," said Barkbelly. "I won't leave like a thief in the night. I have nothing to be ashamed of."

"Nothing? I think you're forgetting something! Two days ago we sat on the porch and you cried your heart out, telling me about that boy on the playground. And now you say you have nothing to be ashamed of? You're a murderer! That's what you told me. You're only here because you can't go home."

"I can go home. I *will* go home."

"Then you're a bigger fool than I thought you were. You know what they do to murderers, don't you? They kill them. If you go home, you will die. They will *burn* you, boy."

"I don't care," said Barkbelly. "I will go home, and do you know why? I want to see my mama and my papa. They might not be my *real* parents, but they have loved me. My mama has been a better mother to me than you will be to anyone."

"Get out," said Rue. "*Get out!*"

"Don't worry. I'm going," said Barkbelly, and he barged his way past her and ran off into the night.

Barkbelly didn't look back. He ran to the end of the garden, jumped the fence and entered the wood. He had no intention of taking the road; the slavers were out there somewhere. He would cut across country. If he ran till morning, he would put a fair distance between himself and the village. Not that his family would be looking for him.

He ran on through the trees. He ducked under branches. Jumped over roots. Twisted and turned. Tried to fight his rising anger. "How could she?" he said to himself, over and over. "How could she?"

He was stumbling now. Running blind. Ripping through brambles. Smashing through ferns. He didn't see the bank until it was too late. He somersaulted over it and landed with a thump at the foot of a tree. And there *was* a foot. A real foot, tangled up in the roots. When Barkbelly looked up, he saw eyes looking down. Bark-brown eyes, two of them, and a gaunt face trapped in the belly of the ashen tree.

"No pain," said Grandpa. "No pain."

And Barkbelly saw the man's body, stretched out like a scarecrow, battling the bark that was eating into it. The hands, twisted and gnarled, with greenery sprouting from the ripped nails. The feet, rooting into the earth, burrowing like badgers.

"No pain. . . . No pain."

"What do you mean?" said Barkbelly. "I don't understand."

"No pain. . . . No pain."

Barkbelly was shaking now. His whole body was shaking. He looked up into the eyes again and the expression was so wild, so unfathomable, so *awful*, he picked himself up and ran. Harder than he had ever run in his life. So hard he thought his heart would punch its way out of his chest and he would die. Alone, like a wounded animal, right there in the wildwood.

Chapter 58

$\mathcal{M}$orning came. Barkbelly sat on a stile and gazed out to sea. He was tired and hungry. His feet ached. But his mind was made up. He was going home.

Two days' walking would take him off the peninsula. Seven days would take him to Kessel. There he would find a ship and be on his way.

He sighed. He could still feel an ache in his heart where Rue's words had struck him. Was she right? Would they burn him? No. They would put him in jail. But Pumbleditch didn't have a jail. He hadn't even *heard* of one before Tythingtown. He remembered the look on Dipper Dean's face. If they all felt like that, they *would* burn him. There would be no Moving On. Considering Grandpa, that didn't seem so bad. But Hyssop had said that Moving On was wonderful. A whole new life. Surely that was better than nothing? Because that was what fire would give him—nothing.

"What are the alternatives?" he said, just like Miss Dillwater. "Let's see, shall we?" This felt good, playacting his way to a final decision. "One, I can return to Pumbleditch. Two, I can stay here. Or three, I can go anywhere in the world."

He pondered. Two was out. The dream was over. Three? He could go anywhere. Farrago! No—the Silverana Sea! Except he didn't feel safe anymore. Captain Kempe hadn't been kidding. He would have sold him in Barrenta Bay. Next time he might not be so lucky.

So it was One. Return to Pumbleditch. There was no escaping it. He had to go back. Not because he didn't have any other option—he did. He had to go back because he had to be able to live with himself, and at the moment he couldn't. If he traveled to the end of the world, he would still be a fugitive. A runaway murderer. He couldn't run away from himself.

"I have to face them," he said. "I have to see Little Pan's parents. Tell them I'm sorry. But they *will* burn me, I know they will. I'm not one of them. I don't want to die. I don't want Mama and Papa to hate me, and they will. But at least I can tell them I'm sorry. And say goodbye."

Ashenpeake Mountain was capped with cloud. A fine drizzle hung in the air. Everything was gray, gray, gray. The men started pushing the capstan; Barkbelly heard the anchor chain rattle. Then, with a hauling of ropes and an unfurling of sails, the ship eased away from her mooring. In the hold, timber lay stacked and packed like slices of ham. No eggs this time. He had checked.

A fresh breeze teased the ship and she gathered momentum, gliding out of Kessel harbor like a snow goose. Barkbelly stood at the stern and watched the town recede. He felt no anger, just sorrow and a profound sense of loss.

The harbor wall slipped by, and suddenly there was a flash of blue and a whip crack of cloth. A golden crab. A silver star. A new flag, flying at the harbor entrance, waving him off. Barkbelly raised his hand and waved back. He remembered. He smiled. He watched the flag until it was no more than a smudge on the horizon. And then it was gone.

PART SIX

Chapter 59

*B*arkbelly stood in Ferny Wood and looked at the cottage. The moss-green door needed a lick of paint. The hinges on the gate looked a little rusty. But there was smoke curling from the chimney and muddy boots outside the front door. His parents were home.

He walked up the path and stood on the step. Raised his hand. Paused with it in midair. Took a deep breath. Knocked.

Muffled voices. Footsteps. A creak of the door. A face: well loved, long remembered.

"Oh!" said Gable. His hand flew to his mouth. His eyes welled with tears. "Oh, my boy!" And he pulled Barkbelly to him and held him as if he would never, ever let him go.

"Who is it?" said Pumpkin. "You're letting in the—oh! Oh, my!" And now there were three of them hugging and holding and laughing and crying. "Come in," she said. "Come in. Sit yourself down. Oh! How I've missed you!"

Barkbelly sat in his old chair by the fire and looked from one to the other. Suddenly he wished he were twice the size so that he could contain all the love he was feeling.

"How have you been, son?" said Gable, drawing his own chair close. "Where did you go?"

"It's a long story."

"And I have waited long to hear it."

"Well, it began in the playground—"

"Who's that?" cried Pumpkin. "Knocking at the door, just when we don't want visitors." She kissed Barkbelly on the forehead. "I'll get rid of them. Don't you say another word till I'm back!"

The knocking was heavier now. Insistent.

"I'm coming!" said Pumpkin, fumbling with the door handle. "Oh!"

The man's bulky frame filled the doorway. His voice filled the kitchen.

"I've come for your boy."

Farmer Gubbin came into the kitchen. The Gantrys protested and pleaded, but it was no use. Barkbelly was taken outside, put into a cart and driven to a barn on the far side of the village. Farmer Gubbin opened a heavy door and led him inside. And there, in a shaft of sunlight, stood an empty wheelcage.

"Get in," said Farmer Gubbin.

Barkbelly stared at him.

"It's for your own safety."

Barkbelly climbed inside. It stank of rat sweat.

Farmer Gubbin slid a padlock through the bars, turned the key and slipped it into his pocket. "I'll be back soon."

Gable arrived fifteen minutes later, dangerously short of breath. He reached through the bars and held Barkbelly's hand.

"What's going on?" said Barkbelly. "Where's Farmer Gubbin gone?"

"I reckon he's gone to the Evanses' house. They've been praying for this day to come."

"How did he find me?"

"Did you come through the village?"

"Yes, but I was careful."

"Careful or not, he must have seen you."

Barkbelly sighed deeply. "Papa," he said, "will they burn me?"

Gable gripped Barkbelly's hand hard. "I won't lie to you, son. I think they will. They haven't been idle while you've been gone. They've made plans. They'll put you on trial, but, to be honest, I think they've decided already."

"I'm scared, Papa."

"I know you are, son, I know you are. And if I could take your place, I would. Believe me, I would. Your mother too."

"I'm sorry," said Barkbelly.

"What for? You've done nothing wrong. It was an accident."

"I'm sorry I ran away. I'm sorry for all the pain and the worry."

"Well, we've had plenty of that, I won't deny it. But you're our son. We love you whatever."

"I thought you would hate me."

Gable smiled. "Son, if I could give you the moon on a stick, I would."

Barkbelly cradled his father's hand in both his own. "This trial . . . who's in charge of it?"

"Farmer Bunkum. Fancies himself as a bit of a speaker."

He was the one whose cider Fish Patterson had peed in.

"When will it start?"

"Tomorrow morning, early." And Gable said no more, but in his heart, he knew it would all be over by sundown.

Chapter 60

Workmen were hammering all through the night. Barkbelly heard them and wondered why they were building a gallows when hanging wouldn't kill him. But everything became clear in the morning, when he was led from the barn to the school. They had built a platform in the playground. The jurors were up there already, sitting on hard school chairs. The villagers were there too—every single one of them, judging from the mass of bodies that packed the yard. When they saw him, their shouts rattled the windows and scared the rooks from the trees.

Barkbelly was led onto the platform and given a seat. He looked out over a sea of faces. Young and old, friendly, frowning—every age, every emotion was there. His past stared back at him. Miss Dillwater. Dipper Dean. Moth Evans. Freckle Flannagan, blowing him a kiss. Farmer Muckledown, Pot Williamson—all the urchin lads, waving at him. Pumpkin and Gable, holding each other, pale as candles.

"Bark! Bark!"

Fish Patterson was bobbing up and down like a fishing

float. Punching his fist in the air. Elbowing the people who dared to drag him down.

Barkbelly beamed at him and waved back.

"It's going to be all right!" shouted Fish. "We're with you!"

"No, we're not!" said someone, and the fighting began.

When Farmer Bunkum finally took the platform, he had to raise his hand for silence.

"Pumbleditchers!" he bellowed. "You know why we are here today. We are here to see justice done."

The crowd cheered.

Bunkum strutted the length of the platform. "Let me introduce the jury. Dust Gubbin, farmer. Boot Marlow, rat handler. Weasel Watkins, farm laborer. Blossom O'Leary, schoolteacher. And finally, Kettle Evans, shoemaker and father of the deceased."

The villagers craned their necks and nudged each other.

"Now, I'm sure I don't have to remind you—"

"But you will anyway," hissed a woman in front of Barkbelly.

"—of the terrible drama that unfolded in this very yard so many months ago. An innocent young boy, Little Pan Evans, was playing with his friends when he was savagely attacked by a fellow pupil. He did nothing to provoke this attack. It was a callous and, I would say, *calculated* act of extreme violence. And it left that little lad dead. Dead! With the lifeblood pouring from him, ruby red, running like—"

"Oi!" A voice in the crowd. "There's no need for that! The lad's parents are here."

The villagers nodded vigorously.

Bunkum snorted and continued. "We all know who committed this foul deed. There were dozens of witnesses. The murderer was an incomer to this village. An outsider. And he has returned. He is Barkbelly."

Bunkum spun round dramatically and pointed a fat finger at The Accused.

"And now I ask him: who do you think you are, coming to our village, bringing your violence and your hatred?"

"I didn't mean to come here," said Barkbelly. "To this day, I don't know why my egg was in Farmer Gubbin's field."

"But it was. And it was found by your adoptive father, Gable Gantry, was it not?"

"Yes, it was. And I will be grateful to him till the day I die."

"That day might be sooner than you think."

Barkbelly leapt to his feet so suddenly, his chair crashed to the ground.

"It was an accident! Little Pan Evans was my friend. I would never, ever have harmed him."

"But you did harm him. You *killed* him!"

"Do you think I don't know that? Do you think that by running away I somehow escaped punishment? Because I didn't. It was always in my head. Tormenting me by day. Stealing into my dreams at night."

"But that is not justice. Not for us. Not for his parents, Kettle and Lace. They lost their son. You stole his life from him. You are a murderer and a thief, and you didn't even have the decency to admit it. You ran away."

"Farmer Bunkum! Farmer Bunkum!" Someone was pushing through the crowd, but Barkbelly was too desperate to notice.

"I ran away because I was scared. I panicked. I didn't know what to do."

"You ran away because you were a coward."

"Farmer Bunkum! Farmer Bunkum!"

"I came back. I want to apologize."

"It's too late for that. You're going to burn, boy."

"Farmer Bunkum! Farmer Bunkum!"

"Oh, for pity's sake! What is it?"

The crowd was parting. Sock Samuels was coming through.

"Farmer Bunkum, sir! There's something you need to know!"

Bunkum glared at him. "Can't it wait?"

"No, sir. Please, sir—there's a massive pair of urchins digging up Little Pan Evans's grave!"

Chapter 61

*S*omeone screamed. Up on the platform, Kettle Evans sprang to his feet, then grabbed the back of his chair for support.

"*They're what?*" growled Bunkum. He turned to Barkbelly. "Is this your doing? Is this some kind of sick joke?"

"No!" said Barkbelly. "I have no idea what's going on."

Bunkum was purple with rage. He pointed at someone in the crowd. "Bring me my gun! This has gone far enough. I will blast those animals off the face of this earth if it's the last thing I do!" He jumped down from the platform and stormed toward the school gates.

"You'll have to knock me down first."

Pot Williamson was standing between the gates, barring the way.

"Move it, old man," growled Bunkum.

The crowd gasped.

"No. Like I said, you'll have to knock me down first."

"And me," said Saddle Yates.

"And me," said Brick Pullman.

"And me," said Shoe Mercer.

Bunkum spat. Behind him, the villagers were getting angry.

"Shame on you," hissed a woman by his side. "He's an old man, with more respect round here than you'll ever have."

Someone pushed Bunkum. There were jeers and whistles.

"Listen!" Farmer Muckledown forced his way through the crowd. "Listen! You all know me. And I know urchins! I can tell you now—digging up graves is not natural behavior. Pot Williamson here will back me up all the way on this."

"Aye, I will."

"So what I'm saying is this. I think we should bring a halt to this here trial until we see what's happening over at Mound Meadow. Everyone who agrees, say aye."

"Aye!"

"Right, let's be off. And no flamin' guns!"

Mound Meadow lay on the outskirts of the village. It was a peaceful place, fragrant with flowers in summer, but today it was white with winter. Circling it was a low stone wall, designed to keep grazing animals out. Now it restrained the villagers, who leaned over it, and over each other, their faces flushed with curiosity.

Farmer Muckledown, Kettle and Lace Evans, Pot Williamson and Barkbelly entered the graveyard. Farmer Muckledown noticed the gate hinges had been sheared off; the urchins had pushed hard. Kettle Evans led the way, steering them behind a clipped hedge.

"Oh!" Lace Evans collapsed into sobs.

Across the way, two enormous urchins were scrabbling in Pan's grave, throwing up dirt and grunting to each other.

"Well, butter my crumpets," said Farmer Muckledown. "If that's not Bramble and Thorn."

Barkbelly stared. Kettle Evans picked up a nearby spade.

"No," said Pot Williamson. "Don't go any closer. I know this is hard for you both, but really—I think we should watch."

Ten minutes snailed by. The urchins took it in turns to dig. Bramble was down in the grave when they all heard the unmistakable sound of cloth ripping.

"*No!*" wailed Lace. "*Not his body!*"

"Hold her!" said Pot.

Bramble came out of the grave. Her snout was red with clay. She shook herself and turned to her mate. Thorn was standing quite still, barely breathing. But then he grunted and his whole body seemed to quiver with effort. The golden spikes on the crown of his head began to shimmer and one of them rose up, like a seedling reaching for the sun. And Bramble took it between her teeth and dropped back down into the grave.

"No," sobbed Lace. "No. My baby."

"Wait," said Pot. "Oh, my—"

There was something coming out of the grave: a strange green mist that crept over the slumbering earth, caressing it, kissing it, waking it. And wherever it went, spring followed. The earth was stippled with green as the shoots appeared. Snowdrops, daffodils, crowds of crocuses. From bud to bloom in the blink of an eye. And still the green mist shaped and shifted, touching a tree here, a hedge there. And now there were roses in the middle of winter, and butterflies and bees, and larks and ladybirds. The graves were freckled with flowers; the air was sweet with song.

But not for long. The flowers were withering and dying. Petals fell sighing to the ground. The sun was smothered by cloud and the villagers felt the earth moving beneath their feet, as if something was stirring. At the graveside, Bramble and Thorn were curling into balls; the ground was heaving beneath them. Above, the sky was shredded by lightning. Hailstones hammered down, big as fists. And from out of the grave came a shape. A shadow. It leapt to the trees in a single bound, and the villagers saw it and knew it was Death.

But their shouts and cries were torn from their tongues by a wind that whipped and ripped through the meadow, toppling the headstones, tearing the trees. And then it began to spin, gathering dust and debris into a temple of air, a roaring vortex that spiraled into the sky and disappeared into the clouds.

"Whoa!" said Barkbelly.

"Look!" said Farmer Muckledown.

A hand had appeared on the lip of the grave. A pale, human hand. And it was moving. The fingers were searching for a hold on the sticky earth. Then there was a second hand. A tangle of hair. A face.

And Little Pan Evans, looking as beautiful as the day he was born, climbed out of the grave. He took a few stumbling steps, then stopped and looked around. He was as slender as a dandelion seed—so light, he would blow away on the wind of a word. But his eyes, lost in lavender haloes, were bright and searching.

He turned to the urchins and smiled. Then he leaned down and took Bramble's furry face into his hands. He kissed her gently on the nose. Then he turned to Thorn and kissed him. The urchins grunted and nodded at him. Then they looked at each other and ran for the gates.

"Let them go!" shouted Farmer Muckledown, still fearing an attack from the villagers. "Let them go!"

And the urchins brushed through the gates and ran off into the woods beyond.

Pot caught Farmer Muckledown by the elbow. "Those two are your best bet for next year's Urchin Cup," he said. "Do you want me to send the lads after them?"

"No," said Farmer Muckledown. "Let them go. I reckon they've earned their freedom. Though why they did that for Little Pan Evans, I have no idea."

"They didn't do it for Pan," said Barkbelly. "They did it for me."

Farmer Muckledown frowned. "Is there something you want to tell me?"

"Yes," said Barkbelly. "But not now."

Over by the grave, Little Pan Evans was still wavering. Slowly his head turned and he saw the watchers.

"Mama," he whispered. "Papa."

Lace pulled herself free from her husband's arms and started to run. Over the path, over the graves, over to her lost son. When she reached him, she fell to her knees and gathered him to her. "My baby," she said. "Oh, my beautiful baby boy."

And Barkbelly, watching the reunion, felt a sob rising in his throat. He tried to swallow it down, but it refused to go. He was finally seeing his dream come true, only it was happening to someone else.

Chapter 62

Barkbelly and Fish Patterson sat on the playground wall
and watched the celebrations. The village green was
covered with tables that sagged under the weight of party food.
Fairy lanterns twinkled in the trees. The village band was playing a reel. Couples were storming up and down, their boots
bouncing to the rhythm of the dance. Welcome-home cards
were pinned to every tree and post.

After Little Pan Evans had returned from the dead, the villagers had been more willing to listen to Barkbelly. It was the
Evans family that forgave him first. They said they had always
worried about Pan playing with bigger boys. An accident had
been bound to happen one day.

It was Miss Dillwater who suggested the double homecoming party. "Both boys should be welcomed back into the com-
munity," she said. The villagers had seized upon the idea
with gusto, and if Pumpkin and Gable thought they were
hypocrites, they didn't say so. Pumpkin had contributed gen-
erously to the feast and Gable had spent the afternoon
setting out tables. But neither of them would be drawn into
conversation.

Whoosh! A rocket shot high into the air above the boys' heads and exploded, showering them in stars. Fish turned to his friend and punched him on the arm.

"It's good to have you home, buddy," he said.

"It's good to *be* home," said Barkbelly. "At least, it is now."

"It's a bit rich, isn't it, all this happy homecoming stuff? Half the village would have burned you on a bonfire and thought nothing of it. But look at them now. Slapping you on the back and saying they missed you."

Barkbelly shrugged. "It's how people are."

"Flamin' heck! How can you be so reasonable? They drove you away."

"You were the one that told me to run." Barkbelly's eyes twinkled.

"I was scared," said Fish. "I panicked. I was wrong."

"No, you were right. You knew what they'd be like. You knew they wouldn't understand."

"Simpletons."

Barkbelly smiled at his friend's indignation. "I'm back now. That's all that matters. And you know, there's a part of me that's glad it happened. Fish, you wouldn't believe some of the things I've seen and done. And some of the people I met along the way—they were brilliant. Course, there were bad times too. Times I thought I couldn't go on. But I did. I'm proud of that, you know."

Fish pulled a sausage roll out of his pocket. "Little Pan Evans showed me his bruise. He's got a puncture wound right in the middle of his chest. It must have really hurt."

"No, he didn't feel a thing. I asked him."

"He *must* have felt it! You can't have a ruddy great urchin spike shoved into you without feeling *something*."

"You can if you're dead at the time."

Fish took a bite out of his sausage roll and chewed thoughtfully. "There's one thing that puzzles me. You say the urchins did it to thank you, right? So why did they just run off?"

"They didn't want to be caught. I can understand that!"

"Yes, but that Bramble knew you really well, didn't she? You'd think she'd have come up to you. Nuzzled you or something."

"She couldn't risk it. And she'd done enough. She'd saved my life."

"It was a close thing, though, wasn't it?" said Fish. "She left it late."

Barkbelly sighed. "Truth is a snail."

"A *what?*"

"A snail," said Barkbelly. He smiled and looked up at the stars. "I'll tell you sometime."

Chapter 63

*B*arkbelly slipped away from the party before midnight and walked through the woods to Mound Meadow. A low moon hung in the sky, bathing the graveyard with a soft blue luminance. Little Pan Evans's grave was still open. Piles of earth lay where they had fallen. The ground was patterned with urchin prints.

Barkbelly looked down into the grave. It was a pool of shadow. He couldn't see what he wanted.

He jumped in and started feeling around with his fingers. A bit of cloth, stones . . . then something smooth. He picked it up and clambered out.

The golden spike shimmered in the moonlight, singing a silent song. And suddenly Barkbelly felt that old familiar tingle. The pattern on his hand was glowing—golden as a treasure map and twice as beguiling. Dazzling visions danced before his eyes. Forest and fern. Sunlight and shadows. Wild-woods. Black beaches. Ancient landscapes. Ancestral power.

And suddenly Barkbelly felt he was leaving his body. He was soaring into the air. Swimming through the stars. Skimming like a swallow. And down below he saw the meadow.

And in the meadow was an open grave. And beside the grave was a wooden boy. And in his hand was a golden spike.

Barkbelly curled like smoke and spiraled down to earth. Caught his breath and slipped back in his body. The spike was still between his fingers. He gazed at it again, memorizing it, as if he knew it couldn't last. Then he kissed it. And the spike turned to dust and blew away on the wind. Up, up, up it went. Over the blue hills. Into the midnight sky. And on, on, on.

Jewel's Story: Truth and the Dragon

"Jewel," said Barkbelly, "what happens in the story about truth and the dragon?"

They were sitting in Jewel's wagon. The wind was howling outside, rattling the door and the little tin chimney. But neither noticed. Barkbelly was holding a skein of wool round his hands while Jewel rolled it into balls, ready for knitting.

"Have you been talking to Carmenero?" she said.

Barkbelly nodded.

"I thought so! 'Truth and the Dragon' is his favorite story. I first told it to him when he stood no higher than my knee, and he's loved it ever since. Even now, fine grown man that he is, he sneaks into this wagon late some nights and says, 'Jewel, I can't sleep. Will you tell me "Truth and the Dragon"?' And I do, and it always makes him happier. Sometimes he'll just lie back afterward and fall asleep like a puppy dog. Let me change over this wool now, and I'll tell it to you."

She pulled another skein from the bag beside her and looped it over Barkbelly's fingers.

"Well now," she said, going all misty-eyed, as she did whenever she was about to tell a good tale. "Like all the best stories, it begins 'Once upon a time.'

"Once upon a time there was a king, and one day that king went hunting. Well, he hadn't gone far when there was a great trembling in the ground and out of a hole came the most enormous dragon you have ever seen. It was huge, with long scaly wings and a thumping great tail. And it looked down upon the king, opened its mouth and roared. Well, the blast of it nearly knocked that little king right off his feet. Then the dragon threw back his head and snorted, and two hot rivers of fire poured from his nose, and when he'd finished there was so much smoke you could barely see him anymore.

"Well, the king just stood there looking at the dragon and then he pulled out his sword. And it was just a short one, mind, but he held it high in the air and he marched right into the smoke and disappeared.

"Now, there was a hill right there where all this was happening, and sitting on it were three friends. They were Thought, Belief and Truth, and they saw everything. And when the king disappeared into the smoke and didn't come out again, Thought flew into the air and wailed, 'Oh! I think the king is dead! I think the king is dead!' and she started flitting all around, because, you see, Thought was a butterfly. 'I have to tell the people!' she cried. 'I'm going to fly to the palace *right now*!' And she fluttered away.

"'Oh dear, oh dear, oh dear, oh dear,' said Belief. 'I believe she's right.' Now, Belief was a beetle, and he stood there in his great hard shell, waving his little feelers in the air. 'I'll have to follow her,' he said. 'She'll be causing no end of trouble, as usual.' And he waddled off, with his armor shining in the sunlight.

"And when Belief reached the palace, he found everyone was in a right old panic. Thought had been flying around all over the place, crying, 'The king is dead! He's been eaten by a dragon!' And when the people saw Belief coming, they all gathered around and said, 'We think the king might be dead! Eaten by a dragon! Do you know? What can you tell us?'

"And Belief the beetle stood up straight and proud. And he said, 'I can tell you this. I saw the dragon. I saw the king. The king drew his sword. He marched into the smoke and disappeared. I never saw him again.'

"'But is he *dead?*' wailed the people.

"'I believe he is,' said the beetle.

"Well, when the people heard this, they fell to their knees and cried.

"Now, you will remember that there were three friends on the hill that day. And when Thought and Belief went off to the palace, they left Truth sitting there alone. And as she sat wondering what to do, the smoke down below started to clear. Then she heard a grumbling sound. It was the dragon talking. And suddenly she could see him, and there he was, shaking the king's hand up and down! He was grinning! And Truth heard him say, 'Thank you, Your Majesty! That piece of bone had been causing me such pain, I can't tell you.'

"And it turned out that the dragon had been eating a goat the day before and a bit of bone had got stuck in his gum. Right between his teeth. And the king had seen it when the dragon roared at him. So he had gone into the smoke, the dragon had opened his mouth and the king had pried out the bone with his sword. And now the two of them were firm friends.

"Well, as soon as she knew all this, Truth wanted to go to

the palace. So she did. But Truth was a snail. She took ever such a long time to get there, though she did in the end. And she found the people crying. They believed the king was dead and gone. But Truth told them the full story and they listened. Some of them didn't believe her, but Truth said, 'The king will be here himself soon. Perhaps you will believe me then.'

"And just as she said that, there was a great flapping sound and there was the dragon flying by with the king on his back! Sitting there like a boy on a donkey! Happy as a king can be. And the dragon was happy because he had a friend for the first time in his life.

"And the king thanked Truth for telling his people the full story. He scolded the ones who hadn't believed her. Told them they were fools. And he told his people to remember that they had to *wait* for Truth—she was a snail.

"And then the king threw a party for everyone. And it went on for twelve days and twelve nights—and I know, because I was there. And when it was over, the king and his people and Truth and the dragon all lived happily ever after."

"Why does Carmenero like that story so much?" said Barkbelly.

Jewel finished rolling the wool. "That's for me to know and you to guess." She smiled. "Think about it."

Acknowledgments

Help, encouragement and support for *Barkbelly* have come from a host of fine individuals, including (among others) a Missus Maddox, an Apron Browning, a Carmenero, countless Taffeta Tythings, half a dozen Wick Ransoms, several Jewels and a Figgis. And so, love and thanks to:

Rachel Murrell, for whom *Barkbelly* was born.

Ruth Hay at the Hay Festival, who gave *Barkbelly* his first public performance. Thanks also to Peter Florence for his stellar support.

Joan Slattery and everyone at Knopf in New York for their wonderful energy and creativity.

Rob Soldat, who inspired sixty thousand words with one timely comment.

Erica Wagner, for her constant belief and encouragement, and for her immeasurable help in promoting the art of oral storytelling.

Storytellers Daniel Morden, Ben Haggarty and Hugh Lupton, for their endless inspiration and advice.

The magnificent Pat White at Rogers, Coleridge and White Literary Agency, London.

Yvonne Hooker, the best editor a girl could wish for, and the entire Puffin crew in London, especially Lindsey Heaven.

And finally, thanks to Ray, for going out.

Cat Weatherill is a performance storyteller, appearing internationally at storytelling and literature festivals, on British television and radio, and at schools throughout the United Kingdom. She grew up in Liverpool and now lives in Wales, a land of mist and magic. Her next book, *Snowbone*, will be a companion novel to *Barkbelly*.

Peter Brown is a new talent in the field of children's books. His debut picture book, *Flight of the Dodo*, was published in 2005. He lives in Brooklyn, New York.

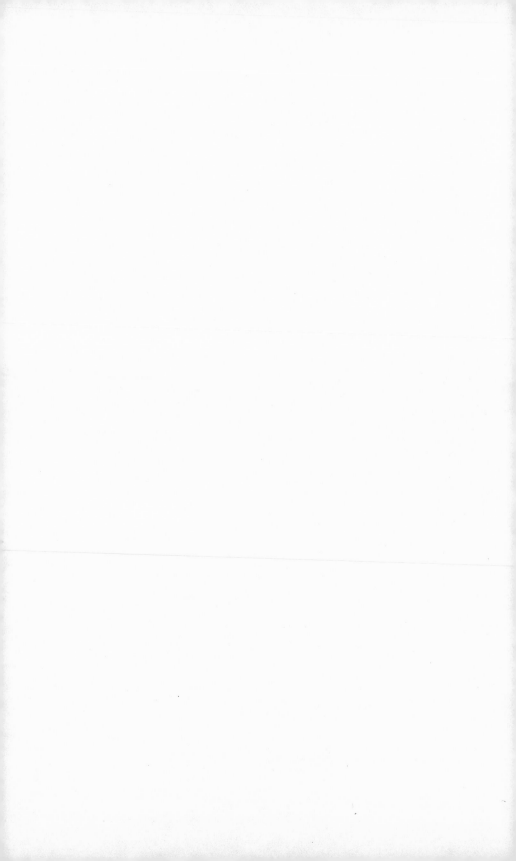